To Glen
Enjoy your taste of Fish Soup
Michelle

FiSH SOUP

by

Michelle Heatley

FISH SOUP

ISBN # 978-1-907984-58-7

First published in Great Britain in 2014 by Sunpenny Publishing
www.sunpenny.com (Sunpenny Publishing Group)

MORE BOOKS FROM THE SUNPENNY PUBLISHING GROUP:

A Whisper on the Mediterranean
Blue Freedom, by Sandra Peut
Brandy Butter on Christmas Canal, by Shae O'Brien
Breaking the Circle, by Althea Barr
Bridge to Nowhere, by Stephanie Parker McKean
Dance of Eagles, by JS Holloway
Don't Pass Me By, by Julie McGowan
Embracing Change, by Debbie Roome
Going Astray, by Christine Moore
If Horses Were Wishes, by Elizabeth Sellers
Just One More Summer, by Julie McGowan
Moving On, by Jenny Piper
Redemption on Red River, by Cheryl R. Cain
Someday, Maybe, by Jenny Piper
The Mountains Between, by Julie McGowan

This book is dedicated to Mum and Dad, who always believed in me; to Brian, who has the patience that all fishermen have; and to Robert and Benn, two wonderful sons who make me proud every day.

Thanks

Fish Soup couldn't have been published without Sunpenny Publishing's hard work and belief in the novel, and a special thanks to Jo for sticking by me. I also would also like to thank the fantastic artist, Dave Cooper, for the glorious cover.

My huge thanks go to my fellow writers and authors at Brixham Writers. You have welcomed, encouraged, criticised and supported me over the years and I am proud to be a member of such a wonderful group.

Finally I would like to give a big thank you to all my family, my aunts, uncles and cousins, and my friends, especially my oldest and closest friend Julie, for their faith in me; and to Clara, my glorious granddaughter, who brings a sparkle to every day.

PART ONE

1. A Good Stock

Each day arrives bringing with it a recipe belonging only to this day. Chicken stew with rice served when the wind blows from the north, and men mend their nets. Pork and clams served in celebration of births counted in years, and births counted in months. Each day has its own rhythm of slicing and chopping, stirring and boiling, to make dishes to be served with the comfort of yesterday and the promise of tomorrow. And tomorrow, before the sun is too hot, it will be time to make soup. A light stock with a hint of spice, filled with snapper, black sea bream and St Peter's fish.

Tomorrow it will be fish soup day.

Cecelia

Twelve tables, apostles gathered on the terrazzo, have been cleaned, the crumbs brushed into a damp cloth. The naked pine stands firm on four legs, the wood stripped bare, scrubbed and wet – like a child's face shined and polished by the corner of his mother's apron.

At my age, older than I care to be, my knees never cease complaining. I feel this chair obstinately press against the back of my legs, refusing me rest. I rub each knee with the damp cloth and try to appease them. The cloth, fresh from wiping the tables, is cool in my fingers, and smells of soap and lemon. It eases the pain gradually, changing it from a raw uncooked throb to a gentle, numbing simmer.

Tonight I must prepare, lay stiff linen over the tables, put a knife and spoon in the correct place and light a candle to offer welcome. I have lost count of how many candles have been brought to life in this place to welcome guests and renew friendships – small flickering prayers waiting to be answered.

The last cloth is laid and the tables are ready, pure, dressed in white for their first communion. The cotton is thin, worn by hand, by soap and by iron. Mama would never rest, insisting every square was pressed to perfection. She sat me on the floor, by the kitchen door, for me to fold the napkins – my hands were not yet big enough to help with larger cloths. Marissa, my sister, five years older than me, had grown enough to help Mama with the wedding-white cotton.

Marissa, orphan of the sea, has left for today. For as long as I have memories, Marissa has been my sister. Mama took her in on the day of the great storm, when Osiris turned blind. They found pieces of the boat washed up with every tide, and blamed her father for forgetting to paint the Eye of Osiris, leaving it dull and sightless. For weeks the fishermen shook their heads. For months the women clicked their tongues, but made sure their own men's boats had Eyes that shone bright.

Forgive me, I forget my manners. Along with the aches and pains earned through life I find thoughts of the past intrude, and my memory is not always as it should be. The spaces between the bead curtain swing with Marissa's shadow and, before I have time to light a candle, the beads announce the arrival of two daughters of another mother.

Isa

'Chloe hurry up!'

'I'm hurrying as fast as I can, Isa!' Chloe growls at me through gritted teeth and gives one of her *where the hell are you taking me this time?* looks. I ignore it.

'I'm sure it's only just around the corner.'

''Bout bloody time.' My sister tugs the solid handle

attached to an orange flaming frenzy suitcase – earth-quake, flood, fire and war resistant. 'I don't suppose when you booked that the web site said anything about taxis, or even some willing local with a cart to help with the luggage?'

She impatiently pulls at the fluorescent case and then, as if deliberately to infuriate her further, the small flimsy wheels – designed for airport departure lounges and marble floored hotels – give one last wobble and lose their battle with the cobbled street.

'Here, let me help.'

I take hold and pull. The weight of it just about wrenches my arm out of the socket; how on earth can one person need to carry so much baggage?

'What on earth have you got in here, Chloe?'

'Just the basics – you know me, Isa. *You* might want a budget holiday, but *I've* got standards, and *this* –' she sweeps her arms wide as if to emphasise the designer *this,* and exclusive that she's wearing; '– *this* takes time to achieve.'

I put down my own small brown leather bag. It wasn't really mine, it was in the bottom of Mum's wardrobe when I sorted it out, and it seemed wasteful to go and buy new luggage for the trip. Between us we push, lug, pull and slide the case up the steep cobbled hill.

'Well where is it then?'

Grateful for the chance to stop, and a moment to get my breath back – I've put on too much weight; caring for Mum left no time for me – I study the tour company's instructions.

'That must be it up there, just before the road curves away.'

I look again at the printed map and picture. The photograph bears little resemblance to the small restaurant. The red-brown tiles on the terrace are chipped, the paint-work peeling. The tables – gleaming and freshly polished – haven't changed, though, so maybe this *is* the place I had hoped it would be...

But the photograph I hold is of another age. There the bougainvillea barely reaches above the door, the vivid orange flowers framing a brightly decorated bead curtain. Past and present collide. Now the climber crawls over the roof and rambles aimlessly over the front of the building; flowers faded to a washed-out peach spill in every direction, and *Casa Cecelia* looks unfinished and frayed at the edges.

I hide my disappointment from my sister. She would only wear her *'I told you so'* face with great pleasure, and then take every opportunity to tell me of the upmarket hotels she has stayed in.

I take one last look at the photograph. The perfect sun lies in my palm; it had seemed the ideal place to forget the past, engender new beginnings. I fold it up and push it, along with the hope of a fresh start, deep into my pocket.

With one final effort we haul the orange monstrosity onto the terrace. Without wheels, it scrapes against the tiles like a spoon scraping an empty bowl, making my teeth itch. The over-packed case leans heavily against one of the square tables – shiny and wet and smelling of soap and lemons – and then, with a thump, it falls.

So without trying my sister has made her grand entrance, upstaging me with a broken case. I'm embarrassed by it all and leave Chloe to struggle alone. I push back the curtain covering the door and a rattle of beads closes behind me.

'Hello!' I call into the cool dark interior. 'Hi, is this where the cookery school is being held?'

I peer into the darkness and can just make out the figure of a woman. As my eyes absorb the shadows I can see she is slightly plump, black hair tumbling with grey, framing a friendly face. She is busy talking, to no-one in particular, smoothing white cloths onto the tables. She turns and I see her eyes, dark and sad; they meet with mine, and a glint of recognition sparkles in them.

Cecelia

Kalimera! Casa Cecelia, named after my mother, who chose to honour me with her name, welcomes you. This is your home for as long as you choose to stay.'

'Thank you. I...we're pleased to be here, aren't we Chloe?' says the older of the two.

'Yeah, thanks,' the younger one grunts, and pushes past the beads.

They look exhausted. It is not the easiest place to get to. Dimitri is becoming too old, yet continues to handle the ferry, and my own aging body protests at welcoming strangers from the mainland in the traditional way.

'Come and sit here by the door. The cool air will refresh you.'

The younger sister has the look of the world in her eyes. She is a woman with weariness on her shoulders, and it is too much weight for someone so thin. The island has called to her, wrapped a chord around her waist and whispered its greetings in her ear. My old eyes can see she does not understand the words the sea has spoken and is deaf to the promises carried in the wind.

'Can we have something to drink? We've been travelling all day and I'm absolutely parched.' The younger sister demands attention and I see her ignore her sister's face – flushed, but not with taking too much sun, the heat comes from inside; anger and embarrassment.

'Chloe, you're not in a five star hotel now.'

She snaps like a twig, this woman who clings to her childhood. I see the unwritten pages in her face waiting to be turned. A shroud covers her sadness and she hides it with the skill of a magician.

'Here is some iced water. Your journey must have been tiring. I have prepared your room so you can rest.'

The young one drinks, like a horse after a long gallop.

'You must call me Cecelia.'

'I'm Isadora, and this is my sister, Chloe.' She tries for a smile, to make up for the young one's petulance. 'As you can see from our names, our father spent much of his time reading the classics.'

'They are names given to shape your life. Each name holds a meaning. Isadora, an ancient name, a gift from goddess Isis. Chloe, a hopeful name, which speaks of green shoots and new beginnings. Your father will have seen this in you when you were born.'

The young one holds the empty glass out to me. 'Don't you have anything stronger?'

'Chloe, please! You're making a scene.'

'You mean I'm embarrassing *you,* as usual. I'm making a fuss!'

They glare at each other, two goddesses throwing thunderbolts across the table.

'I am sorry, the sun has not cooled enough for wine.' I fill their glasses. It is time for them to listen to the island. 'We have to prepare for tomorrow. Today we gather the ingredients for our stock. So please finish your drinks, rest a little, freshen your bodies, and then join me here.' I indicate the door covered with the beaded curtain.

The beaded curtain is an institution. It welcomes all guests to *Casa Cecelia*. It has been there ever since Papa returned from the mainland – I forget on which day. I know I had not grown tall enough to stir the enormous pot, but I was a curious child; I balanced on a chair to smell Mama's soup and nearly fell in. I remember Mama shooing me out of the kitchen, fearing I may be scalded.

On this day, Papa scooped me up in his dark arms, placed me on a chair, and I held the curtain while he fixed it to the door. Sky blue, shell white and sea green beads whirled before my eyes, and when I passed the beads through my fingers – a rosary to count my blessings – I felt each one had been threaded with a purpose.

With the last nail hammered in, Papa had stood back and held my hand as I watched the fish, a picture created within the beads, swim in the cool sea breeze.

Now, the beads are bleached by time and the fish has faded. Over the years its rattle and babble kept me company; although for a while I stopped listening and ignored its chatter when I was deafened by Julio's silence.

Isadora and Chloe ascend the stairs my feet have known for sixty years. While I wait for them to join me again, I listen to their feet dancing in the room above my head. A room I slept in as a girl, knew as a woman, and grieved in as a mother. Their steps are discordant and out of tune, Isadora's dance quick and exhausting, Chloe's reluctant and frightened. Soon their feet find the stairway once more, and they descend.

'Ah, you return and I am sure you do not want to hear any more of an old woman's chatter of beads. You are here to learn the secret of how to make fish soup. If you had arrived in winter you would have discovered how to make a stew filled with warmth. If it had been a saint's day, you would be making the perfect chicken with rice. But you arrived today, and tomorrow I will show you how to make the best fish soup you have ever tasted.'

'I'm so looking forward to it, Cecelia. The guide book said your recipes are unique and your fish soup is exceptional.'

I smile at the sisters. It is good to invite guests to *Casa Cecelia*, it warms my heart, and I am grateful these sisters have travelled far to make my fish soup. I see Isadora, Gift of Isis, clutches a notebook in one hand and a pencil in the other, but do not have the heart to tell her that writing it down will not teach her how to make my soup. She must use all of her senses; see if the stock is as clear as a summer sky; hear if the heat is too fierce or too gentle; smell only the fullness of the tide in the pot; feel the freshness of the fish, and taste, taste – always taste.

'Haven't you brought anything to write with, Chloe?'

'Does it look like I want to spend my time scribbling? I'm here. That's enough.'

'Come on, Chloe. Can't you please make an effort? It's only for a couple of days and you know how important this is for me.'

'Sorry, not feeling too good after that boat trip – this is not the holiday I was expecting. Paul always takes... took me – to some of the best hotels. I miss it, that's all.'

'Miss *it,* or him?' the Gift of Isis asks.

I can see Chloe struggles with the past. It creeps around her, like a weed choking the soil, killing any fresh green shoots brave enough to show. She needs time.

'Before the soup we have to make a stock, a base so full of flavour if it was all you had to eat you would be satisfied. It must be made before the soup has thoughts. It must be a memory of the sea to welcome the other ingredients. We make the stock tonight. And after, we will sit and share chicken with rice, and toast our good fortune at being together.'

Mama had waited until the strength in her arms had gone, taken by a bolt of lightning one winter's morning when she lifted a pot just a little too heavy. I sat at her bedside while she whispered and shared her secrets. Mama told me in a voice very low, with words tumbling over each other – like the tourists who drink too much cheap red wine – all the recipes she kept in her head. It had taken weeks for her to pass on the wisdom of years, and all the time I washed, changed and lifted her. I became a mother to her, as all daughters must become when it is time. I absorbed her knowledge, and she wept at the thought of leaving me. When it was her time I held her hand, and that was all she needed.

'Come sisters, we will now make stock. We will ignore the chattering fish, leave the murmuring beads to whisper to each other and walk the cobbles up the hill where, every day, Marissa meets Stefanos. I will tell you their story when the time is right. The hill leads to the market square, and beyond Julio lies sleeping. First we will stop in the market and buy vegetables.'

Chloe

What on earth possessed me?! How the hell did I allow Isa to bring me to this godforsaken place? It suits her like a loose-fitting smock, old fashioned and faded, not my sort of place at all.

'Isa, where are we going now? So much for a holiday by the sea!'

'Oh please be quiet Chloe, I need to concentrate, it's important I note everything down.'

'Well I can hardly understand a word the woman says. She's been going on and on ever since we got here. Soup, stock, curtains, beads – and I'm sure most of the time she doesn't know she's talking to herself.'

'Shush, I'll tell you as soon as I've noted all the vegetables she's buying.'

Great! Not only is Cecelia incomprehensible to the point of being senile, but I have to traipse up a cliff-face with cobbles worn so smooth my feet slip, in temperatures which substantiate the global warming theory. It's as much as I can do to keep up with Isa. And does she really think she looks good in that old Indian floral skirt, the crumpled tie-dye T-shirt – and those legs, those damn white legs? They've even got morning shadow, can't have seen a razor in a long time.

So there she goes, my big sister, as if she's a disciple hanging on every utterance the old woman makes, and I follow like a puppy with nothing better to do. Since the break-up with Paul, I don't know what it is but I've lost the ability to make any sensible decisions for myself.

'Is this it?'

'Yes, daughter of the green shoots, this is where the goodness of the earth comes to be introduced to the harvest of the sea.'

There she goes again! Green shoots indeed. Better leave them to it and let them go ahead into the market square. Which, while I'm on the subject, in anticipation of there being some sort of night life here, I checked, and – according to Google – this is one of the most authentic Moorish squares in the region. My feet, in expensive woven sandals, are shouting in protest and I can feel the heat of a blister between my toes.

Then I'm there. Slap bang in the middle of the village square. Filling one end is the church with a huge gold painted door and above, looking at everyone who passes, a plaster Virgin dressed in aquamarine and clutching a baby with impossibly pink skin. All of this religious in-your-face bling outshines the plain white painted houses of the village. Opposite the church is the bar, tucked in a corner, as if apologising for being there. The old men, playing dominoes and drinking beer, must have an average age of at least six hundred. There doesn't appear to be any other choice and, what the heck, it might be good for a laugh.

'Hey Isa, fancy going for a drink later?'

'Um, what? I have to focus on what they're saying. This local dialect is difficult to work out.'

'I thought you understood the language.'

I get one of Isa's patient looks before she returns to scribbling in her notebook, no doubt made of recycled paper in some African village and sold at a huge mark-up in an ethnic shop smelling of incense. She's good at giving patient looks. She's spent a life time perfecting the martyr, making me feel guilty for being Mum's baby and for Dad's infidelities.

I stand with sweat dribbling down the small of my back

and my feet blistered where my shoes have rubbed. What was I thinking?

'You could have warned me...'

'Stop moaning, Chloe. You haven't stopped since we got here.'

'Well for God's sake, I've been to some dead-end towns in my life, but this one takes the biscuit. How long do we have to stay here? And I asked if you fancied going to the bar this evening?'

Isa refuses to answer, and hangs on Cecelia's every utterance. That's my big sister for you: avoid conflict at all costs. Cecelia is talking to an even older crone, their arms waving in the way only those with Latin blood in them can, and Isa tries her best to stand between them, busily scribbling in her book. I look at the old crone selling vegetables; her face is crazed like a pot left in the kiln far too long, covered with lines and cracks. I suppose she spends too much time sitting with those baskets of vegetables, carried – no doubt – by that equally ancient donkey tied up behind her, and by the look of the mess in the square it has a severe gastric problem.

Well, Isa can get on with it. I only agreed to this cookery holiday because I felt sorry for her, and guilty that I wasn't there when the end finally came.

'It will be a laugh, the two of us, exploring new places,' Isa had enthused, clicking onto the holiday website. 'A change will do both of us good.'

She'd found out about the 'Gastro Tour' from one of her glossy women-of-a-certain-age magazines. I had to agree to join her – after all, I owed her one for taking me in after Paul's last stunt. And to be quite honest, going on holiday for three days seemed to be a good way of putting distance between us, would give me a chance to leave the last five years behind.

I hadn't imagined that 'Gastro Tour' was another name for *let's put you in a grotty bed and breakfast, and traipse in the hot sun buying vegetables I could buy in an air-conditioned supermarket.* Still, there is one thing to be grateful for: we're only here for long enough to learn how to make Fish Soup. I don't even like fish!

Cecelia

'You make stock in the same tradition as your Mama made it, Cecelia.'

Her hands – blessed by sun and soil – hold out leeks with dark green tops and sweet white stems, garlic to mend broken hearts, and carrots – the simplest of vegetables and the soul of so many dishes.

'What do you have for me today, Grandma?' I pick up carrots, small like a newborn child's fingers, fingers to grasp, fingers to suck, fingers lying soft against my breast.

'See how the soil is light and shakes off easily.' I turn to Isadora looking at me with adoration, and Chloe who is keeping her distance.

The crack of freshness snaps though the air and I hand a piece of the carrot to each of the sisters. 'You will learn how to use every part to make our stock. Here take hold and close your eyes. Breathe in the smell of earth, fresh, and the life growing in it. Then when you think that is all there is, taste it and the sweetness will coat your tongue. This is what we want our stock to be – sweet and full of the flavour of the vegetables, but underneath it holds the smell of the soil.'

'Chloe, Cecelia's right – you won't have tried this before.'

'Isa, you know if it's not tinned or frozen it doesn't count as one of my five a day. *Now* what are you doing?'

'Smelling the carrots, just as Cecelia says.'

'If you think I have travelled...'

'You have to spoil it for me, don't you? It's always been the same, every time we do something I want. Well, you can sulk all you like. I'm going to enjoy these three days, then you can go back to Paul, his five star hotels, his Porsche and everything else you aspire to and, to be quite honest Chloe, you're welcome to them. I really thought this time, just for once, you would change.'

The younger sister is resisting the call of this place with every bone in her body. Each push she receives she stiffens – like a tree refusing to bow to the wind, its branches twisting until, without warning, it breaks and the rest of the forest sighs with relief. Chloe of the green shoots is keeping winter between her and her sister.

It is time for the island to start working its magic.

'Come, take hold of this poorest of vegetables.' I place a piece in her hand. 'Breathe the sweetness, break it and taste.'

Mama had gathered enough strength to share her wisdom and, as the days passed, I prepared the dishes. She approved of my Chicken with Rice, each grain plump with moisture, slowly melting in her mouth. She made me cook Pork and Clams more than once. The pork was too tough or too tender, the clams had been overcooked or underdone, but eventually she gave it her blessing and I made a dish with which to celebrate. Each recipe awoke memories – caught in a net around my heart – and they began to swim free as if they were small fish released back into the sea.

Her last gift, and the most precious, was how to make stock for fish soup. I sat on her bed and covered it with leeks, garlic and carrots. She would slice pieces off and pop them in my mouth, feeding me like I was a day-old chick, until it was time for me to fly. Leeks, with their promise of onion, grown in deep red soil the other side of the mountains. Garlic, every clove a blessing crushed in Mama's hands and rubbed until the room was overpowered by their smell, reminding me of small clove I placed in the cot next to Julio's head. Then finally carrots, firm with the sugar of summer, ready to fill the stock with the body of the earth, helping it to fill the stomach and to keep the soul connected to the soil.

'Listen carefully my daughter,' Mama whispered on the day before she departed this world. 'You are now ready to start making soup.'

Mama then told me the secret of how to make a stock for fish soup.

'First, you take the pot and cover the base with oil, virgin and golden, then add the leeks. You do not want to use onions, they are too strong for a light stock. The dark stems and white base will start to shine, with oil and heat; it is now you add the garlic and carrots. These will flavour the oil. Add herbs – rosemary for remembrance, marjoram to bring love and honour, and bay for prosperity. Take water

from the spring – rising cold from deep in the ear
add it to the pan. Allow the water to heat until it boils, allowing it to steal the flavours from the oil. Taste, and when the soil is on your tongue add enough salt to give the stock strength.'

I did as Mama instructed and it met with her approval.

'It is now time to introduce the land to the sea. Reduce the fire under the pot until the stock holds on to the heat but does not move. Slide in the fish bones and heads. Mario will give you only the best, as his father Alexandros once saved for me. You will see that the delicate bones only take a short time to share flavour with the stock, and you must take care with this. As soon as they swim, and the flesh on the heads turns white, you must remove the stock from the heat and strain the liquid.'

Mama drank the liquid, she savoured it – like an olivier tastes the first pressing – and after I made a few adjustments she gave it her blessing.

'You're right, Isa. I've not had anything with so much taste, and so sweet, before,' Chloe says, surprise awakening her eyes.

I feel the breath of spring in her voice and, underneath the cold winter she has wrapped herself in, I see a small green shoot appear. She disappears into the taste she holds on her tongue – awaking the woman lost for so long – and the warmth of a smile lights her face. When we finish making our soup this daughter, whose mother mislaid her, the child who searches for her sister, will have her bowl filled. Stock is the beginning, a good base, for this goddess waiting to grow from the earth.

Chloe

It must be the soil or something, but I didn't think carrots could taste – how was it Cecelia put it? – 'sweet from the soil', or was it 'soul'? Anyway, it makes my tongue beg for more.

Bloody hell – I am beginning to sound like the woman. Don't be stupid, they are only vegetables, and raw ones at that. I don't know what it is all about but Isa seems pleased, even if she has a dirt smudge under her nose.

Perhaps I should have stayed at the evening class and learnt how to understand the language better, I pick up most but it might be good to understand more of what this Cecelia woman is talking about. Not that I didn't try. I did join Isa at the evening class and struggled up to week three, '*In the restaurant.*' But it really wasn't me and I couldn't see myself sitting for ten weeks with that group of singles! Okay, Paul and I weren't an item any more, but I had to draw the line somewhere. Most of them seemed more interested in pulling, finding someone for a quick shag while they brushed up on how to ask for a beer.

'It's great for meeting people,' my sister had gushed when she signed up.

'Not the sort of people I want to meet! I am here trying to get away from all of that.'

'It's your loss. I want to be able to immerse myself in the country and culture.'

Isa stayed the course, learning every tense, present, past, imperfect, conditional and everything in between. I didn't waste my time, eating soft centres and cookie dough ice-cream and nursing the bruises left by the break up with Paul.

Where are we going now? – I thought at least we'd be going back to *Casa Cecelia.* I could murder a glass of wine. But, Cecelia and Isa are now best friends and I'm here to play gooseberry. That's what Isa does – makes best friends with everyone. Funny how they never stay 'best' for long. She's far too intense, is my sister. It's all or nothing with her. Me? I'll keep my distance.

'Come on Chloe, it's all very exciting. We're off to see where the boats are pulled onto the beach. Apparently we need good fish with sweet bones to make the stock,' Isa informs me; if she was any younger and less fat she would be skipping down the street.

'You mean we have to go back and cook? Look Isa, I didn't sign up for this and we still haven't eaten. My stomach thinks my throat's been cut! There's no way I am going to make fish stock tonight.'

'Don't be so cross, Chloe. We have to get the ingredients for stock. Cecelia explained that in her mother's day they had to make it as soon as possible or the fish would go off, and she keeps to that tradition.'

Isa and Cecelia walk back down the hill, Isa carrying the basket full of vegetables. And me? I feel like a spare part tagging on behind as we walk back down the hill. We traipse past *Casa Cecelia* and down to the beach. The sun hovers just above the horizon as if held by an invisible cord, the waves shimmer deep coral spiked with Bloody Mary red. The waves lie flat and still, and I forget that my stomach is clenching with hunger, lack of alcohol, and the effort of trying to be a good sister. The Island is beautiful in more ways than I could have ever imagined.

'Hey Isa, look at those two.'

Yes, far more beautiful than expected. The views are getting better and better.

'Which two?' Isa lets out one of her very patient sighs. 'You mean those fishermen, the ones mending their nets?'

'Who else? Well the one with the smaller boat, the other looks a bit too old. I suppose he's about as old as Dad would be.'

'Dad was better looking than that,' Isa said defensively.

'I wouldn't know, I don't remember him that much.' I feel a sharp pain inside.

'I know, Chloe.' She puts an arm around my shoulder. The same arm she wrapped around me when I cried out in the night. The warm comforting arm I remember holding me close when Mum threw his things out into the street.

'I think a walk down to the beach later might be quite productive. What do you think?'

The arm is snatched back and the ice barrier falls between us just as it did when I realised Dad wasn't coming back and Mum – who should have been a mother to both her daughters – turned to Isa, leaving me out in the cold.

'You do whatever you want, but I am going to learn how to make Cecelia's soup.'

'And then what? What are you going to do with all this? It's not as if you have anyone left at home to cook for.'

'That's not fair.'

'Nothing is.'

'And Chloe, just remember the reason you're here. I seem to recall you don't have a man at home either now.'

'Point taken.'

'So you'll stay with me at *Casa Cecelia* then? You'll come back and help make the stock?'

'I didn't say that. Anyway there's no harm in window shopping is there?'

'Do what you want.'

'Okay, okay, I'll make the damn soup, but I'm here to get over that shit Paul, and a drink with a couple of locals might just do it. And put your face straight, Isa, it's about time you loosened up.'

Cecelia

From here, stood next to Mario's boat hauled high onto the new slipway, I see where the village ends and the sea begins. New apartments – hot pink against the sky – stand where Emilio once pulled his boat across the sand until it rested safely above the waves. He had painted it in the traditional colours of yellow and blue and it had rested on the large stone cobbles which once sloped down to the water's edge, a road leading to Poseidon's kingdom. Before I lost my innocence boats had filled this shore, all sharing the same colours and the painted Eye of Osiris to protect them. The years have passed and fewer boats are now pulled from the sea. I count on one hand the number of boats dragged over the sand to rest on the small strip of concrete. When they took away the friendly cobbles they told us it was progress.

Each day, when the sun is too hot to work, the young men come from the apartments. They walk through the beaded curtain and sit down to eat. Most of them are boys, younger than my Julio would be, but older than he will ever be. They bring the sun with them, laughter on their lips and in their eyes. They sit at the same table, eat and drink red wine, and wait for the midday heat to move into the afternoon. The beads join in with their chatter and they call me mother. It is then the pain in my knees moves for the briefest moment to my breast.

'This is Mario.' I greet my old friend with a kiss on his cheek, his hair thinner than it once was and his stomach larger than it used to be. 'He will choose fish from his boat to give our stock its heart.'

Mario welcomes us with his shy smile and holds out the bones of a snapper and two sea bream, their flesh already sold to wives and mothers to grace their tables.

'These will be perfect for your stock, Cecelia.'

Mario then turns to the sisters and hands them a small silver fish. Using more words than usual for him, he asks: 'Have you ever smelt fresh fish, put your nose on the damp skin and breathed it in?'

The sisters look at him then with wrinkled noses they smell and look at Mario in astonishment.

'A fish should only smell of the sea,' he continues. 'It should be as if a breath of air, blown from the Azores could bring it back to life. The fish must hold onto the life of the ocean and always remain part of it.'

Mario is a craftsman and can tease the best from the deep. He knows the places where the ancients spread their nets and, as a painter who works only for the sake of his art, Mario refuses to accept any payment.

'A bowl of your Fish Soup will be enough.'

Mario returns to mending his nets and looks at me with the dark eyes of a Phoenician, and I thank him for the fish. It is time to leave the sea behind, and with every step I take up to *Casa Cecelia* his eyes watch and protect me.

The walk from the boats is steep, my knees ache, and each slow step from the sea is harder to take. The sound of the water plays in my ears and the wind seduces me and blows with the memory of Emilio.

The first time I saw Emilio he was hauling his boat over the beach and onto the cobbles. I had been sent by Mama, too busy with her pans to get the fish from Mario, who had taken over his father Alexandros's boat. Alexandros had been imprisoned on the mainland and averted his eyes when Mama walked past. On the day I met Emilio, I remember the string bag cut into my hand and the fish felt too heavy for my arms. Emilio – glowing with the sun – lifted the bag from my fingers. We walked up the hill, and the fish made of beads laughed with us. Emilio handed Mama the bag, raised my hand to his lips and returned to his boat, leaving me blinded with his brightness.

'Stock is the heart of a good soup. We will return to the kitchen, chop, slice, and season, then slowly bring the pot to a simmer. It takes time to make good stock.'

Stir gently. Mama had said; take it gently with Emilio, take your time. You must stir the pot, making sure the stock doesn't boil, that it doesn't spoil. A stock made too quickly is ruined before there is chance to make soup.

PART TWO : FISH SOUP DAY

2. Virgin Olive Oil

Cecelia

Before the cicadas have warmed their wings I lie in the space between night and day and listen very hard. I hear the ghost of Mama lifting the large iron pan – heavy with ore, coke and fire – the burnished metal dulled by the years. The sound of her has been absorbed into the stone walls and I hear her humming with absent-minded satisfaction as she prepares for Fish Soup Day.

Light creeps through the shutters. Once painted blue, they have been faded by the sun and are peeling with neglect. Curling waves of dried paint cling to the cracked frame and when the wind blows from the north they float away, leaving the bleached wood unprotected. I close my eyes and listen to the silence, lying in the bed too large for me. A bed that was too small for Emilio. I arrived in this bed without ceremony or fuss, in the days before Mama made fish soup.

Mama, the daughter of a fisherman, the granddaughter of a fisherman, and promised to a fisherman, had already decided how her life would be. She would tell how, in the days before she wore widow black, she would sit with the other women, nursing her son, and when he had grown big enough he would cast his nets into the sea. She was going to marry Alexandros and help him haul his boat over the beach. She would, with the other women, paint Eyes on the front of her man's boat, and she knew she would have been content.

Mama had not planned for the entrance of Papa. In a town where the advent of a stranger is known before he steps from the ferry and the clicking of tongues moves faster than the telegraph, his arrival had been foreseen. Before Papa had placed a shiny black shoe onto the cobbles, his arrival had been anticipated and Mama and the other young women had gathered by the shore, anxious to see what the tide had brought them. They stood with shawls covering giggling mouths and watched the newcomer walk past, shoes squeaking, suit crumpled, hair held unbelievably solid with plenty of oil.

Mama talked of the time before she was my Mama, of the time when she met my Papa and was called Helena-Cecelia. I remember it made me laugh because Mama had my name, Cecelia, and I loved my Mama because she had my name.

She spoke of Sophia-Maria – daughter of Joseph, the baker from Carcasson – the first to knock on the small office door, bravely holding a basket of fresh bread from her father's oven and wearing her Sunday shawl. She waited while the young man with slicked back hair finished speaking on the telephone. She handed over the basket, her shawl smelling of yeast, and Papa – in the days he was only known as Francisco – accepted it and shut the door. Maria stood alone, her face turned the colour of sunset, and the other girls covered their mouths with their shawls, their eyes watering with laughter.

The day begins to warm the cicada's wings and their high pitched songs fill the olive groves. I fold back the bedspread, made by Mama's grandmother on winter days while she waited for the boats to return. Her busy fingers kept her from noticing the sea change; her eyes watched each stitch, preventing her from seeing white-capped waves smash onto the shore. The steady click of needles drowned the sound of the wind shrieking through gaps in the windows. She knitted, and the blanket covered up the worry of a husband and sons casting their nets into the storm. The wool – gathered by old women from thorn bushes on southern slopes of the mountains and knitted with needles as fine as fish bones – is as soft today as it was when Mama's grandmother knitted it, and has only a few holes made by hungry moths. I feel the warmth of the sheep draped over the end of the bed, place my feet onto cool tiles, and rub my knee.

Isa

'Chloe, are you awake?'

'No.'

'Come on Chloe, I can hear Cecelia moving next door. We really must get up.'

My sister is buried under the covers. A chemical mix of strawberry-blonde and chestnut spill out over the pillow – a cascade of hair spreading over the bleached white cotton. How much did she pay for those highlights? I know it would be far more than I could ever afford, yet I can already see the wisps of grey creeping out like strands of finest silk. But that's Chloe for you – my little sister who thinks she can hold back time.

'Chloe, *will you get up*! It's not my fault you drank too much last night.'

'Shut up and let me die quietly.'

Cecelia moves in the next room, the floor creaks and her gentle voice, muffled behind the rough painted walls, wraps me in a blanket of the past. She sounds like Mum did when she was having a good day, keeping herself busy with too much to say, but no-one to say it to.

'I'm getting up anyway. It's up to you if you want to stay there and miss the day.'

'All right, all right. Just keep out of my hair and let me do it in my own time. You're getting as bad as *she* was, with her telling me what I should and shouldn't be doing all the time.'

The taste of blood is on my lips, sharp and metallic. No point arguing with her when she is in this mood, it's easier just to bite my tongue and keep quiet. My sister has never had a sense of what was right. She moves from one crisis to the next, leaving me to pick up the pieces and keeping it all hidden. Most of my life has been spent smoothing over the cracks left by Chloe's earthquake life and bridging the fissures opened between her and Mum – each one a scar refusing to heal.

Our room is directly above the kitchen of *Casa Cecelia* and so small that our beds almost touch. I have not been this close to Chloe since we were very young. I sit up and look out of the small window. In the clear morning light I see the silver leaves of the olive trees shake in the breeze and, in the far distance, mountains where aubergine shadows hide from the morning sun. Of all the places I have been to – although nowhere near as far as Chloe has travelled – this is the most wonderful. I feel the village has been expecting me; I feel I have come home.

'I'm getting up. I hope that makes you happy. Oh God, if I remember from last night there's no bloody en-suite,' Chloe says, pushing the cocktail of coloured hair out of her eyes.

'Yes and I had to clear it up! Why do you get yourself in such a state every evening? It can't do you any good to drink so much.' I've got to take this chance with her, stop her from going down the same route as Mum.

'Don't lecture me.' Her voice cuts through my fears. 'I suppose the only washing facility we have is that chipped bowl over there?'

Ignore her. I've managed to do that for the past forty years. Ignore the tantrums when she couldn't get her own way and Dad gave in to his "little goddess". Ignore the silences after he left us, and shut my ears to the constant rows she had with Mum.

'I don't care Chloe, not any more. I *like* it here, and intend to enjoy myself.'

Cecelia

The song of the morning cicadas drowns the noise of water pouring into Mama's large enamel bowl – painted with roses around the edge and given to her when she was pure. I wait for the water to settle and smell the lavender soap, and the cool water chases away the night from my eyes. I dry my face and look into the mirror, and Mama's eyes look back at me. They always said I was Mama's daughter, and tried their hardest not to see Papa's mouth when I smiled.

Mama, in the days she was Helena-Cecelia, took little interest in the newcomer. He spent his days in a small office carefully positioned halfway down the hill, where he could count the boats being hauled from the sea. From behind a small square desk with a large telephone placed in the centre, he carefully recorded all the comings and goings of our small village.

Helena-Cecelia's only interest was in Alexandros – son of generations of fishermen. His father had made a fortune during the time of the war by taking partisans to coves known only by the men of the sea. He had invested it in a boat built on the mainland, a vessel with a larger draft than most other boats and built for oceans bigger than the sea beyond the beach. Alexandros inherited the boat from his father and was able to land catches other fishermen had only heard of in legend.

It had been suggested to Helena-Cecelia, by her mother, that Alexandros was a good prospect. She had been told by her aunt that she wouldn't make a better match. And she had been ordered by her grandmother to marry before the old lady died in the spring. Helena-Cecelia's grandmother was determined she was going to die every spring and, with each fresh summer, the doctor was always confounded by her refusal to do so.

I sometimes asked Mama why she hadn't married Alexandros as had been planned, because to have been Mario's sister excited me. Oh, to have had a brother older than me by eight years, a brother with the courage to protect me against the girls who teased and the boys who chanted stupid rhymes:

'Cecelia has ears, Cecelia will hear, so don't say a word or we'll all disappear.'

Mama would pull me onto her lap and tell me of the time before I was born, and of the time she turned her back on the sea.

Chloe

Queen Isadora may want to enjoy herself. I only need to get though the next few minutes, clear my head, forget last night.

'How many days do we have to stay here?'

'The course is three days, we've done one, so you only have to get through today before we leave tomorrow, do you think you can manage that? Now, we're here to learn how to make fish soup and...'

'Yes Isadora, why *are* we here to learn how to make fish soup? Go on, tell me. I mean, it's not that you're going to *do* anything with it are you? Don't get me wrong, so far the trip has been interesting and it has given me time away from Paul, but really Isa – this is all a little bit basic.'

'It's just part of the holiday, and I didn't set the itinerary. I know Cecelia is a little odd, but she is kind, and if you give it a chance you never know – you might enjoy your time here.'

I feel too rough to argue with her and think that probably it was not the best idea to spend most of last night in the bar. It must have been that local fire-water or something, that makes my head far too heavy to lift off the pillow.

It takes a huge effort to prise my eyes open. Look at her; the bedclothes wouldn't argue with my sensible sister, lying round her stiff body not daring to crumple. I sometimes wonder if we are from the same gene-pool. I feel her disappointment, that thin lipped unspoken need – to be better than me, the well behaved child, the dutiful daughter, the caring sister – it follows her like a cloud, ready to rain on anything I do.

'I suppose someone from the bar brought you back? You were making enough noise about it; I wouldn't be surprised if the whole street didn't hear you.'

'You mean Fred? Well, I think that's his name – Fredriki, Fredriko, something of the sort. Yes, Fred brought me back, said he was passing this way before going down to do something. What was it? Paint eyes or ears, I forget.'

'You didn't, *did* you Chloe?' she spits the words at me. 'You haven't – you know... well, you haven't... not again?'

'What do you mean, not again?'

'Nothing.'

'Go on, say whatever you were going to.'

'You haven't,' my sister hesitates as if using the words would make her as bad as me.

'What, you mean screwed him? No, I was as virginal as the statue staring down from the church. I had one too many, that's all, so no need to get uptight about it. He was the perfect gentleman and walked me back.'

I see her relief. When did we become so different? We were close once, me and my big sister. In those days Mum wasn't able to prise us apart, and on good days when she was the mother we both loved she'd sing, *Sisters, never such devoted sisters...* But it was less devotion and more duty from my sister. Mum expected her to look after me, keep me out of her hair, blaming me for Dad finding solace in another woman.

'Look Chloe, just for today can we do this together? I thought this trip would, well you know, help us to get to know each other again.'

Now I feel really bad and it's not the hangover. Isa's not had the most exciting life. After Dad left she was the one who sorted it all out and tried to keep Mum on the straight and narrow, and tried to keep us apart – me and a mother I grew to despise.

'Okay, it's a deal. I'll learn how to make this famous fish soup and I promise I'll not try to pull any more bronzed, tall, dark, handsome villagers with the kind of six packs I've only seen before on Venice Beach.'

'You're impossible!' But my sister is laughing, and for once I feel closer to her than I have for years. She's really pretty when she lets herself go. Although I'll have my work cut out to do something about those clothes. That skirt is going to have to go, should have been condemned years ago, only hippies and old women who stalk the charity shops should be wearing Indian tie-dye.

Cecelia

I hear the sisters, out of tune like badly played violins at a wedding, but it is good to hear movement and chatter in this place even if the sisters are still shooting barbs into each other. I cannot make out the words but I can feel the vibrations as they clash into each other, splinter into a thousand arguments... then, as the morning sun warms the air, I hear them laugh and I know the island is winding itself around them.

Helena-Cecelia, as Mama told me, had been born in this village, with the sea to the south and the mountains to the north, and never strayed far beyond its boundaries. Only girls (as mothers told their daughters) who had no reputation to lose travelled to the mainland. Helena-Cecelia grew up with the sea in her soul. Encouraged by her grandmother, who was going to die in the spring, she began to walk the olive groves with Alexandros.

As was the tradition, the aunt who had never married accompanied Helena-Cecelia and Alexandros. The aunt kept a discreet ten paces behind the couple. She had been promised to a man fighting a war that did not involve him. She had waited and watched while the other men came back, some filled with the tumult of war, minds never to recover; some filled with the excitement of war, never to be surpassed; some filled with the abuse of war, limbs damaged beyond repair. She held onto hope until she was joined by the other widows, the promise of wearing white lace and flowers on her wedding day fading into virgin black.

The olive groves – planted by the Romans from seeds and cultivated in the Garden of Eden – stretch from the edge of our village to where the mountains start. Silver-green leaves float on seas heavy with dark fruit, plump with abundance and peace. Every year branches, taken from the oldest tree, are carried with reverence to be blessed on Palm Sunday. The priest baptises the ancient wood, and the women hang the branches next to the Phoenician Eye to protect their men from danger.

Mama told me – when she was called Helena-Cecelia – how Alexandros, a quiet man and a man who only used words when necessary, would walk next to her in the shadow of the silver trees. His fingers itched to hold her hand but, being a traditional man, he kept them firmly in his jacket pocket, always aware of the watchful eye of their virginal guardian. When he did talk he spoke of the sea, of its changing moods, and of seasons when different fish are caught. Helena-Cecelia said she was content to listen and to know that one day she would nurse Alexandros's son on the shore, and help him to mend his nets.

After they had walked back through the village to the sea, past the office with the telephone, they would pretend to look into Alexandros's boat, which was larger than the other boats, and steal a kiss. Then, with the taste of the sea on their lips, they would part and promise to walk in the olive groves the next evening.

As I sat on my mother's knee I would bury my nose in her soft ample chest. It smelled of rosewater, of garlic and onions, of meals she had served, chicken flavoured with lemon, pork served with figs – and on Friday she would smell of the sea.

On Friday she served fish soup. Mama stroked my head and I asked – because it seemed strange to me – why I was Papa's daughter and not Alexandros's. And she told me of how when she and Alexandros walked down to the boats to steal a kiss, Papa – who was new to the village and called Francesco – would stand outside the office with the telephone and follow them with the eyes of a stranger.

Her voice would barely whisper when she spoke of the day Alexandros left the village. As usual she walked up the hill to meet him in the olive grove, followed by her aunt, who once had walked through the same grove on the thyme-scented ground to be courted by a young man who left the island to fight a war. Mama told me how she waited until the cicadas stopped calling and the evening grew cold. She talked of running down to where Alexandros's boat should have been resting on the large stones along with the other boats. She spoke of how the fishermen, when asked, shrugged their shoulders. They talked of watching Alexandros leave the office with the telephone, they spoke of the man with the slicked hair and crumpled suit standing in the doorway watching the boat – larger than most – being hauled into the sea, and leave on a tide too low to catch fish.

Mama would then wipe her face with a cloth, smelling of lemons and soap, and tell me how the stranger, before he became my Papa, when everyone knew him as Francisco, came to comfort her. He told her that the government needed Alexandros on the mainland and that one day he would return, it may be next week, it may be next year, he was unable to tell. Then, to the consternation of her aunt, he put his arms around her shoulder and pulled her close.

Helena-Cecelia's aunt, who could not believe the forwardness of men from the mainland, followed them as they walked through the olive grove. Francisco held Mama's hand and – as the aunt said when sitting in the square with the other widows – he showed little respect for the ways of the island. Later he demanded of Helena-Cecelia's Papa to give them permission to marry. Agreement was swiftly given; her father knew it would be foolish to disagree with a man from the mainland, a man who sat all day in an office with a telephone, and he along with the others in the village kept his thoughts to himself.

Alexandros returned to the village two years later, and used words only when necessary, and refused to speak of his time on the mainland. He never spoke to Mama again, and if she caught his eye he would bow his head and avoid her gaze. Alexandros married Sophia-Maria, her shawl smelling of yeast, and barely nine months later they were blessed with a son, the son Mama had wished for, and they called him Mario.

I descend the wooden stairs, too steep for my knees. In the kitchen pans hang from the wall, each ready to welcome its own dish, the large round shallow pan for chicken, rice and spicy sausage, the tall deep pan for long pasta made on the mainland and the solid oval pan for fish soup. I lift the heavy cast iron, dulled by years of use, and place it on the stove. Papa – who could arrange these things – had the white enamel gas stove brought over from a city far from here; the other women battered their husbands' ears with demands to replace their own old blackened greedy wood-eating stoves for such a modern marvel.

The early morning air is still cool, and the day must warm before it is time to make soup. I take a tall bottle from the shelf, full of oil pressed from olives, gathered in the autumn from the grove where Helena-Cecelia walked with

Alexandros, where she held hands with Papa and where I fell in love with Emilio. The contents escape the confines of dark green glass and I watch Homer's liquid gold slide across the bottom of the pan.

3. An offering of Garlic

Isa

'Good morning, Gift of Isis, Isadora.'

What name do I give her? A quietness of greeting ponders between us.

'Please, call me Cecelia. It is the name by which I am known to friends. Morning blessings. I trust you slept well?'

Cecelia kisses me and I feel she has chosen me to be the first. Her breath smells of garlic and olive oil and the arms she surrounds me with are covered in a blanket of lavender. She then embraces Chloe, who stiffly accepts. I half expect her to flinch at the touch. She's always backed off from '*that sort of thing*' as she calls it, blaming Mum. We had a mother who chose without care. She'd be sickly sweet in her smothering affection or cold as winter, no in-between. Chloe grew up too soon. My father, always formal with me, Daddy to Chloe – he would comfort her. He tried telling his wife: stop smothering and start mothering!

The kiss and the embrace feel like no other I've felt before. When Dad left Mum pushed Chloe away, and with every false lipstick-covered kiss she bestowed on me, I'd feel a hole tighten inside when she refused to touch my little sister. Cecelia makes me feel as if I was a daughter, welcomed without question. Will Chloe feel the same? I wonder if Cecelia has her own children. I imagine they have left the island; fishing and tourism doesn't buy the modern world. I will ask her. But not yet.

'We eat first, and then we spend the morning preparing for our soup.' Cecelia motions to a table covered with a white cloth. 'I have many things to teach you. Each ingredient will tell you its own story. Come sit, eat, enjoy. A simple welcome to the day is good for in *here*.' Cecelia's hand rests on her heart as if she wants to open it to us.

A plate is placed in the centre of the table. We sit near the door and I listen to the curtain rattle in the morning breeze. I look closer at the bleached wooden beads: a fish swims, and I'm floating between sea and sky.

'What the...'

Down to earth I fall as Chloe picks at the breakfast offering. I give my darling sister a kick under the table.

'Just eat it.'

She stares at the breakfast as if it were laced with poison. The plates, creamy white, large, oval and heavy with age, each hold two boiled eggs, a pale uninviting stale-looking slice of bread, and a bowl of green and black olives.

'I wasn't expecting full English Isa, but really – olives, I ask you!'

'It's just for today and tomorrow. After that we leave early to catch the ferry. Then you can be as rude as you want.'

Chloe picks up an egg and bites into it, and her nose wrinkles.

'See it's not too bad.'

I bite into the rubbery overcooked grey white and the sulphurous yellow crumbles in my mouth. Not the best, I agree; my sister may have a point, eating hard-boiled egg for breakfast isn't right. Soft dippy egg with soldiers, gently fried; melt-in-the-mouth egg with the shining white surrounding the yoke; creamy scrambled egg... in fact, anything would be better than this, but I wouldn't tell her that.

The bread, small and round, is sickly sweet. It tastes as if it's been drenched in honey; it clings to the roof of my mouth and is difficult to swallow. As for olives, I agree with Chloe and we leave the bowl untouched.

'I fancy going for a walk before we start. I need to clear my head anyway. Want to come?' Chloe pushes away her barely-touched breakfast, scrapes back her chair and parts the curtain.

I want to go, really I do, but there's that little voice telling me I should go back to my room, check my notes, make sure I've written down everything so far. I didn't travel all this way get it wrong. How far have I travelled? I am torn. Chloe has never asked me to join her before. All through our childhood she kept me at arm's length forever, pushing me back towards Mum, using me as a barrier. Well, she hasn't got that way out any more and maybe, just maybe, this is where it could change between us.

'Well, are you coming or not?'

'Yes, I'll come. Let me go and tell Cecelia.'

'Okay, I'll see you outside.' She slipped on her sunglasses, decorated with *D&C* in fake diamonds, and hid behind them. I couldn't tell if she was looking at me or not. Maybe that was the point. 'Don't hurry I've got to make a quick call.'

'Not to Paul. You promised.'

The beads rattle as if they are furious at Chloe for leaving, for breaking the promise she wouldn't contact him. They agree with me, this holiday has to be a new start. The fish swims and the beads chatter with disappointment, but Chloe cannot hear anything except her own needs. Despite all my hopes, I can't see her ever changing. She needs to be with someone who'll give her reason to be Chloe. I thought... I had thought that, for once, she wanted it to be me.

Cecelia stands in the centre of the kitchen, pans surrounding her like a halo, as if she knows the words I am trying to choose before I do.

'We're going for a walk.'

'Which road will you choose?'

I hadn't thought that far. It was Chloe who suggested it, maybe she had a plan, an idea of the direction she was headed. If I decide, if I choose which way we would walk, then maybe – just maybe – I can rescue this holiday from the disaster it's swiftly becoming.

'I thought about going out of the village, up there.' I point to where the road disappears up the hill beyond the square. 'I saw olive groves from the bedroom and thought they would be interesting.'

'Ah, it will be good to visit the goddess before making soup.'

Visit the goddess? What does that mean? Cecelia says the word as if it were a prayer. The bead curtain blows open and I can see Chloe clicking shut her phone. Her face hard with disappointment, a shadow of a smile disappearing, and I realise that despite all her protestations she does want Paul.

'So, off to the sea, go and see if the boats are back in, check out the talent. See if Fred thingy is back?' She gusts like a storm, hiding her feelings with ease of practice.

'No. We have to go up the hill, towards the olive grove.'

Chloe stops and looks at me, as if because I'd decided where to go on holiday I'd done my bit and that was enough to be going on with. She opens her mouth, then snaps it shut and follows me. We walk up the hill, leaving *Casa Cecelia* to soak up the morning sun.

Cecelia

On the wall, dusty with old paint, opposite Mama's white enamel stove – brought from the mainland by Papa when she first made soup at *Casa Cecelia* – hangs a bag made of string. Always filled with onions and garlic, it reminds me of Mama.

My Mama knitted the bag when she was a girl. Her grandmother, annoyed with her failure to die in the spring and with time to kill until the following longed-for spring arrived, patiently taught her granddaughter the deftness needed to use a large pair of wooden needles. Helena-Cecelia's grandmother demonstrated how to craft string – the poorest of materials – into a spiderweb of knots and holes. She showed how a humble ball of string could make something useful, with the beauty of simplicity. My great-grandmamma explained with each stitch the value of thrift. Mama carried the bag every day and filled it with vegetables from the market, and hung it on the wall opposite the stove.

The heart of any dish is garlic. I take out a parchment-covered bulb and hear it rustle in my hand – one by one the sweet, pungent cloves are separated. The white veil, covering its virginity, is ready to be drawn back to reveal blush pink. I had felt my cheeks warm when Emilio looked at me, but I was wilful and didn't hide my blushes.

I put one clove in my pocket for an offering, take one for myself, and place the rest beside the stove. With my thumbnail I slowly take off the pink-purple skin, undressing it, until the secretive soft white flesh is revealed, clean, pure, new born and untainted.

The sister will soon meet Hecate. I take a glass of water to clean my mouth – there should be no thought of yesterday on the tongue when breaking a fast. The bread is dry and too hard these days for my teeth. I rub one clove onto the bread and the room is filled with Hecate's perfume. Garlic is not enough; the bread must be softened. The golden oil is slowly absorbed and the fruit of the olive tree infuses with the garlic. It is good to pray to the gods and goddesses of plenty with simple offerings.

On my chair near the door, where the breeze from the sea whispers the promise of another good day and the curtain tells me not to forget the lessons of the past, the cicadas sing in the olive grove. Sat next to the beads, it is easy to wait for the sun's warmth to bring in the day.

The sisters are daughters of their own mother. They cannot decide which direction to go and are lost in their indecision. I breathe in the sacred aroma and feel the prayer in my pocket. The goddess will show them the right path.

Chloe, the younger sister, is lost like Persephone. The underworld is deep in her eyes and she is struggling to find her way back. The older, Isadora, the Gift of Isis, has unborn children in her soul. Their path is clear to anyone who takes time to look, but they can do nothing save argue over which road to take. I see Chloe – daughter with green shoots of spring inside – being pulled by the sea. Her sister only hears the call of the olive grove.

Slowly they turn and, walking apart – an unburied shadow between them – they climb the hill.

I hear Sophia-Maria's granddaughter before I see her. She sings songs she hears on the radio, filled with words from lands far across the sea and played in the bar of the new apartments. She dances around the corner, swinging the same basket her grandmother had carried, filled with soft bread and small round rolls. The tables are always full on fish soup day, and I welcome Sophia-Maria's granddaughter. Sophia-Maria, who had blushed when she first met Francisco, and whose granddaughter now bakes the bread, had never forgiven Mama for marrying the man with the squeaky shoes, slicked hair, who sat in an office with an old black telephone.

'How are you this morning Cecelia?' she asks, and the curtain dances in rhythm with her.

She has been brought up well. The baker from Carcasson taught his family the traditions of the island. She is a modern girl, and yet she understands the ways of her ancestors. I ask her to join me, as custom demands of me.

'Better for the sun. And how is your grandmother? I hear she is not well.'

'She's improving. After grandpapa Alexandros died her heart never fully healed. Dr. Vitrelli has been beside her bed most days and his cures help.'

We stay for a while and we talk of trivial things. Of the neighbour whose goat keeps escaping and eating her Sunday underwear; of the young men who leave for the mainland, only to return on feast days; and how difficult it is for her uncle Mario to make a living from the sea. We drink strong coffee and agree it is good to talk of trivial things.

Mario was thrust into this world on the same day as Emilio. They suckled while their mothers waited for the boats to return, and they played together on the beach, hiding under the nets and walking up the hill to the small school room behind the church. Under the benevolent eye of the priest, who had absorbed the patience of the saints painted on the walls, they attempted to learn. The call of the sea is strong on this island and the priest – knowing what it is to be called by a higher being – blessed the boys and called upon God to keep them safe.

Emilio's father had been older than most in welcoming his first child. His first wife, his only love for twenty years, died when influenza skipped across the sea from the mainland. After a suitable period of mourning, when mothers eyed him up as a prospect for daughters with little hope of securing a good husband, he married again. His second wife – a plain girl with no ambition – soon fell pregnant, and on a day when the north wind blew and the boats remained on the shore, Emilio struggled out of his confines and demanded to be the centre of attention.

Sophia-Maria's granddaughter takes her empty basket, leaving me with my thoughts. The cobbles shine where Stafanos's brush had passed, and the early morning dew dries quickly while the sun gains strength and creeps up the hill. From my chair I see where Papa's office once stood. They locked it when the guns stopped shouting, they cut off the telephone and Papa, who had been a man of importance, his hair still slick with oil, waited with resignation as democracy changed him.

Emilio, who was always eight years older, grew tall, hair bleached by the sun and skin browned by the sea. My years of childhood were passing, young enough to sit on my Papa's knee, old enough to watch Emilio pull his boat onto the shore.

In the evening Papa talked with Mama. I heard him speak of Emilio when they thought I was not listening. Mama said it would be better if I married beyond the sea, found a man who would not judge and knew little of the island, and Papa agreed.

I knew my Papa loved me, and like all fathers he was unable to refuse his daughter. So I sat with him, in his office with the telephone where everything could be seen, and watched the boats being pulled onto the shore. I saw Mario, shorter and darker than Emilio, hauling the boat built by his grandfather on the mainland before turning to help his friend drag it, glistening with gold and sapphire, across the sand. They rested like blood brothers, side by side on the large cobbles, exhausted.

I showed Papa how brightly painted the Eye was on Emilio's boat and with such a boat he must be a very good fisherman. I asked Papa if I could go and speak with him and Papa – who ignored Helena-Cecelia's eyes begging him to do nothing – indulged his daughter and agreed. It was not seemly for a girl to make the first advance, so to avoid appearing too forward (like girls from the mainland), I tipped out the vegetables and took Mama's bag to buy fish from Emilio.

Chloe

Isadora, stop sulking. I only managed a quick call before I lost the signal.' If I didn't know any better I'd think she was jealous. 'He says he's really sorry and he'll make it up to me when I get back.' Jealous or not, she doesn't believe me; I don't believe me.

'How many times have you heard that?' My sister jabs a finger at me. 'And you, Chloe, a so called woman of the world, who has travelled to more places than I can only imagine! You are sometimes too darned innocent for your own good.'

She doesn't understand, she'll never understand, my dutiful pure unloved Isadora. Sure, Paul had never been the best at relationships. But that's where we were so good, he understood me more than I knew myself. Yes, I did promise her that this time it was finished. But it was his voice, soft without the impenetrable coldness I'd left him with, that gave me hope that perhaps we do have a chance. But I'm on this time-shift of an island. I'll just have to wait. The question is, will he do the same?

Got your text, do you really mean it?' Our last conversation before I left, trying not to appear too keen, to swallow the balloon of elation at hearing him speak, bite down as if on a stick to keep me from telling him how much I wanted him.

'Yes babe. Come back home and I promise, it's a new start for both of us.'

He sounded genuine; after all, texts can be too ambiguous. Easy to misread. He'd broken the silence with, '*Hope you are OK. Call me if you have time. Miss you babe.*'

I had to ask: did he mean it? It could have been a friendly afterthought. But Paul, despite his horizontal ease, never did friendly afterthoughts. That what I love, I loved, about him – he would always say it how it was. He said he wants us to have a new start. I do too. But I can't tell him. I can't forgive him, not just yet. My eyes didn't lie. He was with that woman and I had witnessed the betrayal, even if he tried to cover it up saying it was nothing. Paul and Helen at our favourite restaurant. The treachery stung.

'I'll think about it.'

'Don't be too long babe.'

He knows he made a mistake. He'll wait and eventually I'll forgive him, even if it was with *that* woman. She has more faces than this statue. She will have given him her innocent-eyed virginal blonde face, hiding the scheming, hard-hearted witch – the one that cut me in half. The face of my best friend and confidant, turned away from him, looking directly at me.

'It's not what you think,' he blustered when I confronted him about it.

'And what am I supposed to think? You were all over her like a rash.'

'I know you don't believe me, but you must know how I feel about you, Chloe. Hell, I've asked you so many times to tie the knot, and there's always some excuse!'

He's right, of course – it has never been the right time. Fear stops me. Fear of committing myself, of getting off the merry-go-round and saying yes. Fear that eventually he'd leave. What difference would a ring make? A wedding ring didn't stop Dad.

I won't try to call him again if it upsets you,' I promise, fingers crossed behind my back – keep all options open, and it can't hurt to keep Isadora onside. After all, who else is here for me?

'It's not me that gets upset!' My sister's on a roll now; grit your teeth, Chloe, and let her get on with it. 'You are so darned selfish, don't you know how hard it is picking up the pieces each year? I really thought Paul was the one for you; after all, you've been with him longer than any of the others.'

She's right of course. Although if she knew half of the frogs I had to kiss she'd have a fit. Never found a prince – but then I'm no princess.

We walk on up the hill, past the bar with a few old men sat outside concentrating on their dominoes and surreptitiously glancing sideways in my direction. In a place as small as this, word must travel fast. The tales of overindulgence by another drunken stranger are in their accusing dark eyes. The church shines in the early morning sun and the cold marble face of the virgin is wet with dew, eyes rimmed with tears. I want to reach up and wipe them away; it hurts inside to leave her grieving for a son who filled her heart.

We leave the village on the only road out.

'Which way do we go?'

Isadora stands at the cross roads, well not quite a cross – more of a Y, where three roads meet. She looks at me with a desperate lost look. She had it when Simon left her, she held on to it when we buried Mum. It's as if she's realised she was free to do whatever she wants but doesn't know where to start.

At the very centre where the three roads meet – challenging all who walk past – is a statue. The cold marble glows warm in the early light. Her robe drapes softly around her shoulders and she holds a torch high. The statue has three faces, one for each road. Isadora stares at her.

'I don't know, Chloe. I really don't know.'

Cecelia

It is time to make the offering to go to the goddess before the sun rises too high, before it is time to put the pan on the stove. This hill gets steeper with each passing year and I nod to Dimitri. He has travelled far and seen much but is content to sit and play dominoes outside the café where the old men are served by his son. I remember when it was once enough to sit and play dominoes, to drink strong coffee in the morning, cold beer in the afternoon, and to warm the passions with strong spirit in the evening. Things change. Dimitri's son put a television on the bar. The old men continue to drink coffee, sip beer and click ivory tiles. The young men watch football and are unhappy with their lives.

Emilio – once he had Papa's blessing – wasted little time in walking me up this hill. It was not as steep as it is today. Without an aunt to chaperone, we went into the olive grove unprotected. I had forgotten, in my desire for Emilio, to place an offering or whisper a prayer. We entered the shade of the trees and I looked back at the face of the goddess and felt her anger at my lack of respect. The ground smelt of thyme and it welcomed us as we lay down, shaded by silver leaves gently whispering a warning.

I did not hear the wisdom of the ancient trees and, being of an age when Mama had not yet told me of how it was to be a woman, I sank into Emilio's embrace. The thyme covered me in its perfume and Emilio filled my ears with words I longed to hear. He spoke of my body – as he slowly revealed his desire – and told me I was an earth goddess. He promised, as a man of the sea, it was meant to be. When I felt the fire inside as he took me it burned into my soul. As we left the olive grove and as I passed her I looked at each of Hecate's three faces, and my head hung with my shame.

Mama knew – as all good mothers know – I had become a woman. She saw the glowing embers in my eyes, she noticed the marks left by Emilio's passion, and she resigned herself to being a grandmother of the sea.

I wanted Emilio with a longing beyond thought, to marry him and call him husband. I begged Papa to say yes and Papa, who was unable to refuse, said he would arrange it. He stroked my hair and told me not to worry. After he had spoken with Emilio's father – in his office with the telephone – Emilio presented Papa with expensive wine, flowers for Mama and, as is the tradition of our island, asked for permission for me to become his bride.

Isa

'The road to the left leads to the olive grove.' I shiver as the mist holds onto the ground. 'This other one seems to go towards the cemetery.'

Chloe looks straight through me as if I wasn't there; she stares at the statue and it's now she who doesn't know what to do, or which way to go. Not like her at all; I was relying on her ability to make snap decisions – as she always does when off on another adventure involving the latest love of her life.

She circles the statue, pacing round and round, reaches up to touch each face, runs her fingers over the features. The youngest of the faces, smooth and innocent, stares into the dark shadows of the olive grove. Chloe hesitates then moves on. She smiles at the warm calm face of the goddess with the ageless expression of all women who have a past to learn from and a future to welcome. She stops, raises her face and greets the woman who looks steadfastly into the distance, down the road where final journeys are taken.

'I wonder who the statue is, Isa?' Chloe says, her fingers stroking the cold stone. 'I've not seen anything so wonderful before.'

'I suppose it's one of the old Greek or Roman goddesses, they're scattered all over this part of the world.'

'She's very beautiful.'

I move beside Chloe and we stand together to stare at the rose granite, glowing as if the dawn has risen from the centre of the crossroads. The folds of her gown – a testament to the stonemason's craft – drape over the raised arm, torch held high as if preparing to guide us forward.

'Come on Chloe, we really should get back.'

'No need.' Chloe is pointing towards the village. 'Look, can you see, our Cecelia struggling up the hill?'

Cecelia, face showing the pain in her knees, smiles at us, too breathless to speak. From a pocket in the folds of her skirt she takes out a clove of garlic. She's not like the other widows – swathed in black, wearing their widowhood like a badge of honour. Her skirt, scattered with flowers, flaps around her ankles, a meadow blowing in the breeze. The only concession to her age is a thick knitted cardigan to keep out the chill of the morning.

'I see you have introduced yourself to the goddess, daughters?'

'Who is she?' Chloe asks.

Cecelia takes her hand and together they walk up to the statue. She presses a small pungent clove into Chloe's palm, without taking her eyes off the statue, and she looks into the face of wisdom, standing as guardian of the cemetery.

'She is Hecate, goddess of the moon, protector of woman, who sees what we hide inside and what we hold in our hearts. She guides us, and teaches those who honour her how to release the fears we carry.'

I stand to one side, feeling a spike of jealousy that she was chosen first. I see Chloe's face light up as she stares into the face of the statue, and I somehow I know that this has to be my sister's choice. Mine will be different.

'Daughter of the green shoots, take your offering and choose which direction you wish to travel.'

Chloe looks frightened. She stares at the small clove in her hand and I move next to her. We walk around the statue together. Chloe stops at each side and looks at the carved face, then moves on again.

'Come on Chloe, it can't be that difficult, it's not as if it is anything to do with us.' I can't help it; I don't want to be here anymore.

'That's where you're wrong,' she whispers, and looks at me as if I'll never understand. 'It has everything to do with us. If I make the wrong decision, all of this, me and you, we'll stay the same, make the same mistakes for the rest of our lives. I have to change. I want things to be different between us. This is my chance to choose which direction my life will go instead of...'

She's shaking, and places the offering at the feet of the statue. She stands up. She looks different, lighter. It is as if the weight of the fear she has been carrying with her has lifted.

'That's it, decision made. Come on, sis, let's go and make soup.'

4. Onion to hide a veil of tears.

Isa

'What did you mean, decision made?'

Chloe tilts her head to one side, the way she does when she's hiding, thinks I'll not know she's up to something. Even when she was young she'd give the same hide-behind-my-fringe look. She did it when she pulled the head off my favourite doll. I was eight. Cindy had a special wardrobe, long dark hair and pale skin. I'd spend hours dressing her up in her clothes, specially chosen by Dad and presented after another of his long trips abroad. Guilt gifts Mum called them.

'It wasn't me,' Chloe had said, tilting her head to one side, innocent but as guilty as hell. I knew it was her. After decapitation Cindy was never the same, she was sent to the *Dolls Hospital*, but she came back different, cheeks painted red, hair blonde and curly. She became just another doll, and Dad gave up trying.

'I've made my choice. Given an offering to the goddess, just as Cecelia said, and I have to wait to see if it works.' Her head held up hiding no secrets.

'I really don't know what you are on about.'

'So you didn't see where I put it then?'

She never lets me into her head. Keeps an arm's length away. In some perverse headstrong way we're more alike than we want to admit. She'd like to think she's different, not wanting to acknowledge we're of the same flesh and blood, not looking further than the end of her nose. Never saw the secrets I kept securely locked away.

'No, I was watching Cecelia. She placed her garlic at the feet of the statue facing the graveyard.'

We don't speak as we leave the crossroads and walk back to the village. The morning has warmed the air and we walk in silence down the narrow cobbled street. Cecelia greets passers-by like a saint with a smile and a blessing. She gives each one a gentle nod of the head, her eyes briefly closed in prayer.

'Can you smell the bougainvillea?' I say to Chloe, who is quieter than usual.

One last prayer for an old man sweeping the street, stiff broom cleaning the cobbles, and we are at *Casa Cecelia*. The terrace is covered by the intense smell the night releases. I think, and the thought makes the wound inside ache: *Mum would have loved this place. She had such green fingers, spent the spring planting and watering every inch of our garden, covering the small terraced house with baskets dripping with colour. The summers were always good.*

'Do you remember Mum's baskets?' Chloe takes me by surprise. She's never been known to have taken notice of anything other than herself. 'I was a real disappointment to her.' She watches Cecelia disappear inside. 'I don't know why Cecelia insists on saying I've green shoots, can't tell a marigold from a dandelion.'

'Yes, don't I know it; remember when you pulled up all her carefully planted wallflowers, thinking they were weeds?'

'She was furious, but then she always was with me,' Chloe reaches and picks one of the soft peach colour blooms.

'It wasn't your fault – it was the drink most of the time. I learnt enough to help her when she couldn't do the garden anymore.' I always thought Chloe didn't care; she only thinks about herself, doesn't she? 'Come on, we'd better go in. I can see Cecelia going through to the kitchen.'

Chloe stops in the middle of the road. 'What do you mean, you helped Mum when she couldn't do the garden?'

'Just that Mum found it difficult towards the end.'

'I didn't know. I didn't think of her not being able to... I mean, she wasn't that bad, was she?'

I bite my lip. She hasn't a clue, and why should she

have? With Chloe living so far away I didn't want to worry her. It wasn't age that stopped Mum. It's too hard to think about how she was at the end, and anyway, what good would Chloe have done?

'You never asked.'

Chloe, for the briefest of moments, seems to be lost in a past she wants to remember. She smells the flower as if trying to go back to a time when we were all together – Mum, Dad, Chloe and me. Then it's gone, the moment passes and she closes up again, shaking the morning dew off a past she has been trying to escape. The petals fade and fall onto the terrazzo to wither in the sun.

We stand on the terrace, the warmth of the morning drinking up the last of the night. The sound of the cicadas intensifies and the village wakes. The road sweeper stands on the corner waiting; he rests on his broom and I wonder: for how many years he has swept these streets?

'Hi Fred,' shouts Chloe, bashing through my thoughts. 'Isa, there's Fred – the one who brought me back last night.'

'Hello, my drinking friend! – and who is this?'

'Fred, this is my sister, Isadora.'

'Pleased to meet you. Fredriko Salvadori at your service.'

He takes hold of my hand and, with a slight bow, kisses it. Butterfly wings flutter on my skin and I feel the kiss tremble through my body – a tree in the forest shaking in the wind.

Cecelia

The sisters are silent with their thoughts but their faces speak louder than any words. I see Chloe's face uncurling – like a fern sprouting in the spring out of the dead brown bracken – her memories, long hidden, are beginning to be released by the goddess's blessings.

'Chloe, are you satisfied with your offering?'

'Yes, Cecelia. I listened to the words you whispered. Why choose me, not Isadora?'

'She has to find her own goddess to make an offering. Hecate is not right for everyone. Only a few can follow the path she reveals, release the past and accept change. The goddess at the crossroads will help you let go, take you from safe and secure and allow you to travel into what your soul needs to grow.'

'Cecelia, can I ask you something?'

'Yes, daughter.'

'Why did you place your clove of garlic at the feet of the old woman, the one facing the cemetery?'

She has insight and asks a question that is difficult for a mother to answer. I do not think it is time for her to know how I angered Hecate and how the goddess has demanded the highest price to be paid for such disrespect.

'It is time to start our preparation.'

It takes little persuasion for them to enter the kitchen. Chloe, the woman with green shoots beginning to show, is eager to begin. Isadora, precious Gift of Isis, is distracted. 'Your first lesson begins. All good cooks have their own ways, each is different and none are wrong, and you will make the soup your own. My Mama made her fish soup, I make mine, and Marissa will tell you they are not the same.'

Chloe looks at me and I feel unanswered questions waiting on her tongue, but she understands that by placing an offering at the feet of Hecate, the answers will come to her in time.

'Onions? We prepare onions first?' asks Isadora, flourishing her notebook.

The Gift of Isis hesitates too much, is desperate to keep the recipe locked in the past. She has much to learn. But I can see the belladonna of love in her eyes, the same deep blackness I had after Emilio had taken me in the olive groves.

'Come on Isa,' Chloe demands of her sister. 'I thought you would have already got rid of that damn book of yours. All you need to do is look on the table. Olive oil, garlic and onions, not that complicated, is it Isa?'

'All right miss know-it-all, since when did you become a culinary expert?'

Isadora stares straight at her sister, and deep underneath the layers and the barriers placed between them something shifts. Lightness enters them, they argue like children and forget the disagreements adults hold on to, festering sores left open. Children are quick to forget to fight, and become the best of friends.

I can see the Gift of Isis holds so many tears behind her eyes and it is time she shed them.

When Mama needed to cry she prepared onions – peel back the layers to reveal hidden truths of the heart. She would take hold of one of the brown-skinned bulbs from the string bag hanging on the wall and carefully strip the outer layer – paper thin, like a pharaoh's skin preserved for eternity; they would place a sacred onion in the sockets where his eyes were – taking care not to damage the soft flesh inside. With a knife as small as her little finger and as sharp as a gossip's tongue, she would slice through the base and release the powerful eye-watering juice.

The night she heard the truth about Alexandros the onions had bled enough tears for a lifetime. Papa had returned, as usual, from his office with the black telephone. Times had changed, the telephone rang less as old ways were swept away, and Papa did not smile as much as he used to. People were less cautious of him. I loved my Papa, but began to wonder why the men glared at him when passing and the women hissed between their teeth.

Emilio had not long returned from the other side of the island. 'I have the responsibility of three to keep now,' he would say each week. Before taking his suitcase he would give Julio a kiss, ignore my arms and disappear with no word of where he was travelling.

I was unable to sleep the night Mama took hold of the onion knife. Emilio had slipped into our bed and turned to sleep without noticing the desire I had for him. Our child slept with innocence and contentment, protected by the garlic clove placed by his head. I kissed the back of Emilio's neck and I could smell the dark soil of the mainland on his skin. It had the aroma of another place and another bed.

I heard Mama in the kitchen, the sound of a knife slicing and chopping came loud to my ears in the quietness of night and I was curious to know why she was preparing food in the hours after midnight. I slipped out of bed. I could hear her voice holding an anger I had not heard from my Mama before, and the soothing wave of Papa quietly replying. Not daring to disturb them I sat on the stairs, Mama and Papa beyond the bottom step and Emilio snoring above behind the closed bedroom door.

Papa was sat where he always did, on a chair placed by the beaded curtain. He held a cigarette, glowing and unsmoked, between his fingers. I heard Mama's sobs and watched from the safety of the stairs as she removed a thin brown coat from another onion and chopped it into the smallest of pieces.

'Francisco, I saw Alexandros today,' Mama said guarding her words. 'He told me many things I had not heard before. He said it is time I should know what happened. Why did you not tell me?'

Papa flicked the ash from the end of the cigarette onto the terrazzo and without turning his head spoke.

'My family lived a quiet life on the mainland. Papa had ten goats which kept us in milk and meat and each year he would sell the ones he did not need in the market. We were not rich but we had enough. I was raised to follow in his footsteps and walk the mountains with the herd until it was time to bring them down the narrow pass to pastures full of spring flowers. My Mama grew vegetables behind our small home and in the evenings she sang songs of the mountains.'

Mama – her hands covered with the smell of onions and washed with her tears – sat opposite Papa and placed her arms on the table.

'Why have you never spoken of this?'

'After the war, fought in the north, the people thought they deserved more than they had before,' Papa continued. 'Partisans began to move in our mountains. They hid their weapons in our caves and demanded food to keep them fed. My Papa was a man who did not appreciate change and when he discovered a cave full of guns, ready to kill, he informed the authorities. They were swift in their action and captured several of the partisans before they had time to disappear into the secret valleys high in the mountains.'

I held my breath and time stood still while Papa told Mama of the memories he had kept safely locked inside for so long. Mama, face streaked with the tears, wiped her eyes with cloth smelling of soap and lemon.

'The partisans came to us three days later and dragged Papa into the garden. They spent time asking him questions, demanding with feet and fists, where their comrades had been taken. He wasn't believed when he said he did not know. They broke bones and split skin and ended it with a bullet into his head.'

'Oh Francesco,' said Mama, fresh tears joining the old.

'They came for me next. They had decided a fourteen year old boy was man enough and should answer for the failures of his father. Mama begged them, told them that I knew nothing, pleaded with them to spare her only son, and then offered to make an exchange.'

The cigarette shook in Papa's fingers. He stared at the glowing tip as if it was a smoking gun, then dropped it to the floor where it burnt for a moment before being crushed underneath a polished shoe.

'They took Mama with them, and when she returned she was not the woman who had left. They had used her body as if they were greedy for meat; she kept their beds warm and after they tired of her they allowed her to go free.'

Papa lit another cigarette and drew long and hard on the tip. His face glowed for a moment and I could see the anger of a fourteen old boy who had seen things no man should see, and Mama wiped her face again.

'What has this got to do with Alexandros?'

'His father made money from selling guns to the partisans.' Papa spat the word across the table and Mama flinched as if he has struck her. 'He is as culpable as his father was in the death of my Papa and the ruin of my Mama.'

Papa stubbed out his cigarette and the beads rattled as if they wanted to call him back, to tell him he has his own family, a wife with love and forgiveness in her heart and a daughter who adored him for the Papa he is, and not the boy he once was.

Chloe

I can't believe it! Me, peeling onions! I look at Isadora trying her best not to let the tears trickle down her face. How many of them are real?

'I never knew how much these things made your eyes sting,' she sniffs, chopping another bulb into tiny pieces. 'And just look at you, Chloe. If Mum could see you now!'

'I know, we'd be scraping her up off the floor. She despaired of my lack of any domestic skills, and no interest in cooking. Do you remember when she showed us how to make cupcakes?'

'Do I remember? Yours resembled pancakes,' she giggles.

'She did her best, didn't she Isa? She had been determined I was going to be able to cook for a man as soon as I caught one.'

'How wrong can you get? You didn't need to be an angel in the kitchen, just a –'

'Go on, say it!' *Just a whore in the bedroom.*

She thinks she's overstepped the boundary, that faint line that separates us. She'll never know it was how I survived. Each different one made me feel wanted and loved, at least for as long as each lasted. Hotel rooms, booked for a night or a weekend, identical rooms, on the edge of identical industrial towns or, if I was lucky, a capital city served by a budget airline. At first I believed they wanted to be with me, stupidly failing to understand I was second best, when a wife, a girlfriend, or even a mother was not around for a few hours or days – men with time to waste and money to spend. Each one short-lived as they tired of me. I moved on each time, the same men but with bigger bank balances.

'You were the one always great in the kitchen, Isadora.'

I get one of her patient looks; she returns to chopping the onions and I still can't quite work out if the tears are real.

'Mum insisted,' Isa sighs. 'She said you would never be any use in the kitchen – she saw too much of Dad in you. *Your sister will never be a good wife, not like I tried to be,* she told me. *I could have been the best wife, but I married the wrong husband. Of all the men I could have chosen, it was your father I promised to love, cherish and obey. Listen to your mother, Isadora. Don't go with the first man who asks you; save yourself for that someone special.*'

I listen, her voice in rhythm with the slice of the knife; it has an edge to it as sharp as any blade.

'I did save myself, didn't I Chloe? While you were off in some exotic place with one of your men, I stayed. I can chop, slice, boil, simmer and bake like an angel, ready to be a good wife, and where did it get me? I'm what in days gone by they'd term a *spinster*. I've ending up looking after a mother who drank herself into oblivion, was abandoned by the only man who might have asked me, and here I am, desperate to find out how to make fish soup.'

I don't know what to say. We've both spent the best years of our lives doing the things we shouldn't have. Following dreams and waking up to find out that's all they were, just dreams. I see the tears dripping of the end of her nose, real tears, and she seems grateful when I pick up a small cloth and wipe her face. The smell of soap and lemon seems to comfort her, and we both turn to chop another onion.

'Don't you think all this very cathartic crying for no reason gets all the crap out of the system? What do you think, Isa?'

'Yes, I suppose so. Who are you crying over then – Paul?

That's one slice too deep, it cuts straight into me. I don't think I'll ever get over him but I can't tell Isa that. I know he wants us to try again, he's said as much on the phone, but do I really want to start all that again? It's not the fact that he was with Helen, she's a bit of a tart anyway and it takes one to know one. No, it's just that I thought he was the last. At my age – knocking on the door of forty and finding it already open – I'd had enough of sleeping around. And to be honest, it doesn't look quite as good in an older woman, taking younger men to her room, making sure the lights are kept low. Paul knew my past and he didn't hold it against me. "You are what you are, Chloe, and I love you no matter what." I really miss that.

My sister picks up the cloth and gently wipes the tears from under my eyes.

'Call him. I know what I said earlier about leaving him behind, but perhaps it's time to take a chance.'

'Thanks, Isa.' She smiles and that thin line that separates us fades and I step over it and give her a hug. 'I'll do it when we have a break, if I can get a signal.'

Cecelia

After Papa's anger had grown as cool as the evening, Mama sat with him. From my place on the stairs I saw her take his hand.

'Francesco,' she said in a voice tinged with the stab of a blade. 'Alexandros told me things he said I should hear. He said now it is the time of change and we no longer have the curse of the dictator.'

Papa lit a final cigarette and this time he breathed in deeply and filled his lungs with dark tobacco smoke.

'It was something I had to do,' he said, as puffs of blue grey smoke disappeared into the night. 'Alexandros's father should have thought of the consequences of selling guns to the scum who roamed the mountains.'

'But Alexandros was the son, like you, he had nothing to do with what his father did.' Mama removed her hand and sat as stiff as a man waiting execution. 'You knew how much I loved him.'

Papa nodded.

'You knew we were promised to each other and we were to be married.'

Again he nodded.

'He told me they arrested him as soon as he landed on the mainland and it was you, you who told him to go.' Mama took a deep breath. 'He said they kept him locked up and, while he listened to the screams of others who had been accused of crimes against the state, he feared for his sanity. Alexandros told me he had almost lost his mind in that awful place. He said after they had finished with him they took him inland, locked him in a prison surrounded by wire, far from the sea.'

Papa bowed his head.

'Francesco, what did they do to him there? He would not tell me.'

Papa took one last pull at the cigarette and looked Mama straight in the eyes.

'It is how it had to be at that time. There had to be total loyalty to the Party and if examples had to be made then that is what had to happen. It prevented anyone from thinking that they could damage the system.'

'Is that why you came to our island?'

'Yes. The leader said it was necessary. It was important that all parts of the country were monitored. There was to be someone who was loyal to the Party in each town, each village, each island.'

'So you married me to become part of our island.' Mama hesitated. 'Did you ever love me?'

Papa scraped back his chair, rattled the curtain and disturbed the fish as he strode outside. 'Enough, woman! You now know why I came here. You have heard of my parents who died at the hands of cowards. But yes, Helena-Cecelia, I love you. I loved you the moment I stepped off the boat all those years ago and I saw you walking down the hill from *Casa Cecelia.*'

Exhausted by hearing so many secrets, I returned to Emilio. His body was warm and I slid into our bed with the confusion of a young woman who loved her Papa. A Papa, who had strong dark arms to sweep her up and give her comfort, a stranger who was holding onto the past. I snuggled up to my husband and wondered how much he loved me, and what secrets a husband will keep from his wife.

Isa

Chloe may as well have some happiness, we've both been miserable for too long. This island, *Casa Cecelia* itself, has a soft energy, it gives me a good feeling and it seems as if a blockage is shifting. I know Cecelia can see it in us. She looks over us like a mother proudly watches an infant learning to walk. Step by step, we'll learn how to make our own fish soup.

The relief in Chloe's face warms me and, although she's never needed my permission, it's important to her this time. I like Paul, he was just right for her, but she couldn't see it. When I think back to the time she started to show the cracks in her life, the night Dad left for good... *No-one noticed her sitting on the stairs, watching him carry his suitcase out of the door, a pale face peering through the bannister. Mum had pushed past her, deep in her own loss, without a second glance. I saw her – looking like a china doll with no expression – staring after the only man she truly wanted to be with.*

After the fury, the angry shouting, the final slam of the door, I'd tucked her into bed, sleep scratching her eyes, confused by something she didn't understand.

'Is Daddy coming back?'

'Soon darling, soon,' I lied. Ten years old and I knew how the world turned; a lifetime of hurt had passed before me that night. It was too much for a child to have to understand.

'Tell Daddy I love him,' she'd murmured, rubbing the sleep pricking at her eyes and seeking comfort in a well-sucked thumb.

I sat with her most of that night, listening to Mum crying, and knew our family had been broken as easily as a bottle falls from the fingers of an alcoholic.

'What are you thinking about?' Chloe holds the knife like a thought; it hangs over an onion as if she were a reluctant executioner.

'Not much really. About when we were young and the night he left.'

Why now? We've not spoken of that time. Perhaps Chloe was too young and then life got in the way; I had to protect her from Mum's hurt. He'd abandoned us; that's all she needed to know.

'He never came back. I waited and waited. No birthday cards, no Christmas presents – it was as if he'd disappeared from the face of the earth.'

The face stares out through the banister.

'It hurt you the most, didn't it?'

I can't tell her.

All the cards, the presents, the letters, shoved in the battered brown suitcase hidden in the bottom of the wardrobe. After the funeral I was petrified she'd want to stay, to help sort everything out. If she had known what Mum had done, how she cut us off from him? It wasn't hard to persuade her to leave, even if inside I was begging her to stay. It gave me a chance to make it right. It took an evening to burn them all.

'Come here.'

For what seemed the longest time Chloe rests her head on my shoulder and I stroke her hair. The smell of onions on my hands mixed with the rich scent of salon shampoo but for once, she doesn't seem to mind.

'You know earlier, at the crossroads?'

'Yes.'

'When I made my offering to the goddess, Cecelia said Hecate – that's what they call her here – can see the past, present and future. She told me the goddess was powerful; she helped Persephone escape from Hades and she would do the same for me. I think she's right, I think you're right, and maybe I should listen to Paul before I decide what to do.'

'I think so too, Chloe.' I kiss the top of her head. 'While I was waiting for you I saw Cecelia place her garlic and I could hear her asking for Julio to be watched over. Who do you think Julio is?'

'Probably her husband, there's no man around here anyway.'

Chloe, always confident and rushing in where I dare not go, flicks her hair and turns to Cecelia.

'Yes, daughter of the green shoots?'

She smiles at Chloe as if she had been waiting for the question and my sister's face lights up. It holds the fleeting joy she had when Dad would take her in his arms, before she sat on the stairs watching her world fall apart all those years ago.

'When we made our offerings to the goddess, you spoke of Julio.'

'Julio...' Cecelia whispers the word. She passes a hand across her face and motions to Chloe to move close. 'Julio was my soul, my heart. He was made of me and of my ancestors.' She places a hand on her stomach. 'He grew inside this empty womb and lightened my life. He was my son.'

A silence hangs like the pans hanging from the ceiling, wombs waiting to be filled.

'Cecelia, have we chopped enough onions?' Silence is better filled; it doesn't allow anything else to intrude. I filled the spaces when Dad left, and soon Chloe stopped trying to find them. 'Cecelia did you hear me?'

'Yes, Isadora, Gift of Isis. Sometimes the thoughts of the past intrude, and they should to be listened to.'

'I'm sorry about your son, was he very young?' Chloe asks, and I wish she hadn't.

Cecelia, no older than Mum would be if she was still here, bends her head and the heaviness of her memories holds her in a grip so tight she is unable to move. The moment is suspended in time – frozen forever like ice in the deepest mountain crevices. Cecelia sighs, and as the breath escapes her lips – still holding the fullness of youth without the narrowness of age – she whispers her son's name again.

'Julio. I had Julio for eight years, which is more than some. Mario had married not long after I had said my vows. Angelina had conceived under the same summer sun as I had with my precious Julio. We carried our cargo safely, until winter arrived and the time came for us to become mothers.'

She runs her hand across her stomach, the joy of child-birth held in its roundness, in the fullness of her breasts and in the width of her hips. Cecelia's face shows the pain of a question which needed such an answer.

'We began our labour on the same morning,' Cecelia continues. 'Julio entered this world and the pain all women feel when giving birth was quickly forgotten when he sucked at my breast. He was born furiously pink and angry, like his father. He had the eyes of Papa and the sweet mouth of Mama.'

Cecelia moves her hand from the empty womb and rests it over her heart. The constant shrill of the cicadas is silenced and I am sure I can hear her heart beating. 'That night the moon was hidden behind clouds and the sea spat its anger onto the shore. Angelina was a modern woman who had been raised on the mainland. She hadn't learnt our ways, and had not made an offering of garlic to protect her unborn child. For two days the storm blew, and Dr. Vitrelli was stranded on the mainland. The goddess – who gives smooth passage to the underworld – called that night and took Angelina and her unborn child with her before dawn could bring light.'

I hold my breath. Chloe wipes her face and the spell is broken. Cecelia picks up the last finely chopped onion and scrapes it into the pan. The oil sizzles and spits. Slowly the white flesh becomes translucent and a sweet smell rises and fills the room.

'See how the oil takes away the sting and bitterness from the onion,' Cecelia whispers. 'Onions help tears to fall, they hide heartbreak. A lifetime of tears is quickly dried.'

5. Tomatoes – Apples for Love

Chloe

Isadora breathes in. The smell of onions softens with the garlic and olive oil. Tears have washed her eyes and they shine as if the sun has bounced off the sea.

'Smells good.'

'Yes.' I see Isadora smile and I smile back and we remember better times.

Maybe it's being here, away from the things that hurt us. In Cecelia's kitchen everything smells and tastes better. Perhaps it's the vegetables, tasting of the soil in which they grow in an earth of different gods, or possibly the kitchen filled with the aroma of the olive oil, garlic and onions. It makes me want to smell them again and again and I want to stay here until I've had my fill.

Cecelia stirs the large pot, lifts out a wooden spoon worn smooth and shining gold with olive oil. She looks at Isadora, hesitates then turns to me.

'Here, taste.'

She holds the spoon to my mouth as if I was a child that couldn't be trusted to feed herself.

'This is the base, the foundation of our soup, ready to be introduced to the other ingredients.'

Cecelia places the spoon onto my tongue and I begin to understand. My tongue absorbs the knowledge of how it is to bring together simple ingredients to make one single taste.

My sister is scribbling away, nose in that damn notebook. She's shutting the world out again.

'Come on Isa, you try some.'

'Hang on, in a moment. What order were those ingredients put in the pan? I have the olive oil, but not sure how much, then was it onions and garlic or garlic and onions?'

'Does it really matter? For God's sake, all I'm asking you to do is just taste the stuff.'

I don't understand her – never have really – she's so determined to write everything down. Lists for everything, that's what she does, rather than living life she had to write it. Lists for shopping; lists for clothes; lists to remember to make lists – and now she's so intent on writing down the recipe, she's missing the point of being here.

Will you listen to me going on? I'm beginning to sound like the sensible sister. The one who has her life sorted, when in reality it has been my list-making sister who's always been there to mop up the spillages before I slip over again.

Isadora was too young to take me on and deal with the crap Mum dumped on her. Ten, going on twenty, she had to grow up fast. I got off lightly, being so much younger. It hurt though; it was me who Mum blamed for Dad doing a runner, and so she simply ignored me. Isadora dealt with my fury – boiling like a cauldron inside – leaving me as spiky as a thornbush. I made sure Mum would need thick gloves if she ever had wanted to touch me.

'Here, open your damn mouth.'

I take the spoon from Cecelia and pop a small amount onto my sister's tongue. She closes her eyes and swallows. Slowly she opens her eyes, the colour of cornflowers, and smiles. Her mouth smiles, her eyes smile, her nose wrinkles and her whole face changes. She looks at me as if she is greeting a long lost friend.

'Now, in what order do they go?' she says, picking up her pen.

'You are impossible, Isa! I'll give you what order they come in.'

I take the notebook, snatch it out of her hands and shut it. It snaps like a breaking twig and I am determined that this will be the last time she will bury herself inside it.

'Good,' Cecelia nods her approval. 'The base is now ready to be filled with the fruit of the Incas. Xtomatl it was called in ancient times, *Poma de Moro* – the Moor apple from the land of pasta, and the land drenched with the syrup of love. They call it *Pomme d'Amour*.'

'That means love apple, Chloe,' whispers my sister.

I'm not stupid. Even I know she's referring to the tomatoes piled high on the small scrubbed table. I give her a quick flick with the dishcloth and once again her whole face lights up with a hundred smiles.

Cecelia

Laughter bounces off the pans and it is good. It is so long since the kitchen heard this much joy. Mama laughed at me when I tried to copy her and stir the soup in the same way she did.

'Daughter, you must be your own woman,' she insisted. 'I am made from my Mama and yet I am not her, and you, Cecelia who holds my name and is made of me, must be the woman you were born to be.'

Emilio had laughed when he rubbed my stomach, growing bigger with every passing month. 'My son grows strong; he will be just like me.'

I recalled Mama's words and prayed I would have a daughter who I could teach to be her own woman, who would learn how to make fish soup and not carry the burden of trying to be someone else.

I married Emilio before the life growing inside me was visible to the outside world. They would know eventually, all women know that a baby born before its time is small; my child was to be round and fat as if it had served its full term. Our wedding day was as expected. The men of our island came out of fear to respect Papa and raised their hats in silent salute to him. Papa, who lived in the time when he sat in his office behind the desk with a telephone, was a man who demanded respect. I was proud he was my Papa, and unlike the other men whose ancestors had anchored themselves on this island. My Papa was not a hostage of the sea. My Papa worked each day halfway down the hill, speaking into the black telephone, watching all who passed by.

After the ceremony Mama made pork and clams, served on tables covered with white starched cotton, a candle placed in the centre of each one, twelve reminders of my love for Emilio. Each guest honoured my Papa by pinning gifts of money to my dress. After the guests had left Marissa and Mama cleared the tables. Emilio scooped me into his arms and carried me – with a little difficulty because I was heavier than I had been in the olive grove – up the stairs to our bedroom above the kitchen. He held me in his arms and my heart was overflowing. I was so full of love for him that I couldn't stop smiling.

'Cecelia,' he whispered in my ear, like the wind caressing the Cyprus trees high in the mountains, 'I'll take care of the money.'

My husband of a few hours carefully unpinned every note given in respect for Papa and put them one by one in a large leather suitcase. My husband – how good the word sounded as I said it – my husband laid me on the bed and kissed me, as he had when we had rested on a bed of thyme in the olive grove. He undressed me and saw the roundness of my belly. His eyes froze; the spark of passion died, and when he kissed me it was not the kiss of a lover but the kiss a mother gives a child.

Emilio left the next morning, carrying his wedding suit and the large leather case. He took the road to the north leading out of the village, forgetting about his boat pulled onto the shore. Over the months his boat remained where it had been abandoned. The paint peeled in the sun and the Eye of Osiris became dull. When Emilio returned he told me he was no longer a man of the sea, he had become a man of substance and as such would find different places to cast his net. He brushed away my protests with a hard hand and hung a different suit on the door, and placed a pair of polished shoes under the bed.

When it was time for our child to arrive I asked Emilio – as tradition demanded of a wife – if we could use some of the wedding money to buy a crib. I felt my baby push his feet against my ribs and knew he would need a solid place to sleep. Christofe, the boat builder, had offered to make a vessel to carry the child. Mama busied her fingers making sheets made from a cotton tablecloth cut down and trimmed with lace, and I told Emilio that the crib would not cost much.

The slap came as a shock the first time he raised his hand to me. As the weeks went by I learned how to hide the marks. I wore long sleeves to cover bruises and brushed my hair to fall over blackened eyes.

Julio was born the same morning as Angelina's stomach had tightened. I laid him on the bed beside me and I showed Emilio how much I loved him. Knowing I was at fault, I apologised for asking for too much of him, for being the cause of his anger, and he forgave me.

Mama was too busy in the kitchen. She had filled *Casa Cecelia* with the laughter of those who came to taste her food, too much to notice her daughter's hidden bruises. Tourists had discovered our island, and in the hot summer evenings they would sit at the square tables. They ate chicken and rice and ordered bowls of fish soup, and they filled our small village with voices loud, and Mama did not hear my heart breaking, or see my silent tears.

Papa had become a hermit. He spent most of his days in his office, the telephone ringing with an urgency it had not had before. He burned papers in a small metal bin and looked over his shoulder when he walked up the hill to *Casa Cecelia*.

It was only my sister who noticed the change in me, and when I could bear Emilio's anger no longer I sought comfort in her arms. Marissa stroked my hair, as she did when we were young, kissed my forehead and gave me the strength to welcome my husband like a wife should. She bided her time, understanding the nature of a man who can turn his back on the sea so easily.

Emilio only returned home when the weather was good, the sun shone and the sea was smooth. As a good wife I welcomed him back without question. He carried gifts, pasta for Mama – only made on the mainland; whisky for Papa – more expensive than a wooden crib – who gratefully accepted it, allowing the fiery liquid to numb more than his throat. To me he presented the largest roundest tomato I had ever seen. The skin was dark red, the colour of lips when they had passion in them, and I knew that the poor soil of this island could not grow such fruit.

'They call them love apples over the sea,' he said to me, and I wondered why he travelled to the mainland to bring me love. It was known that women who lived beyond our sea were different; they did not have the same respect for another woman's husband. I held Julio to my breast and promised him he would not grow to be like his father.

Isa

Cecelia hands me a tomato, then offers the same gift to Chloe. I feel the smooth skin, cool against my fingers, and embrace it – a cocktail of orange and red, tough enough to guard the soft flesh from damage; I hold it like a disappointed woman with a skin so thick it keeps a heart from breaking.

'What do you want us to do with them?'

'Gift of Isis,' Cecelia smiles, 'the fruit has a protecting shell. You will learn to release the softness, full of flavour. First it is necessary to break the skin with heat.'

Cecelia lifts a pan of boiling water from the stove and plunges in the tomatoes. Chloe copies her and drops hers straight in. I rub the cool skin against my cheek and I don't want to let it go. Cecelia swiftly scoops out the scalded contents with a large slotted spoon, and places them on the table. They are wrinkled and look old before their time; the skins have lost their vibrancy. I keep my untouched apple of love close and youthful.

'See how the flesh is revealed, a secret love hidden behind a tough exterior, waiting to be released. It is the love of a mother for a son, or a girl for a boy, laying her heart bare, when love first strikes.'

The skins start to split, leaving red open sores, and Cecelia quickly scoops them out of the pan. With practiced hands she pulls away the skin, leaving the flesh raw and naked lying on the table. I see Chloe, who is totally absorbed by the whole process, grab a handful of the peeled tomatoes; she squeezes her fingers and the juice drips through her hand and fills the waiting bowl.

'Wow, Isa! Hey, look at all of this.'

She holds up her hands, showing off as usual.

'Well hey, look at you.' She ignores the cut in my voice, all it does is slice my tongue, but I can't stop myself. 'You never did make much of an effort in the kitchen.'

Same as always, Chloe has to be centre of attention. This is *my* holiday. She forgets it was *me* who invited *her,* felt sorry for her. She was the one who was so upset about the split with Paul. Now she's spoiling it, showing off, showing off to Cecelia, pretending to be a goddess in the kitchen. Well, it's just not fair. I won't give in this time, sit back and let her wash all over me – no, it's time that Isadora, Gift of Isis, stood up and came out of the shadows.

'Here, give some to me,' and I grab a handful of the soft, squishy flesh.

Between us we scald, peel and pummel the huge mountain of tomatoes, abandoning the skins as if they were autumn leaves scattered by the wind. Our hands drip with juice and the slippery insides slither through our fingers as we squash, mash and crush them into the large white bowl.

Chloe took it hard when Dad left. The love of her world deserted her that evening. Her four-year-old heart never had a chance to mend; the first of so many breaks. I felt guilty, and resentment at being torn in two. I had to choose between my sister and our mother. I desperately wanted Mum to love me. I needed approval that, as the eldest child, I was important. And Mum won, she always won. What could I do? I felt sorry for Chloe, but I basked in the love Mum showered on me, and Chloe was a tough kid. Well, that's what I told myself.

'Isa, did you ever wonder where Dad ended up?'

Juice oozes from my fingers, dripping into the bowl like tears. Why is Chloe asking about him now?

'Not really,' I lied. 'Mum said he ran off to punish her. She didn't speak about him after. Isn't it all too late for that now?'

Chloe starts to colour, her face becoming a red as the tomato she holds in her hand. She could never hide from me, her face burning with untold truth. She stood, head held to one side, cheeks as if they'd been brushed with rouge.

'I went to see him.'

'How? When? We didn't know where he was, so how could you visit him?'

'Mum told me where to find him.'

Now I know she's lying.

'Really...'

'Yes, really. It was when you started seeing Simon, you were all loved up. Mum was having one of her better days, and seeing as you'd abandoned her – and for a man, even if it was slimy Simon which by the way she thought was the worst sin you'd ever committed...'

'What happened?'

'She knew where he was all along. He lived really close, only three streets away. All that time, and only just around the corner.' Chloe hesitates and looks at me, her dark brown eyes soft and open, and I know she is telling the truth. 'Anyway he wasn't too pleased to see me, hustled me inside before the neighbours could get a good look. Nice house, nice wife and two very nice boys.'

I drop my hands, feel the unbroken tomato in my pocket, and my fingers tighten. *Brothers, we have two brothers.*

'He even had the gall to ask why I never replied to his letters. Asked about you, if you were okay. Then he showed me the door.'

Chloe's fingers clench and the tomato gives way under her grasp, juice slides through and drips onto the floor, another heart broken.

'When was this?'

'On my eighteenth birthday. I wanted to know the truth, and now I do. He's a liar, just like Mum always said.'

I want to tell her about the box in the wardrobe, but what good would it do now? It was thirty years too late.

'You know, Mum didn't always see things straight.'

'I know that, Isa. But I saw with my own eyes, he was embarrassed to see me. And you know we never got any letters, birthday cards, he couldn't even do that. I went to see him because...'

She hugs herself, and tomato stains spread over her white T-shirt.

'Because it was my fault he left.' The words tumble from her lips like water over a precipice. 'I was his little angel and I loved him. It was him who tucked me into bed, took me to the park, everything. I don't remember Mum doing any of that. And I'd given him every piece of my heart, so it was my fault – I took him away from her.'

I can see her face peering through the bannisters looking at him with misery, disbelief, and something else – hope. Hope that one day he'd come back.

'It wasn't your fault, Chloe.' I reach out and touch her arm. 'Mum had problems. *Post natal depression* they call it today; back then it was just *nerves*. She had mood swings – one moment all over us, the next shutting herself away, finding comfort in a bottle of vodka. That's why Dad did everything for you. If it was anyone's fault, it was mine.'

I could have done more, should have been a big sister. I was only ten. I'd had six years of them both to myself, Mum and Dad and me, perfect in our love. Chloe's birth changed all that.

'But that still doesn't explain what Dad did.'

'I suppose some men... some men hang on, hoping things will improve. Our father wasn't one of those; he was as weak as she was. He told me I was a big girl and to look after you, on the day he left.'

'And you did, Isa,' Chloe unfolds her arms and I wrap her up in the hug she craves. 'You tried to look after me – I just didn't want you to.'

I smell her hair, just as I did when I finished bathing her and dressed her in her pyjamas, and ignored her when she asked where Daddy had gone.

I have to tell her.

'He did write.'

'You're only saying that. He didn't love any of us; just himself.'

I tell her about the day after Mum died. The house had taken on a silence which hurt my ears. I had to create noise. Clean the house; take apart the life I'd lived. I'd started with her room, stripped the bed, cried over the dent in the pillow which she wouldn't ever fill again. Packed her clothes into large plastic bin bags: charity shop, recycling skip. Kept a few things for me. It was then I found the case.

I told her of the birthday and Christmas cards.

'Were there any presents?'

There hadn't been; maybe once, but not in that small

battered brown case. Chloe asked if I still had them. What could I say? Tell her I'd burned every last one, the pain of loss clouding my eyes, the anger that even in death she had kept him from us?

I simply told her they were lost when we cleared the house. Easier for both of us.

'Thanks, Isa.'

'For what?'

'For telling me he did love us. And I think Mum did too, wanted to protect us. If she'd only have said... but now it's too late to tell her.'

The deep knot just above my heart began to loosen.

'You said it was your eighteenth birthday when you went to see him. Wasn't that when you...?'

'Left home, yes. You and Mum seemed fine together, so it was my time to go.'

'And you didn't give *me* a second thought did you?'

Chloe stiffens. Well, she should know! Maybe *I* wanted to leave, take off, travel, see what it feels like to be wined, dined and made love to. She had all of that and what did I get? A fumble with Simon in the back of his Ford Escort, losing my virginity on the fake leather seats, and rushing home to find Mum in one of her moods, dark and menacing. Simon was patient, and I thought he loved me.

'No, Isa. I didn't, and I'm sorry about that.' She leans over and her lips brush my cheek. 'We... I suppose I always thought you'd be fine.'

'We can't change what has happened, as much as we want to,' and I hand her another tomato.

Together we pummel the soft flesh until the bowl is full of it. Occasionally our hands collide. The resentment and hurt is squashed with each round red fruit, and a calm love surrounds us.

'Its good fun, isn't it?' I eventually say to Chloe, her arms up to her elbows covered in tomato juice.

'You bet. No wonder all those people go crazy at the festival of *La Tomatina*. I would really love to do that, fling tomatoes at everyone in a scarlet orgy! All that lovely juice.'

Chloe licks her fingers, then wipes her hands down her very white, very expensive linen trousers. The red stains make them look like she's been involved in a chainsaw film

– not that I've seen one, mind you, I was more an *Upstairs Downstairs* sort of person – but she doesn't seem to mind.

Then it comes to me. I know what I have to do.

'Hey Chloe, you go and get cleaned up. I'll follow you.'

The curtain whispers and I sneak out, pushing the beads to one side so Chloe and Cecelia cannot hear. Good – at least there's a signal.

'Chloe?'

'No, it's me – Isadora.'

Chloe's mobile phone warms my ear and I don't know if it is the radio waves burning out my brain or the conversation I am having with my sister's ex-boyfriend.

It doesn't take long, and I push the mobile back deep in my pocket just in time. The curtain announces Chloe's arrival with a fanfare of beads.

'Isadora, where are you?'

'Over here, just getting some fresh air.'

'Come on you, Cecelia's ready for the next ingredient. It's chilli.'

We walk back, past the bougainvillea, the guilty secret pushed deep into my pocket. At the edge of the terrace, on a cracked tile, is a flower. The petals, creamy white touched with pink, are so delicate that when I pick it up it feels as if it would disappear in my hand like a sigh. Carefully wrapped around the delicate stem is a small scrap of paper.

To the sister with the eyes of summer sky. It would honour me to walk with you. When the midday sun is high I will be here, where this flower greets you. Fredriko.

'What have you got there, Isa?'

'That man, the one we met earlier, Fredriko. He wants me to meet him.' In my hand the scent of the flower, a mix of summer sun and dark velvet night, twists around me.

'You mean *my* Fred? Come to think of it, he did say his name was Fredriko.'

'Well at least one of us has pulled.'

Chloe snatches the note out of my hand and examines it, then she shrugs and I'm sure I see a flash of jealousy cross her eyes.

'Don't be stupid. Women of forty-six don't pull, we make friendships.'

'Looks like it to me,' grunts my sister, as if she is disappointed that it's me who was given the flower.

In silence we go inside. It's good to get out of the heat and I place the flower on the table next to the beaded curtain. Cecelia, hot from the kitchen, joins us. In her hand she carries tomatoes, sitting like jewels on her palm.

'These will add freshness to our lunch.' She stops and looks at the flower and her face loses the smile, like a summer squall crossing the sea. 'That is a beautiful flower, Gift of Isis, but it is from a plant not from this island. Blooms such as this only grow on the mainland, by people who fill their bellies with pasta and thick sauces. I have only seen one of these once before, given to me in apology by a man who could not control his fists.'

'It's lovely, isn't it? Fredriko left it for me. He's going to call for me at midday.'

As soon as the words leave my lips it is as if I had plunged a knife into her. Cecelia's lips become thin, she looks hard and unforgiving, and the tomatoes fall from her fingers, hitting the tiles with such force they break.

'Fredriko Salvadori?'

'Yes, that's him.'

'He is from bad stock; you must not see him. I forbid this for as long as you are guests in *Casa Cecelia.*'

'But it only...'

'I have spoken. That boy is not to have a welcome in this place.' Cecelia hustles back into the kitchen, leaving the tomatoes bleeding on the floor. 'Come sisters, you have much to learn.'

Chloe follows her, but I cannot move. Cecelia has been so good and kind to us, but I feel something moving deep in my heart, a flutter I have not felt for years. I follow them into the kitchen and pull my sister to one side.

'What do you make of that?' I whisper.

'Just another of her strange ways, ignore it. Look Isa, you've paid to be here, you can do what you want.'

'I don't want to upset her.'

'Get a life, live dangerously – it's not as if you have men falling at your feet every day.'

I want to hit her, but she's right, this is probably my last chance.

6. Chilli to fan the flames

Cecelia

It is time to add heat to our soup. Chilli, left to dry over the winter, rises in temperature with each cooling day. When it has become brittle with fire, it is ready to be crushed in the spring.'

Isadora looks confused. The impatience she feels is shown in her eyes, washed with the blue of the sea when the midday sun reflects on the water. They are ready to douse any flames in her heart.

'When will we add the fish?'

'Daughter, Mario, who gave us the bones for our stock, will gather his nets and when the afternoon begins to move into the evening, he will pull his boat onto the beach. My friend will then choose the best of his catch to bring for our soup.'

'So the chilli will be the last ingredient before we add Mario's fish?'

'Yes, daughter. The morning before we serve our soup is nearly finished, and now we will rest, as our soup will rest and gather flavour. It is important to understand that the best soup must have a perfect base. Chilli is essential, and for me the most important.'

Isadora nods without understanding. She is in too much of a hurry to live the rest of her life – a mayfly emerging from years of being a nymph – she thinks that everything must be rushed, the soup must be made quickly, and love will be found in the petals of a flower.

Emilio returned from one of his many journeys beyond the mountains. He brought gifts – a wooden train in his brown case for Julio, and a disappointed look for me. When Julio had tired of the train – a toy of the mainland – his thoughts turned towards the beach, because the sea was strong in him. He asked his Papa why he didn't have a boat like Mario's, yellow and blue with the Eye of Osiris to protect it. His Papa said he had important things to do on the mainland, and I hid my face, afraid Emilio would see my disbelieving eyes.

While my beautiful son slept, with cheeks as soft as freshly baked bread, I asked Emilio what he did on the mainland and his answer was held in his quick fists.

I found Marissa, folding starched table cloths, listening to the gentle chatter of the wind blowing through the beaded curtain and the clatter of pots as Mama prepared mussels for German tourists sat on the terrace.

'Cecelia, my sister, no man should raise a hand to his wife,' she said softly and held my hand to feel my pain.

'I don't understand why he is doing it. Why would a man change so much?'

My sister ran her hands over my bruised cheek; her eyes did not need to see for her to feel the heat where his finger marks lay. She stroked my hair and placed a whisper of a kiss on my forehead.

'My eyes might not be able to see the joys of this world, but I see more than you do, my sister, blind Cecelia. You only see the good in your heart and are sightless to things which hurt it. Your name was chosen well and, like our Mama who had the same veil pulled over her eyes, you will never see Emilio for what he really is.'

Marissa had drifted on the wreckage of her own Papa's boat. She had been taken to sea in a vessel that did not have the protection of the Eye. After the storm from the east had finished blowing its fury, Poseidon had taken his fee. Her Papa – his body a sacrifice to feed the fish – paid the price for his mistake. Her Mama had clung to the wreckage, grasping at life long enough to save her daughter. Marissa became my sister the day she was washed up on our beach; the salt and sun had burned out her eyes.

My sister, who sees more than those with sight, told me

to stay and listen to the fish swim amongst the beads. She climbed the stairs to speak to Emilio.

I did not know what was said between them, but when Marissa returned to the table, she continued folding the clothes and merely said it was done – Emilio would not raise a hand in anger again.

She told me years later – when Emilio had settled on the mainland – that she had said as a son of the island he should respect our ways. She advised him that although her eyes did not see the same sky as him, her day and night were as one. Marissa had told Emilio that a man walking the dark roads alone could easily lose his way. She described the mountain paths he took when travelling north in detail.

Emilio, who was not a stupid man, agreed that the ways across the mountain were treacherous and promised to do nothing that might cause him to take the wrong path.

Isa

'Chloe, do you think I'd better call it off?'

'Call what off?'

I pull my sister to one side, not wanting Cecelia to overhear. She'd looked at the flower with... hate? No, not hate, *loathing,* as if it had been given by the devil himself.

'This meeting with Fredriko. If we were staying for longer it might be worth going. But we leave tomorrow and – well, you know...'

'You mean he'll want a quickie, then move on to the next?'

'No – yes – oh I don't know, it's been so long since I did this sort of thing.'

'If you don't go you'll never know will you?'

Cecelia intrudes into our whispering as if she can read my thoughts. She takes a large pinch of dried chilli flakes from a jar. Stuck onto the glass is a label faded by time. I can just make out a bee balancing on purple clover. The jar once filled with sweet honey now holds a million sparks of fire.

'Here, Gift of Isis, take these flakes and feel the heat awaken your mouth.'

A small pinch is placed into the palm of my hand; dry and dark the skin, thin and delicate as a dried flower. Scattered amongst the delicate wisps of chilli pod are the fiery seeds, red, orange and yellow dots, so light a breath would blow them away.

I lick my finger, dip it into my hand just enough to capture the pieces of dried chilli, and put them into my mouth. The heat, gentle at first, starts to warm my lips and then my mouth begins to feel it is dancing – a stamping flamenco, passionate, swinging crimson skirts of fire on my tongue.

'Sugar water will douse the fire of the chilli,' says Cecelia. She hands me a tall glass, then she takes another pinch from the jar and drops it onto Chloe's hand.

My mouth begins to calm. The fire from my mouth smoulders, cooled with a swallow of the cold sugar-water. I wonder: if this fire had been there when Simon left, I would have fought harder. I wouldn't have stood back and let him do what he did. Anger rises inside, and after all these years the hurt is as raw and painful as a chilli on my tongue.

I should have told him he was a lying cheating bastard, said I was worth more than a weekly fumble in the back of his car, but I didn't. Simon had been my first, and ended up being the last. There was no way I was going to let anyone do that to me again. I gave myself in the back of his battered car. The sort of thing a girl of seventeen would do, not me, at the grand old age of twenty – too long a virgin. I stuck to the fake leather seats in the heat of the summer while he puffed and panted. I didn't know any better, didn't expect any better.

I told myself Simon didn't do flowers and chocolates (not that I didn't hope for a hint of Milk Tray man). He was kind enough, but it became all too predictable. I had to sneak out, even at my age, so Mum didn't know; it was always best to keep her calm because it was me she'd take it out on, not Chloe. He'd take me to the cinema, we'd see one of the many disaster films pulling in the crowds, yet I could not see the disaster sitting next to me. I wanted *Love Story* and "love is never having to say you're sorry". Afterwards he'd treat me to a steak and black forest gateaux in a Berni Inn, followed by the inevitable. Simon would fumble to fit the condom – filling the car with the smell of rubber – and I would be banging my head against a window running with condensation.

The first night Simon didn't call, I didn't think anything of it. After silence for two weeks I plucked up the courage to go and see him. I should have said he always insisted on calling me from a phone box – told me he didn't have a telephone; those were the days before mobile phones. I found his car, British Racing Green with Go Faster stripes down the side, parked in our lay-by, next to an old sofa and bin bags with their contents spewing out. It was what the old folks called Lovers Lane, in innocent holding-hands times, and the youngsters now called Condom Ally. I couldn't see in, the windows were dripping with a grey condensation, hot bodies and fast breathing, and I knew I was not the only one he brought to this place and mine wasn't the only bum to stick to the vinyl seats.

I didn't give up on men, not totally. There were plenty at the local council offices where I worked, checking parking fines, but none who gave me a second look. I took up going to evening classes: French, Italian, pottery. I learned quickly, rebuffed advances and offers to walk me home, knowing that they were either married, divorced or very very strange. I settled into my life of being single, always hoping of course. Mum became more and more dependent and I put all thoughts of moving out to the back of my mind – drying up like the flakes in that jar.

I take another gulp of sugar-water. Sod it. I'm going to meet this Fredriko, I take another pinch of dried flakes straight from the jar and pop them into my mouth. They hit my tongue and I feel my body spring into life.

Cecelia

Emilio came home less and less. On one of his visits he saw how straight and strong his son had grown, tall like the wheat growing in the fields. He kept his fists hidden from the eyes of Marissa, who always greeted him with the sisterly kiss of my protector. On Julio's eighth birthday, my son was so excited at being nearly a man he begged his

Papa to show him how to cast nets, and his father promised to take him out on his boat.

I had already planned the celebration for the anniversary of his birth: pork and clams, and it angered that my son preferred to be with a father who was only ever present in name. In my silent rage I ignored the wind from the east, and how the Cyprus trees bowed. Hurt boiled inside me when I remembered the love I had for Emilio and how he had thrown it away, and it blinded me from seeing anything else.

'I'll take the boy fishing, it will be good for him,' Emilio announced, as if it was something a father and son did every day.

I watched as he pulled his boat, faded by the sun with the Eye merely a memory in the peeled paint, and he took Julio out onto the flat grey sea. Emilio had forgotten how the sea lies quiet and still when it listens to the distant storm. Mario called to his old friend to take care and told him it was not a day for catching fish. But my husband had become arrogant by travelling to the mainland. With Julio waving his joy and excitement at becoming a son of the sea, Emilio pulled at the oars and headed into the wind whispering from the east.

It was too late when I heard the waves crash against the rocks, shark-tooth sharp, where Marissa's father's boat had been wrecked. Time, being unkind, had passed quickly. I ran to the beach. Mario, who had felt the sea move, was standing at the shore. I shouted into the salt-soaked wind until my voice refused to call Julio's name any longer. Mario held on to me, and I allowed him to comfort me.

The storm – as fickle summer storms do – soon blew itself out. I looked at the calm sea as far as eyes can travel towards the empty horizon. It was not long before Mario spotted Emilio's boat. He recognised the shape – it is well known all hand-built boats are as different as the eyes of a new born baby – and I thanked the Virgin for bringing my boy home safely.

I called out; my voice trickled over the waves, and as the boat sailed closer I could hear no answering greeting. I waved my shawl, hoping Julio would wave back, remembering the soft wool I had once wrapped around his warm body, singing him to sleep, but it flapped in the wind unanswered. Gradually the boat with paint peeling – a remembrance of colours, yellow and blue – came nearer, the Eye of Osiris a shadow on the bow. I could see one of the oars broken, and Emilio hunched over.

Emilio, pulling at the one good oar, shaded his eyes from the glare of the sun, and looked at the fear in my face. Mario held me close. He wrapped his arms around me tighter than Emilio had ever held me; whispering in a voice low and soft, he tried to calm me.

'You should let me help him pull it up the beach,' his breath warming my ear as he guided me away from the sand.

I pulled away. It was how it used to be. For a moment I imagined that Emilio was the fisherman I had longed to marry, who would teach his son the secrets of the sea. Mario tried to shield my eyes, but I had already seen the small limp shape lying motionless in the back of the boat. Mario helped Emilio pull up the boat – a casket carrying Julio's body to my waiting arms. It was Mario who lifted him out of the boat and carried him in his dark Phoenician arms up the hill to where my Mama stood to welcome her grandson.

'It was the storm, it came from nowhere,' Emilio said.

I refused to listen in the heat of my anger and the slow awaking of my grief. I struck his chest with my fists so hard he staggered back.

I hit him again and again, bruised his arms, clawed at his face and pulled his hair, anything but to feel the pain of my heart splitting apart. I didn't want to hear his excuses of how the wave, higher than a house, lifted the boat and they were both flung into the arms of Poseidon. I refused to listen to how he had held onto Julio while the god's white horses reared and struck him with their hooves. I ignored his grief, and how he mourned for his son.

After Julio was laid to rest – under the watchful gaze of Hecate – and joined generations of sons of the sea who had also been trapped in Poseidon's nets, I closed myself to the world and Mama fed me fish soup. Emilio had been swallowed up by his own grief and left our island. I didn't notice his absence, and slowly the soup began to work its magic and I returned to my Mama, who welcomed me to her kitchen.

Many years later I heard from those who had travelled beyond our sea that Emilio had found another woman. They spoke of a woman who ate pasta and did not know how to cook fish. And I became a widow of the sea.

Chloe

Bloody hell, that's hot!

'Daughter of the green shoots, you should be careful and only take the smallest amount into your mouth.'

'You could have warned me... it's like my mouth's on fire!'

What's she doing, trying to test me to see if I'd listened? How was I to know she was expecting me to try just a couple of flakes? It's so damn difficult to keep up with her; she keeps going off at a tangent – where's that jug?

'Isa, give me that water, quickly!'

The inside of my head is exploding with fireworks and my tongue has lost all feeling. Isa shoves the jug of sugar-water at me and I down three glasses before I can talk properly. Water – I've never had so much of the neat stuff before, always saved it for diluting Paul's twenty-five-year-old Irish malt. None has passed my lips since we split up, the taste reminds me too much of him.

'You won't do that again in a hurry.'

I stick my still-burning tongue out at Isa. That just about sums us up. One takes just the right amount of chilli and spends her life lukewarm, and for me it's fireworks or nothing. I can't remember – well actually I can if I really want to – all those spectacular displays lighting up the sky; although of course there was the occasional damp squib to bring me back down to earth, a burnt-out rocket found in the garden.

After I had been to see Dad, that was it for me; no point waiting for Mr Right, they never come along when you need them. My first conquest set the pattern and it had been so easy, all it needed was a pair of skin-tight jeans, a T-shirt, and no bra. It wasn't that he was anything special. I really *wanted* to see if I could take any man, just like that! Call it revenge, but I don't think it was; more complicated than that – retribution for Dad leaving me.

It was uncomfortable in the back of his old rust-bucket of a car, and as I said, he wasn't anything special. Trouble was, *he* thought *I* was, and dumped my sister unceremoniously. He seemed quite hurt when I told him there was no way I was going to spend my weekends on my back, sticking to his seats and bashing my head against the steamy window, all for a steak and a glass of Liebfraumilch. And for that brief moment when he hurt more than I did, the pain dulled. I soon found bigger and fatter fish to net.

'More water?'

The fire in my mouth works its way up to my nose, setting the internal sprinkler system off, and it takes more than one wipe with the back of my hand to staunch the flow.

'Those are some hot chillies, Cecelia!'

She stops and smiles at my discomfort, and sprinkles a generous pinch of flakes into the pan.

'Daughters, you now know what too much heat does. It is the skilful cook who can add enough to give the soup a bite, to awaken the tongue, and it is the careless woman who adds more than is necessary. Not only will it kill the flavour of the fish, but it will awaken the devil inside.'

After I dumped Simon I moved steadily onwards and upwards. Sure, there were the frogs, usually married, trying to spice up their dull little lives. There were the few sharks lying beneath the surface; the wife who walked in on me going down on her husband – the stupid fool, he thought she was doing aerobics every Thursday – only her weekly aerobic session was in the back of the local plumber's van. He wasn't to know on that particular evening the plumber had been out to a burst pipe, and I've never seen a man deflate so quickly.

I thought I'd found the right one with Adam. He was such a sweetie, shorter than me, but made up for it in so many other ways. We moved in together and had a great time travelling the world with his television production company. There were times, of course, when he travelled alone, and for once I didn't even see the signs. He was always thoughtful, calling me with promises: *missing you babe,* and *I'll make it up to you next time.* It was only after

– and men are so damn stupid – he left his mobile phone bill lying around. It didn't take long to check, he'd made hundreds of calls to France and the States, more than he'd ever made to me. The woman living in Paris, her ridiculously heavy accent, told me all about her "darlink Adem". Then there was the very camp guy living near Venice Beach who was "so ever so NEVER going to trust his precious Adam, never so ever again."

It had been a narrow escape. I did make sure it was the end of his travelling road; all it took was one email – sent from his computer – and copied to his homophobic boss. His frequent flyer rewards were soon cut off. I did feel as if I'd been cut inside – a small twist of the knife. I could see every time I hurt someone it came back on me twice as hard.

They were all pieces of chilli cooled by sugar-water, no fireworks with any of them. I thought fireworks were for the Fourth of July. It was only when I met Paul that the pyrotechnics really started.

I down another glass of sugar-water and my mouth begins to regain some feeling..

'To harness the fire you must grow only the finest chillies,' Cecelia continues. 'See the pots on the terrace? Each year I plant some of the seeds saved from last year. Daughter, Chloe of the green shoots, can you see how the flowers have begun to lose their strength, and just behind each tired white bloom is the beginning of this year's crop?'

'Yes.' I see small shiny pods hanging on the plant. 'You wouldn't think anything so tiny could hide such a punch.'

'It takes time, daughter.' It warms me like the chilli flakes when she calls me daughter, and I begin to listen to her, really listen, not just looking interested for the sake of my sister. 'The sun will introduce heat as the plant grows and, like Icarus, they will keep reaching skyward until they fall to earth. The fruit changes from deep cool green; heat fills it, changing it to orange, then finally bursting into a flaming red. Then it is ready to be dried, bringing warmth to dark winter days.'

Paul, oh my dear Paul, where are you when I need you? You'd love all of this, each ingredient telling its own special story. Oh, I understand it will be down to me to make the fish soup taste as good as I can. But if you were here, maybe we could to do something with this. I had thought when I gave my offering to the goddess that things would change, that I would change, but it's just not working.

I remember the first time I met Paul. *Calgary*. How could I forget? Olli was the man of the moment, with his floppy fringe and a yacht in Antibes. He'd decided we should spend the winter skiing. He was good fun, nothing too serious. I had learned my lesson with Adam, but Olli had more money than sense, and a father who didn't care but who footed the bill.

Skis and me did not really make the best of companions. On my second run I turned too sharply and went over on my ankle. So there I was, foot strapped up, sitting in the bar nursing an ankle the size of the bloody mountain I fell down, when:

'Poor old you, what have you been up to?'

I was in no mood for sympathy and it took a few seconds to notice who had been speaking. Shorter than I'd expected from his deep voice, he ran his fingers through his hair, a mix of sun-bleached strawberry blond and schoolboy ginger, I never did take to ginger-haired men, but it suited him. His face, scattered with freckles, would have immediately turned me off, but I didn't notice the ginger or the freckles – only a pair of green eyes, flecked with gold, and a voice that tumbled with laughter.

'What the hell does it look like?' I was not going to be seduced that easily. 'Icepack, support bandage, an ankle so fat it's got dimples, might be a bit of a clue!'

He threw back his head and laughed, then looked at me and his eyes were fringed by the darkest longest lashes I had ever seen on a man. He looked fun, more fun than I was having at that moment, so I patted the seat next to me... and that was the start of me and Paul.

'Paul Wilkins.' He held out his hand. 'Another gin?'

The next hour passed quicker than any downhill run, we talked and talked. Not the trivial stuff Olli and his mates spent hours discussing – who's got the latest spinnaker, and the best way to wax a snowboard. Paul was genuinely interested in what I had to say. I told him about how I was getting bored of travelling, living out of suitcases. I even told him about Isa, back at home with Mum, and he said she sounded like a great sort of sister to have around, which took me back because I'd never thought of her as a great sister.

'And what about you?' I asked, wondering who this bloke was who didn't seem have the slightest interest in skiing.

'Not much to me, I'm afraid,' he shrugged. 'Came here with my sister – she's a bit of a tyrant, determined to see me hitched before I hit forty. I've been introduced to most of her single friends, most pleasant enough, but the horse-faced female she brought here with her is frightening.' He pulled a face and whinnied, and bounced up and down as if astride some huge steed.

'Mind the bloody leg,' I protested, as shooting pains shot through my ankle.

'Sorry – here, let me kiss it better,' and before I knew it Paul leaned over and covered my mouth with his, and all the pain in my foot was soon forgotten. I sank into his arms and felt for once that my lips *belonged* to someone. I didn't want it to stop, which was a first. I know it's a bit of a cliché, but he took my breath away; and it wasn't just that neither of us wanted to stop. It was more that I felt totally comfortable with him, and for a long time I was not looking over my shoulder for the next conquest.

'Look Chloe,' he'd said when we finally came up to breathe. 'I don't want to be here and it doesn't appear that you're having such a great time either. How about you and me catch the next flight out and go somewhere nice and hot?'

And that's how it started. Me and Paul lighting the blue touch paper, leaving Olli and the horse-faced woman to the ice and snow while we headed for the heat.

Cecelia

The sisters are beginning to blend, to hear each other's voices and listen to the story the soup tells them.

'We have now reached the time when morning moves into the afternoon. The base of the soup is ready, and as all good cooks, you must taste it.'

Chloe, of the green shoots, and Isadora, Gift of Isis, each dip a spoon into the pan, and together the sisters taste the soup. The older sister, always guarded with her emotions, sips the deep red liquid from the end of her spoon and Chloe, a woman who plunges into life without thinking, tips back her head and swallows the soup too quickly.

'Mmmm, that's really good.'

'And what is it you taste, Isadora Gift of Isis?'

She thinks, and licks her lips. 'The tomato, onions and garlic... I can taste them, but at the same time they all blend into one with a hint of the olive oil, and then...' and she takes another sip. 'There is something else just underneath the surface, warmth, would that be the chilli?'

'Life, there is *life* in it,' interrupts Chloe.

She is right. Chilli adds more to the soup than heat, it brings it to life. There must be a balance, it is like walking a tightrope: a heavy hand, and the soup burns the tongue; too light, and it has no flavour. Fish soup must have a base subtle enough for the harvest of the sea to be tasted, but there must be just the right amount to awaken the senses.

'Yes daughters, our base is ready. And now we have introduced life into our simple ingredients, we must rest. The heat of the day is when we must be take time to get ready for the afternoon. Our soup will then welcome us back. You will remember the taste, and you will never take fish soup for granted.'

7. Isis and Osiris

Isa

'Well? How do I look?'

I have to ask; the insecurity inside makes me question everything. Chloe puts her head to one side. She'll lie to me, tell me I look fine. Her head moves from its secretive side to the other and she looks at me hard. I feel like I'm being assessed, standing before one of those awful television fashion gurus; standing, everything exposed, in the moment before the poor victim is told – ever so kindly – that style has passed them by.

She obviously doesn't think much of my choice. I love the skirt; creamy white layers scattered with rose buds and finished off with a row of *broderie anglaise* along the hem.

'Mmm,' she grunts. 'Too much milkmaid-chic for my taste.'

'What, then?'

Chloe mutters something about silk purses and sows' ears and dives into the luminous Armageddon-proof case. The vacuum-packed colour-coordinated wardrobe she insisted on bringing is carefully placed on the bed, until finally she pulls out a selection of carefully folded sarongs.

'Nope, too small,' my sister comments on each one, holding them up to the light. A ritual dressing, and I feel like a sacrificial lamb. 'Definitely not!... This one is far too expensive...' Silk rainbows float onto the bed. 'God forbid... Hah! Here it is.'

Chloe holds up a gossamer-thin piece of silk, sugary pink and sparkling with sequins around the edge. Surely she can't expect me to wear it? There's no substance, nothing to hold to, far too insubstantial for me!

'You did bring your cozzi, didn't you?'

I reach into my own battered case – I didn't have time to go and buy a new one, and anyway, once the contents had been burned it was after all only another suitcase – and pull out my own sensible swimming costume with cross-over straps. It looks dull next to Chloe's carefully folded all-in-ones, two-pieces and minute bikinis, each with their own matching wrap. I hold mine, safely black to hide the lumps and bumps, with sewn-in support keeping my boobs from going freestyle, behind my back.

'It'll have to do,' Chloe concedes, pulling out a bright costume. She holds it against her, checking in the mirror as if wanting to ask it, *Who is the fairest of them all?* 'None of mine will fit you anyway,' she says, checking the mirror one last time, then: 'Right Isa, now to get you ready for your hot date.'

'It's not a hot...'

'Of course not,' Chloe laughs. 'Now, on with that,' and she points a finger at the costume dangling from my fingers – as if it was something unpleasant that had washed up on the beach.

The fitting of the sarong is such a palaver. First Chloe drapes it across my front, adjusting it so my cleavage isn't hidden; she twists the ends, pulls them behind my head and knots it, and I feel like a trussed-up birthday present.

'And to finish...' Chloe pulls out a matching cerise straw hat and plonks it on my head. She stands back, looking me up and down, as if I'm a work in progress, but eventually she appears satisfied. 'Best I can do. Right, off you go and see if you can land yourself Mr Right.'

Fredriko waits, back pressed to a white wall facing *Casa Cecelia*, a moth hiding from the light. My fingers rattle the beads.

'Gift of Isis,' Cecelia calls from the kitchen as the sound of the fish swims to her ears. I must leave, pretend I haven't heard and hurry to get to Fredriko before he decides to fly away. *And I wish she'd stop calling me Gift of Isis instead of using my name!*

'Isadora,' she calls again, and this time I have to answer.

'Yes, Cecelia?'

Cecelia leaves the kitchen, her face red with heat. She takes my hand and leads me to a table next to the beaded curtain. She glances towards where Fredriko stands; the shadow he hides under crawls over the terrazzo and falls across her face.

'Take your time daughter, there is no need to rush.' She nods to where Fredriko nervously shuffles his feet and he glances up, looking more uncomfortable than a grown man should. 'You must be wary of such men, strangers to this island. He has the soil of the mainland running through his veins.'

I feel her hand grip mine and sense she wants to say more. I see Fredriko getting impatient and I must catch him before he flies.

'I will, don't worry Cecelia. I am old enough take care of myself.'

She averts her eyes and presses her lips together until they are as thin as ribbons tied around her face. I know she doesn't believe me. She takes one last long look across the street, sighs and makes the sign of the cross.

'I ask you not to meet with him, but...' Cecelia's face softens and her smile brings kindness to her face. 'I see you are in the time of the heart, it is a time when the ears cannot hear and eyes cannot see. It was the same with me once, before my love grew cold. My Gift of Isis, you will only listen to your heart telling you of what could be; your eyes will not look into the future to see the truth of today.'

I don't understand; I know she is warning me, but of what? I fidget with the sarong, trying to cover up the large amount of flesh still on view.

'Thanks Cecelia. I know you want me to take care.' I look over to Fredriko and my heart jumps to my mouth. 'Why don't you like him?'

She takes my hand and presses it against her chest. 'This poor heart was broken many years ago and you, Isadora, have a heart which is as delicate as mine once was.' She gives my palm a kiss and returns to the kitchen and the fish whispers my departure, swimming on its sea of beads.

If I could fly I would, but instead I try my hardest to walk as elegantly in the sarong as possible. I pass an old woman feeling her way down the cobbles and nod in her direction. She carries on counting the doors until she climbs the few steps up to *Casa Cecelia*, without giving me a second glance. Curiosity whispers at me to turn and see who she is, but Fredriko peels himself from the white-painted wall and my eyes become transfixed as he strides up to me.

'You accepted my gift,' he smiles.

'Yes, it is beautiful.' I'm unsure if I should say more.

He holds out his hand and I see his dark skin flushing a shade deeper. From behind his back he produces a flower, the same delicate shade as the one he left on the terrazzo.

'Here is another, for you to keep next to your heart.'

'It's lovely. Where do you find them? Cecelia said they don't grow on this island.'

He laughs, a solid laugh which makes me feel I could grow to love this man, feel safe with him. 'When I arrived, adrift as strangers often are, I wanted to remember where I was born. Every evening my Papa would pluck such a flower from the garden and present it to Mama before she filled our plates with pasta. Before I left the mainland I dug up one of the plants from Mama's garden, placed it here in a different soil. It grew and I can hold Mama and Papa close.'

Fredriko places the stem behind my ear and arranges the soft petals, I feel his breath warm against my face and his fingers tickle my cheek as he gently draws them away and stands back.

'Yes,' he whispers. 'It is perfect, delicate like your skin, like this cheek.'

His finger touches my face, hot with midday heat and his closeness. He takes hold of my arm; my skin tingles with his touch and together we walk towards the sea.

At first, after the flower conversation, we don't seem to have anything to say to each other and the silence between us is thicker than a wall. The cobbles merge into the hard concrete of the slipway and my steps sound far too loud. I feel grateful that Chloe didn't notice I'd kept on my old comfortable brown sandals, or she would have insisted I wear something glamorously painful. I was having enough trouble keeping the sarong from slipping.

We step onto the beach and the sand muffles our feet. I hear the sea stroking the shore, whispering against the sand, the call of a lazy gull circling overhead before dipping across the waves. Then the silence is complete.

'Over there is my boat.' His voice sweeps away the stillness between us.

'You have a boat? I thought you said you were from the mainland?'

'Ah, it's a long story.'

'I've at least three hours to kill. I'd love to hear how you came here.' I hide my face, flushing red like I was on my very first date. It's been a while, I admit, I'm a bit rusty and out of practice, but I really do want to spend as much time as I can with this man, the one who chose me instead of my sister.

The sand is gloriously golden, the colour a palate lighter than the line of rocks hunched around the bay. Fine grains pour into my sandals – like in an egg timer – scratching my feet. I reach down, undo the straps, kick them off and feel delicious ripples of warm sand between my toes.

'Come. Sit with me.' Fredriko falls onto the sand, like an angel tumbling from heaven.

Small talk comes easy to some. It's easy for my sister, never stuck for something to say, but not for me. Everything I want to say catches in my throat. My mind races with all the words I have held onto for so many years, but somewhere between my head and my tongue they get lost, as if there is a wall of stone holding it all back. Unable to think of anything, I lie down on the sand next to Fredriko and listen to the waves holding their own conversation with the sand, and feel his body quiet in its insistence, waiting to speak to mine.

'Your sister calls you Isa, can I also call you by that name? I do like Isadora, but Isa suits you better, it is less harsh.'

The silence is broken, and my tongue loosens. 'Yes.' And the years of being unable to say what I want to disappear, as easily as sand trickling through my fingers.

I bury my hand into the warm beach and feel down to

the cool sand where the midday sun has been unable to reach. The sand begins to shift and I feel his fingers touch mine. Fredriko turns and fixes me with his dark brown eyes, and I sink further into his spell. I examine his face, absolutely every detail of him, trying to engrave him like a photograph inside my head: from eyes shining with dark honesty, to his crooked smile held by lips I want to taste. He twists his fingers around mine and turns to look at the horizon.

'I have grown to love the sea, this sea.' His voice washes over me like a spring tide. 'I grew up in a town as big as this island is small, and is as far from the sea as a town can be. When I was young my Papa travelled from home a great deal and I remember, as only young boys can, he would return late and bring me gifts. He would creep into my room, when he thought I was asleep, and I smelled the sea on his clothes. When he left I would dream of boats I had never seen.'

I listen to this man I've only just met telling me his story, and all the time his hand explores mine, touches every finger and traces around my hand, leaving the shape of me in the sand.

'Carry on,' I insist, and want this moment to last forever.

Fredriko smiles and moves closer, bending his head so near there is only a whisper of a breath between us. His smells sweet, of basil and mint, and his body has the freshness of the wind blowing over the waves.

'Papa stopped travelling when I was in my tenth year. The sea left him and his clothes held the perfume of pasta made from wheat grown in a soil many miles from the sea.' Fredriko stares intently beyond the horizon, as if he could see the place he once called home. 'I once asked Papa to take me to the sea, but I saw fear in his face, and although I was only a child I thought myself to be a man. I remember him holding me as if I were still an infant and told me to forget the sea.'

'So you became what? Someone who works on the land?'

I find my hand alone and my heart sinks, it buries deep into the sand, pressing the feeling out of me. Why do I always manage to do it? No matter how hard I try, always end up saying the wrong thing. I want the fine golden grains to swallow me up. The thought I have said something to upset him is too much. I hide in my misery, take myself to the place where I am most comfortable, alone.

'No!' Fredriko laughs, and gusts away my fear as he falls back onto the sand. His laughter is loud and I don't know why but I join him. Tourists splashing along the shore must think we're mad, the two of us lying on the sand drowning the sound of the wind and waves with gusts of joy.

'What?' I giggle. 'What then?'

Fredriko takes a deep breath and strokes my fingers. 'I trained as an engineer and travelled, building roads.'

'Then why are you here, if you're not a fisherman?'

'Patience, dearest Isa, I have not finished telling my story,'

'The life of an engineer, an engineer of roads, took me to many places, and in one of these I met and married Daniella.'

It was like having cold water poured over me. He is married! I had thought perhaps once, just once, I had met someone who wanted me and only me. I should have known! I feel my insides summersault. Men think that it's fine to take hold of someone's heart and play with it for a while. Chloe had the right idea, love them and leave them, no ties no hurt.

I brush the sand from my legs and stand up. 'I've got to go. Thanks for the lovely walk, perhaps we could meet again for a drink maybe?'

I can't say it. What I truly feel. The damn words just stick in my throat. I want to say, *What about your wife?* and, *Do you really think I can be taken in so easily?* Tell him to *find another single forty-something to give flowers to!*

But I can't, and start walking back towards *Casa Cecelia.*

'But Isadora, she is not –'

'She's not here to check up on you?' And it begins to spill out, the years of disappointment and resentment at not doing what *I* want to do. Cecelia was right when she told me to be careful of men like him. 'Did you really think you'd find yourself a lonely woman to pass the time with? Well let me tell you, Fredriko Salvadori, if that's your real name: you tried it on with the wrong person this time.'

I did it! I said what I had to and told him! So why don't

I feel good about it, and why is he looking confused? I suppose he thought I would go off to lick my wounds, as if I am a deer wounded by the huntsman – and not fight back.

'But you have got it all wrong,' he calls as I stride off, as elegantly as I can with the stupid sarong flapping around my legs. 'I *was* married, we divorced four years ago. Isa, please stop, I like you so very much!'

'You mean...' I stop, and the sand burns my feet and tears prick my eyes.

'Yes,' and the voice whispering in my ear holds the harmony of a sea breeze. 'I do not have anyone – or I *did not* have anyone – special in my life. That was, until I met you.'

Fredriko reaches down and takes hold of my hand and, oh so gently, kisses it. He caresses my arm and his hand moves up until with the crook of his finger he lifts my chin. The touch of his lips, filled with the sea breeze, is soft and warm. I run my tongue over his mouth and the taste of salt lingers, and all I want to do is always to be able to have the sea on my lips.

'Come – sit down, and I will tell you everything.'

I sit on the sand but cannot bring myself to sit too close, not at the moment. It would be tempting fate and I can feel the old Isadora, the safe Isadora who doesn't take risks, sit down next to me.

'As I told you, I travelled, and it was far too much for a wife to put up with. Daniella was a girl when we married, with all the hopes of a girl who had been raised in a traditional way. She wanted little from me, a husband who came home every evening and a child to hold close. I am ashamed to say I was not what she wanted. A man who travels also finds temptation in every new town. I was easily bored and too weak to resist things that excited me. I drank too much spirits and made love without any care.'

'You don't have to tell me all of this.'

'Ah Isa, but I do, because if I am to fall in love with you it must be as an honest man.'

I let him continue, and I hear the music in his voice. It is so different from the clash of cymbals and the staccato rhythm Simon played in the back of his car. Fredriko speaks softly, as if soft pipes play; the sound circles me and looks for a way through the barrier guarding my heart.

'I returned to the home of my birth when Papa became ill. It began with the small things; he forgot to polish his shoes and walked outside with his slippers on. As time began to eat into his brain, he was unable to recognise where he lived, he would accuse Mama of trying to poison him. He would lash out at her. After we had forgiven him once, the second time we knew he had to be looked after by the nuns, who care for such lost souls.'

'Oh, I'm so sorry!' I take hold of his hand. 'I know how dreadful it is to lose a parent before it's their time to go. My Mum was the same, and I cared for her until she left this world.'

'Then we both have had to be parents, you to your mother and me to Papa.'

We sit with the ghosts of what used to be, when the minds and bodies were whole, and with the unspoken knowledge that one day it might be our own fate.

'Life is so fragile,' I say and he nods.

'We have to savour every moment.'

'Your Papa, when did he pass away?'

Fredriko finds my hand again and I feel the pressure of his touch. He sighs, and his fingers are still and thoughtful.

'Papa is still alive. The nuns care for his every need and Mama, who never stopped loving him, goes to see him daily. He lives in a world of the past... and that is how I came to be here.' Fredriko searches the shore, as if he could see his father waiting across the beach, where his boat lies. 'Papa now only remembers when he was young, memories of the boat he had before he became a man and storms blew him to the mainland. He calls me Mario, and we talk as friends. He talks of how as a boy the sea called louder than the lessons the priest taught.' He hesitates, as if he hasn't spoken to anyone about it before. 'I would sit and listen to him speak of a young girl he fell in love with, and I watched my Papa weep as he remembers how he broke her heart and took her only love from her. His speech is confused, but I understood enough to hear the sea in his soul, and decided to honour his youth. And I now catch fish in the boat my Papa once did.'

Fredriko reaches for my hand. 'Come I will show you.'

8. Persephone lost in Hades

Chloe

Three hours. Hundreds of seconds to fill the space, and I've wasted so many, anything to prevent silence from intruding. I placed my garlic; all she has to do is answer – give me a sign.

I could call Paul. Maybe it's down to me, not a statue at a crossroads...

Even *Casa Cecelia* holds its breath. The hiss of water hitting fire, the clang of heavy iron pans, has stopped; the silence presses on my ears and I miss Isa. I should be used to this, being alone. There's nothing quite as lonely as lying next to a man – spent and exhausted – while he squanders the next half-hour making excuses to his wife as to why he's going to be late.

With Paul, I was never alone.

A splash of water will wash away the stickiness of the morning. Onions, tomatoes, garlic, oil, chilli, all cling to my skin and bring Isa closer. Tears, love, prayer, all washed away with lavender soap.

Forward, Chloe, no looking back.

What to wear? Definitely not the bikini. It was a mistake not to book the spray tan before we left. It'll have to be an all-in-one. Spacehopper orange? What made me buy *that?* Then there's this peppermint green, meant for the spa and sauna... No. It will have to be the aquamarine, shaped to cover only the necessary – a perfect choice.

To wear a hat, or not to wear a hat? I look at my hair and scoop it up. Mouse brown roots, the colour I had wished away along with the child I had been. Jean-Marie will have his work cut out when I get back; a morning wrapped in foil will soon get rid of the memories.

I pluck a stray hair from my eyebrow and pull out the scarf Paul bought in Goa. Pale sorbet where the wax held away the dye swirls in the raspberry silk, like scoops of ice-cream. Paul had haggled with the insistent beach seller while she pushed red, purple, green scarves under our noses. A flutter of pink, not Barbie or Mills and Boon, it held the colour of a warm evening and a distant horizon, and after several minutes Paul and the scarf seller came to an agreement.

Cecelia is talking. Her voice, indistinct, weaves through the floor. She has so much to say, keeps her whole life alive by telling it. But, like all of us, I feel she is holding too much hidden. I know parts of my life will never be talked about, living with me in corners, buried under stones like worms, slithering away to hide when the stone is kicked. Times I was so desperately unhappy I'd drive, fast, not caring, screaming where no-one could hear, and other times when I was filled with so much happiness that no words could outshine them.

Paul was both. Together we moved in harmony, we knew what each other needed and gave without even thinking about it. Until, and that's why I'm here, I caught him with Helen, in our favourite restaurant, holding her hand. The scene goes over and over in my head, a film on playback, looping round and round. *Why would he do that?* I know I couldn't give him the answer he wanted, but he didn't waste any time, did he?

He came after me. It was too late. I'd never been one for hanging round when a bloke had done the dirty on me, and I wasn't going to make an exception for Paul. Garlic at the crossroads; all I have to do is tell him.

Gold sandals with diamante straps, the finishing touch. Right, have I got it all? The look? Mirror says yes. Money? Enough. Mobile? Where is my mobile? Must be in my bag. I shake out the contents onto Isa's bed. I didn't realise how much I eat on the run; my sister will have a fit. The tight clean bedcovers are scattered with a half-eaten sandwich (dusted with penicillin), biscuit crumbs, and a very sticky and rotten mess which I think was once an apple.

Where is it? I search through my bags. The empty handbag, contents spewed out over Isa's bed; my best bag, thin straps with gold detail, vanity case, everything for the five star hotel – unused; flight bag, only essentials.

I had it when I tried to speak to Paul this morning, and I'm certain I brought it up. I pull at the bedspread, sending Isa's clothes scattering over the floor. The fabric lands hard on the floor, too hard for a gypsy skirt. It's heavy in my hand, and after a quick inspection I find it. Tucked inside, my mobile, guiltily hidden in the flounces and lace.

What did she need it for?

Ah daughter of the green shoots, you are very much the elegant lady!' Cecelia's eyes sparkle. 'Perhaps they are a little too bright for our little island?'

Thanks for the back-handed compliment. I expect she means well. She's like all who are more comfortable in the language of their mothers. The words seem right but the meaning tangles until it says something quite different.

'Sister,' Cecelia turns to an older woman sat next to her, 'this is the one I told you about. Chloe, the youngest, who has come to make Mama's fish soup.'

'Hope it wasn't all bad,' I say, and Cecelia looks confused.

'No daughter, we do not talk of bad things.'

'No, it means... it's a way of saying things,' I end lamely, and hold out my hand. 'Nice to meet you – Marissa, isn't it?'

Marissa looks through me, her eye unfocused, staring at a world only she can see.

'Oh, well... I'm off to the beach for a few hours, I'll see you later.'

'Daughter, sit for a while, indulge an old woman and her sister.' Cecelia shows me to the empty seat with a sweep of her hand. 'Share a refreshing coffee with ice.'

The beach can wait for a few minutes. I sit down and feel the breeze blowing from the sea, and for a moment the only sound is the rattle of the curtain hanging over the door. Marissa looks at me but her eyes seem to have no sparkle. Cecelia's flash with a dark olive light.

'Marissa, my sister, has eyes which clouded many years ago,' Cecelia says, noticing how I can't keep my eyes from the pale face, high cheekbones and delicate lips. She sits by the curtain, as she must have every day for years. She doesn't belong here. She's older than Cecelia but her hair is fair, with no grey to age her. It is scraped back and pulled into a knot behind her neck. Cecelia sees me staring at her sister and continues: 'When I was too small to notice such things there was a great storm. It lasted for many days and the fishermen were unable to bring in enough to feed the village. It was winter, and mothers worried how they could nourish their children; there was no fish, and soup made from leaves and the few vegetables had not substance.'

Marissa nodded. I held my breath; it was as if she was holding onto the images of the past. 'Yes, it was a bad time, and you my sister were little more than a baby. Your Papa made sure you did not endure the pain of an empty stomach. Our bones became bigger each day, and Papa could not bear to see Mama refusing to eat, saying she would fill her bowl later, while ours were filled until they could hold no more.'

Cecelia reached over and patted her sister's hand. 'Mama told me that my sister's Papa had travelled from lands far to the north, where the hair is fair and eyes are always blue. He decided to defy the anger of the waves. Marissa's Mama tried to stop him, but a man will do anything to feed his family. When she knew her husband was not to be stopped she joined him – she was a girl from the island and knew the places where danger lurked just below the surface. Marissa, before she became my sister, could not bear to be left alone and jumped in before they could stop her.'

The two sisters hold hands across the table, and Marissa encourages her sister to continue.

'It was on that night she became my sister. Despite her Papa's strength with oar and sail, and despite her Mama's knowledge of the sea, they had forgotten – because it was not her Papa's tradition – to paint the protecting Eye on the boat, and the sea took it along with her Mama and Papa. The salt damaged Marissa's eyes, and although Doctor Vitrelli tried every cure he held in his bag, her eyes faded.'

'Oh, I'm sorry!' It doesn't seem enough to say, I am stuck for the right words.

'Oh, do not be sorry, Chloe.' Marissa smiles at me and for an instant I am sure she can see me. 'Over the years I have seen much more than my sister has ever done.'

Cecelia squeezes Marissa's hand, and words don't need to be spoken. There is a gentleness between them, and I find myself wanting to have this more than anything.

Marissa breaks the silence. 'I can feel you need to leave, and hear the sea.'

I thank them, and leave the two sisters drinking iced coffee, talking as sisters should, to find my sister and keep the promise I made to the goddess.

I escape with a haste that embarrasses me and begin to walk down to the beach. My sandals slide on the cobbles and I have to stop several times before I end up flat on my face. Just above the small area where the boats are usually pulled up, the diamante straps give out and I bash my toe.

When the air has turned a lighter shade of blue and I've run through every expletive in my vocabulary, I lean against a crumbling wall and rub my foot. The mist of pain clears and the throbbing eases. A collage of posters covers the wall. Layers of circus elephants, faded and peeling; notices for elections, the candidates long since voted for; adverts for brands of cigarettes no longer smoked... each one jostling to be seen. I look closely, anything to avoid walking on the toe slowly turning a violent shade of purple.

The years of yesterday's announcements have been pasted onto the rough boarding covering windows at the front of a low square building. I peer through the gaps in the chip-board. Inside – lit by slices of sunlight from the broken roof – is the wreckage that must have been a small office. The table, upturned, is surrounded by strewn papers and looks as if it has been like that for years, I squint to see more, but other than a broken telephone wire hanging from the wall there is nothing else.

The pain eases. I stand by the door, planks hammered across. *Casa Cecelia*, the terrazzo, the bougainvillea are clearly visible. In the other direction, the beach, the slipway, boats and nets can all be seen. A great position and would make an ideal bolt-hole.

He wanted us to escape, Paul wanted to settle down,

and that frightened me.

'Just you and me babe, leave the rest of the world behind us.'

But I didn't want to leave the world, not then. I was having too much fun.

I look up and down the hill again and try to imagine what it would be like to sit here, to look through those windows. Nothing would move in this village without being seen.

The sand is hot, but at least it's soft enough to walk barefoot. I scan up and down to see if I can see Isa. She should be easy to spot, but neither sarong nor my sister are anywhere to be seen. On my own, and it doesn't feel right. At the far end of the beach a flurry of beach umbrellas are rocked by the wind. I draw closer and see the rows of neatly toasting tourists on large white plastic sun-beds. Out of habit I adjust the wrap so it floats just behind, revealing enough thigh and breast to arouse interest.

On closer inspection of the sun-beds, half are occupied, the rest reserved with garish beach towels. And it doesn't look too promising. I stop myself from staring at a large woman who is filling her bikini to overflowing; there should be some regulation against that, too much freshly-burned stomach on view. A family with impatient children whining for their parents' attention take their frustration out on the sand, until eyes filled with tears and grit are wiped and a hug is all it takes. *It was all it would have taken and she couldn't even do that for me.* I stopped crying soon after Dad left, started building the wall between us.

'Morgen.'

He lies on a sun-bed, with no umbrella to shade him.

'Morning.'

'I think I have not seen you here before,' he says, his accent heavy and thick as if he has been eating too much bratwurst. 'You are staying at Villa Nova?' He points towards a large concrete apartment block, a bright pink cartoon vision of a Spanish village.

I shake my head. The tanned body with implausibly tiny Speedo is not bad at all. By the way his limbs hang over the edge of the sun-bed, he is well over six foot, with big feet – and you know what they say about men with big feet. The Speedo clings and I can't take my eyes from his other oversized attributes.

She's only a stone statue, no goddess. Feel a bit silly now, and what the hell – promises are made to be broken.

He rises from the white plastic. He's huge, and I thank the gods or goddesses who arrange these things for the solid piece of muscle standing in front of me. He has that firm bulk of a rugby player before it disappointingly turns to fat, and I forget everything else. Although there's one let down (there always is with his sort) – his hair. Shaved short at the sides, left long at the top, makes his head look impossibly square – something like Terminator meets the Addams Family.

I take a deep breath. Where am I staying? It wouldn't be good to tell him I'm on a cookery course with my sister, would it?

'I'm staying in a small guesthouse in the old village. I do think staying with the locals makes a holiday feel more authentic, don't you?' I hear myself, pompous and full of myself. Chloe. Not the woman with green shoots, not the Chloe who made a promise. Soup is forgotten.

Even so, it's like casting pearls to swine, a tumbleweed of thrown-away words. I thought it was quite a good opening for conversation, but my words pass two foot above that strange hair cut, as if his mind was on something other than conversation.

'Would you take a drink with me?' he asks. 'You call me Wilfred, yes?' He strides towards the building.

Of course, I jump at the chance. I've nothing to do and boredom breeds mischief. I need something to forget about Paul. I know he said he wanted to start again, but he still went with Helen, and what the hell – it might do me some good, get my head in the right direction, not always focusing on him.

'Love to.'

The third glass of heavy red wine has me feeling dizzy, and his constant talking doesn't help. He insists on telling me how lovely the island is, although I do wonder how much of it he has seen. He boasts that his holiday apartment is really cheap, and keeps saying that his body is tanned all over and if I want, he will show me. I really don't want to view his all-over-tan, no matter how far down it goes, and find his conversation decidedly one-sided. As much as the toned body does it for me, the man is a total pain – and the last thing I need just at the moment is another pain in my life.

'I really musht be going,' I slur. My tongue clings to the side of my mouth, and the words tumble around.

I didn't think I'd had too much to drink, but as I stand my feet refuse to obey. I miss my footing and fall – a slow motion film of a fall – landing in a heap on the floor. Wilfred scoops me up, balances me back on my feet and escorts me towards a low marshmallow block.

'Let me help you, *fraulein*,' he says, half-carrying me, his hand gripping my buttocks and boobs.

'Now now, none of that, Wilfreddy!' My legs want to run, but they are as muddled as my head and his hands keep roving.

'You should refresh yourself.'

He's right about that – I could do with a splash of water to clear my head. 'Come, my apartment is not far.'

Why do I never see the warning signs? There's that little voice saying, *Change course!* And, *Don't go down that road again!* My voice? I listen hard, and think I hear a whisper in the wind from the crossroads... I am too far gone to listen, and allow Wilfred to lead me up the echoing corridor and through one of the many identical mahogany doors.

The apartment is stark and practical. The white stucco walls close in, moving back and forth. Under my feet the tiled floor has a life of its own.

'I think I'd better lie down...' I don't feel well; the cocktail of sun and wine is making curds inside, and I feel very sick. 'I'll have thish bed.'

Wilfred's breath, short and sharp, doesn't register. I have switched off, moved inside to a place I want to be. Even when he strokes my arm and starts to undo my wrap, I lie there. I am a million miles away, in a different bedroom with the man I really want.

I float in a haze. The edges of my body can't respond, each nerve-ending numbed. The haze clears and I am lying next to Paul, I feel his warm breath on my neck and turn. I want him to scoop me in his arms, wrap them around me and never let me go. I can't remember... was it this I asked for?

'Mmm, Paul,' I hear myself; I want it to be true.

'No, it is me, Wilfred!' – and I plunge back to reality.

The silk wrap is yanked off. The flimsy costume is no match for a determined strong pair of testosterone-fuelled hands. Impatient fingers knead my breasts and his breath burns, a lion over a kill.

Then he bites my shoulder.

'N... No!' I sober up very rapidly. This is not what I want. 'Get off me!'

He ignores me. All too quickly I'm pinned down on the bed, the Speedo long since abandoned. I feel him hard against me, pressing against my stomach while he struggles to pull my costume down my firmly clamped thighs.

'Stop it, you bastard!' I shout, trying to resist his attempts to prise my legs open, and feel his fingers dig into soft flesh, eager, bruising.

'Now now, you do not mean that.' I thwart another thrust. 'I know of women such as you – what is it they say, a cock teaser.'

He thrusts his tongue in my ear, then tries to kiss me. It doesn't seem to matter how much I struggle, he takes no notice. He pins me down with an arm held across my chest.

This can't be happening to me! Not the woman who loves them and leaves them. Me, who at this very moment – with Wilfred's red face dripping sweat as if his skin is leaking over me, hands pawing at my naked flesh – know that I *do* want to be with Paul!

I promise the gods, the stars, even the plaster virgin that if I get out of this I will be a different Chloe.

'Come on, you know you want it,' he pants.

'I might want it, but not with you!' I spit the words into the red face.

He tries to kiss me again. This time his tongue, like a lizard in the sun, is flicking. He forces it into my mouth and I take my chance. My teeth sink into the soft surface, harder, harder, until for a moment he releases his grip and I manage to wriggle my arm free.

'What a little tiger,' Wilfred says. A smile crosses his face. I move my free hand down, feeling a dark tangle of hair. He relaxes. 'Ahh, that's better.'

I always thought a good manicure would pay dividends. I think they must be able to hear him howl back in *Casa Cecelia*. Wilfred rolls off the bed, clutching his balls. There is one thing I have learnt over the years, and that is how to squeeze – or in this case, dig – my nails into a man where it hurts.

I pull up my costume, grab my bag and wrap, and make the quickest exit out of a hotel room I've ever made.

The beach welcomes me, and I feel safe. An overwhelming sense of relief hits me in the solar plexus; my legs wobble and give way. I can't stop myself, and collapse on the sand, shaking. Bruises start to appear on my arms and thighs, and I pull my wrap as high as possible, trying to hide the marks, and sit in the space between heaven and hell.

I feel around in my bag, take out my mobile; it's time to honour my promise. But there's no signal. Somehow I have to call Paul, tell him I'm coming home. Whatever has gone wrong between us, it's nothing that we can't work out.

The line of rocks at the end of the beach is higher. Maybe I'll get better reception there.

The wind is still; no breeze from the mountains. I'd hoped the goddess would have given some sign – after all, I'm fulfilling part of my promise.

9. Osiris and Isis

Isa

'She was a total wreck.' Fredriko looks at the boat the same way some look at sleek sports cars, and others at beautiful women.

'She's beautiful.' The hull is smooth and warm. I run my hands along it. The wood flows under my touch; lemon-curd yellow and lagoon-blue float under my fingers. The paint shines as if it has been dipped into the sea, capturing its very essence.

Pulled up onto the beach, it rests and looks the same as all the other boats, yet different. A closer look and it's easy to recognise a boat for the sea. Wide wood planks carefully crafted, broad at the front, then sweeping back, gradually narrowing – looking sleek and eager to be on the water. At the place where it first meets the sea the vessel curves into the narrowest of points, sweeping skyward as if to challenge wind and waves to do their worst. Even though I've lived my life far from the sea, I see how perfect this boat is.

'Did you paint her yourself?' I ask. I stroke the wood, and wonder why boats are always called 'she'; then I see love in Fredriko's eyes.

'Mario helped me.' He touches the wood the way I want to be touched. 'The old man knows the colours of this island.' Fredriko's hand begins to follow, just as he might follow a shoal of fish before casting his net.

Between the sun and the sea, narrow lines, sea-spray white, sunset red, run from the very front to the back.

'These are my colours.' His hand catches mine. 'You see

how each boat is painted slightly differently?' Our fingers touch. 'It is done so everyone knows at a single glance the fishermen who are at sea. If one is lost, and the boat broken by a storm, his family will know to mourn.'

The air cools for an instant and I shiver. I can't bear the thought that one day this boat could be destroyed, and the beautiful man next to me, his hair darker than midnight tangled with the moon when he moves – this man, full of life, could one day be lost to this world.

Fredriko locks his fingers with mine and together we explore his boat. I examine his hand, the palm large, generously strong for hauling nets. His fingers are long and thin, not hard and calloused from mending nets, as if they belong to an artist.

'What's this?' I ask. Our hands stop at the very front of the boat.

'Ah, it is the Eye of Osiris.'

He guides my hand around the carved Eye, a painted hieroglyph from ancient Egypt. We trace round its kohl-black outline and I touch the clear white of the Eye, looking straight out to sea.

'The Eye of Osiris protects all fishermen. Mario once told me it is important to keep the Eye painted, keep it bright and clean, to see all danger that may be ahead. It protects everyone the boat carries, returning them home safe from harm.'

'You don't really believe that, do you?' I can't understand how this man, who has worked as an engineer in our modern world, could accept such an old superstition.

He raises my hand to his lips and gives it a kiss. 'My educated mind tells me it is foolish, but I am also a fisherman, and grateful that someone looks after me.' Fredriko pulls a small wooden cross hanging on thin leather from under his shirt. He kisses it, then pulls me closer and rests his head against mine. 'Men sometimes must believe without question.'

We stay as close as two bodies can be, there is no need for words. Fredriko replaces the cross and pats his boat, as if to reassure himself she is his.

'When I found this boat the Eye could hardly be seen. It was as if it was waiting to have its sight restored. When

Papa talked of the island, while the nuns cared for his every need, he spoke of a woman he once loved, how he couldn't stay and how she was unable to see him. He said how easy it was for an eye to become clouded. I did not understand him until I arrived here.'

I feel how much he loves this boat. We lean against each other, I remembering the whisper of a mother's kiss and he feeling his father standing close. I smell salt on his skin, and feel the wind in his breath, and the past starts to lose its hurt.

'Isa, Isa, my lovely Isadora...' He whispers my name. It flutters around me like butterfly wings, and I feel the breeze from them skip across the waves. He breathes deeply. 'You have spent the morning in a kitchen, haven't you?'

I pull away. I'd forgotten how strong the smell of garlic and onions must be.

'No, no, come here. I love the smell of a woman who can make a man's stomach happy. What have you cooked, my Isa?'

'Fish soup, well, the base. That's the onions and garlic you can smell. We have to finish it this afternoon. Cecelia, you must know her? Lives in *Casa Cecelia*, she's the one who is teaching us. This afternoon she'll show us how to prepare the fish, maybe some of the ones you've caught. Hey, why don't you come and eat it with us tonight?'

Fredriko strokes my hair, but he is distant and he holds his body away from me.

'No, I do not think I would be made welcome.'

'Of course you will!' Despite the fact that we are so close, a chasm has opened between us. 'Cecelia's such a warm-hearted woman,' I continue, confused at the change in him. 'When you get to know her, she'll welcome you in. She always seems happiest when she has people around her, listening to her stories.'

'Not with me. I have never been welcome. Come, let us not spoil our time together; let me show you how wonderful it feels to be in a boat crafted by a skilled hand.'

Fredriko, the fisherman, Fredriko, the man I am falling in love with, pulls the boat down the slipway over the beach until it meets the sea. The yellow hull bobs on the waves and Fredriko leaps in – like a flying fish skipping over the water.

'Jump in!'

I try to copy, slide effortlessly into the boat, but the stupid sarong catches on the side and I fall into the bottom. Fredriko covers his mouth, trying hard not to laugh. He reaches down and pulls me up, and I concentrate on preserving my dignity by adjusting the swathe of fabric, garish against my skin, attempting to remember how Chloe had tied it. With my back to the sea I begin to relax as Fredriko heaves on the oars.

'You are very beautiful.'

I try to look elegant, sat at the back of his boat, as if being dressed only in a black swimming costume, a see-through garish pink sarong and a large matching hat, is the most natural thing in the world, when in reality the nearest I have been to being on the sea was paddling at the seaside. Mum, Dad and me, before Chloe changed it all. It wasn't her fault, but it was never the same after she arrived.

Fredriko stops rowing and points along the coast. It is so different, detached from the land; I feel free.

'From out here you can see everything.' He raises his arm and I look to where he is pointing. 'Over there is the village. You can just see the terrace of *Casa Cecelia*.' His arm sweeps across the coast to dark crags in the distance. 'Beyond the line of sand there are caves known only to fishermen. Mario took me there, showed me where to catch the large fish which swim in the shadows.' He lowers his arm. 'Would you like to go? It is beautiful there; the sea is a blue beyond description. The caves are cool, a place to go when the sun burns too hot.'

I nod, and smile brilliantly. I would love to go, more than anything. I sit back and hear Chloe telling me to *enjoy the view*. Fredriko flexes his muscles; his shirt, open to the waist, reveals a chest made broad and strong by fighting the waves. I watch as sinews tighten. His mouth is set firm, and he pulls the oars.

The village disappears far behind. *Casa Cecelia* is now a white speck in the distance, and the boat follows the line of the beach. Along the shore brightly coloured umbrellas flap in the wind. The holiday apartments shimmer in the heat, and pale-skinned tourists ignore the strength of the sun.

The oars slicing into the water, the waves slapping against the boat, the occasional grunt as Fredriko pulls the oars back, all beat a gentle tempo so relaxing... I shut my eyes and lean against the side of the boat.

'Before we go into the caves, may I ask you a question?' Fredriko says, taking a strong backwards pull.

'Yes.' My eyes open just enough to see how close we are to the rocks.

'Would it be too presuming of me if...' He stops rowing and rests on the smooth wooden oars.

'If?'

He moves, the boat rocks, and he is sitting next to me. We are as close as only sisters and lovers can be. I close my eyes again. This is what I've been waiting for all my life. I feel his arm around my shoulder.

Doubts claw the pit of my stomach. If I let this happen now, will it be the same as before? Will he find out I'm not what he wants? What if he moves on, finds someone else, someone more like my sister? I pull away and it feels as though a chasm has opened between us.

'I am sorry, Isa. I had thought you liked me.'

'No, no its not –' I protest. 'Oh Fredriko, I... I do, so very much. You're... I've never met anyone who makes me feel this way. It's just... I never thought anyone would look at me in that way again.'

'Isa, Isadora,' and he turns my chin with one finger and places his lips over mine. I feel the knots of doubt in my stomach loosen, but it is still too soon for them to be completely untied. It feels so natural to respond. His hands stroke my legs and all the passion I have saved inside begins to flow out.

I explore his body, feel the solid muscles of his arms, run my fingers through the dark hair covering his chest, and he pulls me tightly against him. I feel his urgency as he lowers me down into the bottom of the boat.

'I want you, Isadora,' he breathes.

Yes, yes, I want him too. I want this more than anything, for him to take me, in his beautiful boat with the Eye of Osiris watching over us. But I can't.

'It's too soon.' I run a finger over his lips and as he sits up. I feel I have lost my only chance. 'Please understand.'

Fredriko leaves my side. His knuckles are white when he takes hold of the oars, and without another word he begins to row back towards the shore. The waves slap against the side of the boat, rocking it from side to side, as if trying to shake us out of our silence.

Fredriko takes a deep breath, looks at me with his soft brown eyes, and a smile spreads across the lips I can still taste.

'You are right. We are not like the young who are always in too much of a hurry. We have age and time to grant us the wisdom to wait, and I will wait as long as you want me to.'

The boat floats on the water, but I don't feel the waves, I'm deaf to the sound of the boat cutting into the sea, and the oars pulled with steady strong strokes. I can't stop smiling and we look at each other, exploring the faces we want to spend time getting to know.

'Look.' Fredriko nods towards the shore, a frown fading his smile. 'Even the stupidest person would know it is dangerous to climb along those rocks.'

'Where? I can't see anyone?' I look along the jagged line sticking out to sea.

'To the left of that outcrop. A woman, right on the edge.'

'Oh my God, Fredriko, she's slipped!' I see a flash of aquamarine disappear below the surface. 'Quick, we have to get to her!'

10. Hecate and Persephone

Chloe

Oh God! No, it can't end this way! I gulp a lungful of air and sink under again. Which way? I am unable to find my direction, whether I'm swimming up to the surface or all the way down to the bottom. My lungs scream for air. Weed wraps around me, pulls me to a place I fear the most; it tangles around my legs, grabs my arms and touches my face – like the fingers of the dead.

I kick at the Kraken dragging me down and the sea flings me to the surface, as if I am an uninvited guest at the party. I suck at the fresh air; the waves pitch and toss me about, a piece of driftwood. All I can do is swim as I have never done before, keep my head above water. The swell lifts me up, takes me closer to the cliff I fell from, and I see jagged, shark-toothed rocks getting closer.

A huge wave picks me up, and with the force of a fist throws me at the spiteful rocks. Then I taste more than thick sea brine coating my tongue; the sweet warm taste of blood flows into my mouth as the rocks bite and snarl at me. All I feel is the sea holding me up, and then it carries me away from danger – a guilty lover trying to make amends.

It's funny what passes through your head when you know: *this could be it. This is the end.* It's not what you think, my whole life doesn't pass in front of my eyes – it would be far too long, and the sea is too impatient for that. It's the little things which float along with me.

I gasp again, suck air into aching lungs, desperate to stay alive.

How the hell did I get here? There's Wilfred, holding me down, pressing against me... and Paul. That's it, I was trying to call Paul. Where are the gods and goddesses when you need them? Cecelia had whispered in my ear when I made the offering of garlic, *Choose carefully, daughter, and Hecate will grant you anything she feels you need...* her hand pressed mine before I made my promise: *Be careful, she is powerful and can take it away from you if she is angered.* When I placed the offering at her feet, the goddess touched my heart and at that very moment it felt that someone else was watching over me. Cecelia warned me Hecate would only show me the right path. Fat chance of that now!

Why was I on the rocks anyway? Isadora had left me, chasing her own dreams, and I felt more alone than I ever had. I couldn't get a signal on the beach. My head spins and things are getting fuzzy, mixed up. I do remember the phone ringing, and me praying he'd answer at any moment.

'I'm sorry, I can't pick up the phone, but leave a message and I'll call you back.'

His answer message. His voice sounded good but I was pissed off. After all the effort I'd gone to, climbing the damn rocks in my best wrap, and he couldn't be bothered to answer. I imagined him looking as my name appeared on his phone, and him pressing the red button, rejecting the call, rejecting me. *I hadn't thought about where I was, balanced on the narrowest of ledges; all it took was one careless step and the cold water hit me like a train.*

I can't keep this up much longer. I'm in some huge washing machine, being flung backwards and forwards, and I desperately try to swim to open water. All my instincts tell me I'm going in the wrong direction; it's as if I'm being guided by something or someone, leading me away from danger.

The water is icy cold under the surface. It drags at me, and I slow down, unable to keep moving. My head throbs and I swallow more and more of the foul-tasting seawater. All the time it rocks me – like a baby in its mother's arms – until I give in, and close my eyes.

Chloe!'

Why is Isa shouting? Can't she shut up and let me sleep? Never gives up, does she? *Get up Chloe, you'll be late for school; wake up Chloe, you should be at work; hurry up Chloe, we are making fish soup...*

'Chloe, hang on, we're nearly with you!'

I open my mouth to tell her to leave me alone, she can make the damn soup on her own. A wash of seawater covers my head and suddenly I know I'm not in bed, and my sister is screaming.

'Faster Fredriko, she's sinking again. Chloe! CHLOE!'

Strong hands grab my arms and haul me out of the water like a prize catch. I reach down to pull up my wrap, but it's long since been taken by the sea. I push the hair out of my eyes and search for the pink batik silk scarf, but Paul's patiently bartered gift has gone as well. I shiver, feeling wretched, naked and vulnerable, a small fish lost in a huge ocean, alone with too many sharks waiting with teeth ready to tear me apart.

A shirt is put over me and I open my eyes, and Isa and Fredriko – minus shirt – look down at me.

'Fancy meeting you here,' I say. The red wine, the narrow escape with Wilfred, the large amount of seawater swallowed congregate in my stomach. I swallow, but nothing can stop the volcano churning inside, and I am violently sick.

'Oh Chloe, what have you done? Look at you!'

Isa cradles me in her lap and gently brushes the hair from my eyes, and with the edge of the shirt wipes my mouth and looks even more frightened than me.

'I'm sorry Isa, I truly am...'

'There's no need to be sorry, my darling, at least you're safe now.'

I lie back and feel the boat rock as Fredriko pulls hard on the oars and hear the sea – which wanted to take me – slap against the side. The sky is clear and cloudless. The taste of bitter bile rises again; this time it sticks in my throat and I realise that I'd got myself into one scrape too many.

Isa, my lovely sister who has spent her life mopping up after me, wipes my mouth. She cared for us all – Mum after Dad left, and now me. She looks down at me, a mixture of fear and relief in her face and I know she deserves more than this. Silently I vow that from now on I am going to try to be the sister she deserves.

'Mario,' Fredriko calls as the boat shudders to a stop, the bow digging firmly into the sand, solid and safe. 'Help me pull the boat further up.'

The sand crunches under the boat as Fredriko and Mario pull it away from the sea and high onto the beach. I am scooped out – as so many catches have been scooped from the bottom of the boat – and carried in Mario's arms, dark from sea and salt, to the safety of *Casa Cecelia.*

'Hurry up. Fredriko, tell him to hurry, she'll need a doctor.'

I shut my eyes and hold tightly on to the old fisherman, tighter than I have clung to anyone, gripping him like a frightened child. I hear the soft sand under his feet, changing to the slap of the concrete, the scrape of cobbles, as Mario's steady and solid feet carry me up the hill towards *Casa Cecelia.* Isa's sensible sandals flap alongside, worrying, desperate to keep up, urging the old man to be quick, to hurry, to get me to safety. Just beyond, far into the distance, I hear Fredriko's quiet feet getting fainter, as if they're reluctant to walk the short distance up the hill.

Daughters, what has happened?'

The beads on the curtain clatter and Mario pushes past Cecelia and Marissa. On the table a pile of freshly folded white cotton cloths are swiftly forgotten. The curtain rattles with worry as first Mario, then Isa, push it to one side. I hear it chatter into silence, no-one else pushing past to disturb it.

'Upstairs, Mario, take her upstairs.'

Cecelia fusses, pushing Mario up the narrow staircase, then quickly sends him away and tucks me into bed.

'Come, Gift of Isis, sit with your sister. Dr. Vitrelli will be here directly.'

'Where's Fredriko? I have to speak to him.'

'No, you must sit with your sister.' Cecelia is insistent, and pushes Isa into the seat next to my bed. Through half-open eyes I see hardness cross her face as Isa's eyes flick towards the door then back to me – torn between duty and her heart.

'Go on Isa,' I tell her. 'You can't do anything until the doctor gets here.'

'But daughter, you must –' begins Cecelia, as Isa brushes past her. I sense panic in Cecelia's voice, and with one last smooth of my bed she hurries out to follow my sister down the stairs.

The room, once stark and empty in my eyes, feels safe, and I am comforted by the simplicity. The open shutters allow a shaft of light across the scrubbed wooden floor – a lighthouse shining a beacon across the ocean of wood. The singing cicadas fill the room with sound, and I lie back on my pillow and listen to the island.

Above the high-pitched insect song I hear voices float up from the terrace; they creep through the window and all I can do is listen.

'It was fortunate you were near... accept my gratitude... but now you must leave.'

Cecelia talks without feeling, as if she were sending away a stray dog.

'Please, Fredriko,' I hear Isa call, and it sounds as if her heart is breaking.

I cannot hear Fredriko's reply. His voice is soft and sad; all I can hear is the wind rattling the beads with such violence it is as if they are being torn down.

Isa is still crying when she sits on the bed next to me.

'How are you feeling?' she says, biting her lip to stop the tears.

'Pretty rough, but I'll survive. What was all that going on downstairs?'

'Nothing.'

'It didn't sound like nothing. Are you going to tell me, or do I have to get out of this bed and ask Cecelia?'

'Look, I said it's nothing.' She swallows hard, and I see her desperately bringing back the old, sensible, no drama Isadora. 'Anyway – what do you think you were you doing on those rocks?'

It's my turn to be evasive. 'Trying to get a signal on the mobile, this island must be in a black hole.'

'And who were you trying to call?' Isa glares at me with

an *I know damn well why you were trying to get a signal* look.

'If you must know, I was trying to call Paul.' Time to own up. 'Fat lot of good it did! I was going to tell him ... well it doesn't matter what I was going to tell him. All I know is, he couldn't be bothered to answer.'

Isa begins to fidget, then proceeds to wipe my forehead a little too vigorously.

'Careful with the Nurse Nightingale act!'

She looks shifty, averts her eyes, and I know she's trying to hide something.

'Now, Isadora, you'd better telling me what's being going on.'

'Earlier,' she begins, 'after we had all that fun with the tomatoes, when you went upstairs, I called Paul.'

'You did *what!*'

'I did it for you, Chloe.' Isa holds the cloth between her hands as if it would give her some protection. 'You've been so miserable without him, I just thought...'

'It wasn't up to you to think!' I'm furious, sit up far too quickly and the room begins to spin. I fall back on my pillow. 'It really wasn't.'

Isa looks away, searches the room as if she could find the answer, staring at the floor, the sheeps-wool rug, the chipped enamel bowl, her hands, her feet... She looks anywhere but straight at me. She reaches over to take hold of my hand. I am so angry I snatch it away, and her face crumples. Huge tears roll down her face.

'I never can get it right, can I, Chloe?' she sniffs. 'Even Fredriko doesn't want to see me again, after what Cecelia said to him.'

Her hand is shaking. I reach out to her, take hold; she grips mine, squeezes it so tight the end of her fingers start turning white, her cornflower blue eyes swimming in misery not of her making.

'That's your problem, Isa, you try too hard, and sometimes you can't make it right for everyone. Sometimes wrong is how things have to be. Dad was wrong to leave, Mum was wrong to need you so much. You have to let me get it right – or wrong – for myself.'

I try my hardest to think of her, of how she must be

feeling. I've never thought of my sister as needing me. My mind yo-yos between being the new Chloe, who is a good sister, and winning back Paul – how I want to be with him, and wondering if after all of this we will be together again. I think back to the crossroads, and turn to give all of my attention to my sad, inconsolable Isadora.

'If he's worth anything and if he really wants you, loves you even, he won't listen to anyone else.'

'Oh, I know he loves me, he told me so, but...'

'Well then, there are no buts, go to him!' I flap my sister away and push her off the edge of the bed.

'He said he was leaving, Chloe,' she sobs, remaining on the floor, unable to get up. 'Cecelia told him his sort, men from the mainland, don't belong here, she even threatened that one word from her and he wouldn't receive a welcome anywhere in the village.'

'Go on, silly – find him, tell him you don't care what problem Cecelia has with him.'

She sniffs, and a watery smile starts to light her face. It's about time my dutiful sister stopped worrying, and thought of herself.

Listen to me, I'm beginning to sound sensible – it must have been all the salt water I swallowed addling my brain – or (and I think back to giving the offering of garlic), maybe there is a goddess out there and we just have to find her.

'But you've not seen the doctor yet, I can't leave you.'

'You can and you will. I'll be fine.'

I watch her float through the door and remember how it felt to be walking on air, when love struck me.

The sounds of the island float over me and I lie back, hear Isa push through the beaded curtain, and listen. Cecelia, her voice hard and angry; the rhythm of Marissa speaking softly – like a breeze blowing through the window – calming her sister, and slowly their two voices melt into one, mingle with the wash of the sea, the wind blowing through the olive grove, and I can't imagine any other place I'd rather be.

Except maybe... my sister called Paul, did she?

11. A Handful of Herbs

Cecelia

'She must rest,' Doctor Vitrelli says, puffing down the stairs. 'She had a few cuts and bruises, but they will heal quickly, with a poultice of lavender. The trauma of falling into the sea may leave more permanent scars, ones the eye cannot examine, I have left a bottle of sleeping pills next to her bed.'

'I will take her some soup later, it will help to restore her.' I thank the stars today is fish soup day. I show the doctor out through the beaded curtain. 'You must come and join us tonight and accept a bowl in thanks.'

'You know how to tempt a man, Cecelia.' He looks at me with his steady grey eyes, wanting more than soup but knowing it is all I will offer. 'I accept.'

The heat in my face begins to cool. I watch the doctor climb the hill, then disappear round the corner where Stephanos always waits for Marissa. Doctor Vitrelli is a man who still turns a sensible old woman into a blushing virgin; his dark curls have turned grey and stiff, his olive skin is scattered with the brown marks of age, but his eyes are as young as when they first saw me.

I turn, listen to the fish apologise for the harm the sea has done, and climb the stairs.

Doctor Vitrelli is not a man made for this modern world – he takes his time, considers his every diagnosis with patience, in the way of the bright quick lizards warming themselves on the terrazzo in the morning sun. He treats each patient with such attention to detail for it sometimes to be a burden. Doctor Vitrelli feels the pain of this island, and carries his cures in a square black bag.

He was not always so diligent. When he was young he carried his newly-framed medical certificate with too much pride, and came to this island with the zeal of a missionary. His parish stretched far: the south, where boats carry travellers to and from the mainland; the mountains, wild and sparse where goats outnumber people – and to our village. When he was young he travelled in a car with tyres as bald as Dimitri's head, treating the sick with pills purchased from new pharmaceutical factories on the mainland, and he ignored the ways of the island.

On the edge of our village, before the road divides under Hecate's gaze, the old woman once lived. She had been taught by her mother how to be wise in the use of herbs – as Aesculapius instructed Hygeia and Panacea. But her knowledge was shunned in favour of Dr. Vitrelli's new medicines. She had used Virgin's Lily, to mend the hearts of passionless men; she'd made infusions of fennel for colicky babies, lavender to calm the soul, and grew herbs whose names have been lost to memory. In the enthusiasm for the doctor's round white pills, the skill held in her hands was shunned and forgotten.

On the night of the storm, when Julio was born, Doctor Vitrelli had travelled to the mainland – to replenish his dwindling stock of medicine – and it was the same night Angelina began to feel her stomach tighten. Mario, torn between new and ancient ways, begged the old woman for herbs to help his wife deliver their son safely, but she could not help; her garden was choked by weeds.

To lose a patient would have been penance enough for the overeager doctor, but the unborn child – never to suckle at his mother's breast – was too much for this man of medicine to bear. He swallowed his pride and spoke with the old woman, who never held a grudge and was generous in sharing the knowledge of herbs. Doctor Vitrelli helped her clear the garden, uncovering new growth, and he learned the skills she held in her hands.

Eventually she was carried up the hill under Hecate's gaze, and Doctor Vitrelli planted rosemary for remembrance, and moved into the house with a garden filled with herbs.

Chloe lies with her eyes closed but I can tell she is not asleep.

'Chloe, daughter of green shoots, are you listening?'

'Mmm,' she murmurs, refusing to look at me. 'Please go away, I know you mean well, but I need to be alone.'

I respect her wishes and turn to leave, but the floorboards betray my steps, like the groaning planks of a boat too long at sea.

'Sorry, Cecelia, I don't mean to be unkind. Come back. I'm sure company will do me good.

'It is good you are safe,' I tell her, and sit beside her.

'All down to Fredriko, if he hadn't been out in the boat with Isa I'd be feeding the fishes by now.' Chloe opens her dark eyes, warm chocolate brown and soft like the gentle eyes of the cattle grazing on fresh mountain grass. I know she can see the anger in my face. She said the name that should never be heard in this room, this room where I gave birth to Julio, she does not know how much it cuts me each time I hear it.

'Your sister was worried for your safety.' I feel it is time to move the words we speak away from the subject of that man. 'You must rest – it is not good to talk too much.'

I sit with Chloe and a wave of warmth floats into my breast, awakening the feelings I had so many years ago for Julio. This daughter who once belonged to a different mother begins to become part of me, just as Marissa – saved from the waves – became my mother's daughter. This Chloe, this daughter who was nearly taken by the sea, brings me back to motherhood.

'Cecelia.'

'Yes, daughter.'

'Why do you dislike Fredriko? I've never seen Isa cry as much as she did when you sent him away.'

'It is a story of the past and cannot be changed.'

'Why not? I don't understand. You welcomed us, me and Isa, with no questions. You didn't know who we were – and I see how you welcome everyone who comes to *Casa Cecelia*, so why not him?'

Emilio keeps the wound in my heart from healing, and my sweet Julio will never be able to rest. Mama's grandmother, as she had always predicted, died in a spring the winter refused to surrender, and had not anticipated being joined in the lonely piece of ground at the edge of the graveyard so quickly. I buried Julio next to her and planted herbs, as is the custom, on his grave. When Mama's time came she was laid next to her grandson, and I travel alone up the hill to where Hecate, the ancient, watches over and keeps Julio safe.

'Cecelia, are you going to tell me?'

'Tell you what, daughter of the green shoots?'

'Why you hate Fredriko so much.'

'I am sorry, my daughter, but such questions cut me, as easily as a knife.'

I look at Chloe, whom I would wish to call daughter, and feel the conflict between my heart and my head. A mother shares the depths of her soul with her daughter, as my mother shared hers, and I know it is time to speak with Chloe, the sister who has not been disloyal to the memory of Mama and Julio.

'The doctor insists you rest.'

'I'm fine. I've had worse.'

I see her hide the bruises on her arms. She has lived a life full of heartache, and the marks left inside, where no bruises can be seen, will be the hardest to heal. Yet the healing green shoots are beginning to flower, and with help this girl, this woman, has the strength to recover.

'If you think you are strong enough we will sit in the sun and pick herbs for our soup.'

The soil of my garden is poor and only plants which expect nothing more than the damp brought by the morning, and the heat of the sun, will grow here. I bring a chair and place it next to Mama's herbs.

'Daughter, you sit here. The sun is too strong in the hours after midday, but now it hides behind this wall and it is cool to sit in the shade.'

'Thanks,' she says, and I hear the strain in her voice and the effort it has been to walk. 'I didn't realise how much it has taken it out of me.'

'As the good doctor said, you must rest. But you are here to learn how to make soup, and while your sister is chasing what she thinks will bring her happiness, we will pick herbs together.'

I think back to their arrival, the two sisters determined to remain the persons they had become. They did not know that this island is quick to uncover the reality they were born with – like a magician pulling doves from under a cloth – and the sisters are now flying in different directions. 'We have already made the base, the spirit of the soup, and now we have to prepare it for the fish, with a gentle touch of leaves chosen for their flavour.'

12. Rosemary (Rosmarinus officinalis)

Cecelia

'Mama planted rosemary to keep Papa's memory alive.' I reach and pluck at the bush. 'She was given seeds by the old woman, in the times before Dr. Vitrelli, and was instructed to surround her garden with this prince of herbs.'

'I remember this smell,' says the daughter of the green shoots, and places a small finger-length sprig under her nose. 'We had a bush of it in the garden, right at the bottom, where it had become overgrown. I think it'd been planted long before Mum and Dad moved in. I've only just remembered! It's strange how some things stay with you forever and others seem to disappear as soon as they have happened.'

'Yes, daughter, this plant has many blessings.'

I had planted one of Mama's bushes on Julio's grave. It covers him with a blanket of its perfume and welcomes me with needles of silver green – sharp to the eyes but soft to the touch – and I talk with him and tell him of how his father betrayed his memory. When the flowers bloom – as blue as the Virgin's cloak laid over the bush as she fled from Herod – I pluck them, and I keep a sprig next to me to remember my only son.

'I used to hide in the garden when Mum and Dad argued.' Chloe rubs the needles, filling the air with its purifying perfume. 'Isa always tried to stop it. She'd stand between them, trying to prevent the inevitable. A bit like Canute ordering the sea to stop. This smell, it reminds me so much of pine, balsamic, and the stuff they rubbed on my chest when I had a cold.' She cups her hands to her nose. 'It brings it all back – and hiding under the bushes again.'

I agree, the old woman knew her skills well. Mama, even though she had not seen Papa after he was taken, would come and sit where we sit now, and rub the rosemary to release good memories.

'For months after Dad left I would return to that place,' her voice whispers, as though if she spoke too loudly the memories would disappear. 'It was as if I breathed in the smell it would be all right, I'd go back into the house and Dad would be sat in his chair waiting for me.' Chloe, the little girl grown into a lost woman, picks at the leaves and drops them one by one onto the floor. 'It didn't work. I grew too big to crawl under the bushes and had to find different ways of hiding and trying to forget him.'

I hand her another sprig and as she takes it I hold her hand.

'Daughter, it is good to remember. This plant has so many uses. By using the smallest amount it will give the soup a deepness of flavour. It does, as you have found, restore memories, bringing them back with gentleness. We hold on to the good, keep them close to our hearts, and the bad are cleansed. It has one last gift known only to those who experience the power of the herb. Rosemary, used wisely, will help the heart become faithful.'

Emilio had ambition beyond this world, and to keep him close I sewed dried rosemary into his pillow. I thought of the ancients who used rosemary to dispel evil spirits, and I wanted my husband to keep his heart only for me. But Emilio's dreams were too strong and he could not smell the herb while he slept.

'Here, daughter, pick the very tip and put it in the basket. The base of the plant is old and too tough for use, as hard as my heart has become. For our soup we need the fresh new leaves that have not lost their youth.'

'It's a pity I didn't have any rosemary a few months ago.'

'Why, daughter of the green shoots?'

'Paul,' she says, as if the word is a sigh. 'He was too quick to move on when I refused him.'

'Ah, your heart is remembering what it feels for this man.'

I hand her another sprig of the herb. She holds it under her nose and closes her eyes – a penitent with incense to aid her prayers.

'When we first met, I'd expected it to be like all my other short-lived love affairs, a bit of fun. We were both experienced in the way these things happened, no ties, no commitment, just friends having a great time. But... he grew on me. Do you understand what I'm saying?'

'Yes daughter, your heart told your head to forget.'

'Exactly. Don't get me wrong, we still had a great time, but it went on longer and I moved in with him. It was great for five years, and then he...'

I wait; it is hard for her to talk of such things, and she rubs the rosemary between her fingers, opens her eyes and looks at me. Her dark brown eyes hold the light of remembering too much.

'He became too serious, wanted us to get married, and I couldn't give him the answer he wanted. So I pushed him away, remembering how it had been with Mum and Dad, and I didn't want that to happen to us.'

I squeeze Chloe's hand and gently take the bruised leaves from her grasp.

'Sometimes, daughter, what we are afraid of seems to be huge, as if a dragon breathing fire blocks our way, but if we turn to face it we find that this ferocious beast is little more than a small lizard sunning itself on the rocks.'

'He, Paul, said he wanted us to try again, but now he won't take my calls, and after all he said, I don't see him rushing to be with me.'

Chloe shakes her head and I see the blinds come down to cover her emotions. Silently, each locked in the past, we pick the herb of remembrance and fidelity.

13. Wild Marjoram (Origanum Vulgare)

Cecelia

'To pacify the soup we must choose the Joy of the Mountains. Marjoram makes love to the tomato, and together they sweeten and caress each other until they become one.'

Chloe plucks the oval leaves, bright and fresh, golden green with a hint of fire, and rubs them between her fingers. She is learning quickly, and her name fits her more each day.

'It smells like... I know this will sounds silly, but it smells like the pizzas we'd order when Paul wanted to watch football. I couldn't be bothered to cook, so we would sit together and...'

'Yes, daughter?'

'It was nice that's all, doing nothing but doing it together.'

'You will taste this herb in all dishes where the tomato is needed. Some use the strength of basil to help the taste of the red fruit, but this herb is more subtle and can only be recognised by those who have picked it.'

Mama collected wild marjoram in the summer, filling her basket with leaves full of sun and dew, before the herb had dressed itself in purple flowers and Mercury had taken away its strength.

'I took one of the plants from the mountain where Mama had once picked wild leaves, and planted it here. My knees had begun to protest at being asked to climb the mountain paths to find herbs. You can see how it has spread over the years; it is an easy plant to grow.'

'Then you dry it for the winter.'

'How do you know that, daughter?'

'I saw the jars of dried herbs lined up above the stove, and bunches of herbs hung to dry along the wall. All those lovely summer flavours, ready to be released.'

She is gifted, and she understands what is needed to bring a dish alive.

'We will pick just enough for our soup today, the year is too young to pick more in preparation for winter,' and Chloe, without being shown, plucks the sweetest leaves and places them in the basket.

Mama and Marissa had woven a wreath of herbs. They hung it on the bedroom door the morning of my wedding. They had risen early to pick wild marjoram from the mountain and – taking care not to bruise the leaves – threaded round flowers gathered from the meadows. Before we walked to the church they kissed me, cupping my face in their hands in a blessing, and I was filled with the sweet scent of love and the spicy aroma of desire. The same gentle smell greeted Emilio when he carried me to my bridal bed.

After my husband of only a few hours had turned his back on me, his passion cooled by the changes in my body, round and full – the body of a mother in waiting, I tore down the wreath and washed the leaves with my tears.

Mama had taught me – in the days before I belonged to Emilio – how the mountain herb, good for tomatoes and for sweetening fish soup, would sweeten a marriage with love, honour and happiness.

I kept hold of my love for Emilio, even when I suspected he slept in different beds, while his son grew inside me. I told myself that once he laid eyes on the child, and saw his own reflection in the child's face, he would forget to take the road to the north. I forgave him, made excuses for him, because some men do not appreciate how a woman's body changes to nurture and feed. I hoped that his love would return and lie next to me beneath the fresh cotton sheets smelling of rosewater, thyme and lavender.

For Mama it was different. She was honoured every day by Papa, and when he was taken to the mainland – for sitting in an office with a small black telephone – she knew in her heart he would always respect her with thoughts of love.

I looked at my Emilio and wondered what sort of man he had become.

'Cecelia,' Chloe's voice breaks my thoughts of Emilio and I am grateful, 'I think I should go and find Isa.'

'The doctor said you should not exert yourself.'

'I'll be fine, don't worry,' she says. 'I want to see her, make sure she's okay and she's found Fredriko.'

'No, daughter, I insist!' These sisters must not change what should be, and this island will never welcome that man.

I move towards her from the shadow where the sun covers the soil, and I find myself blinded by the sunlight, fierce with the midday heat. I stand, blinking like a child. In my haste, my hurry to hide the past and keep the future from changing, I forget the weakness in my knee and stumble. Chloe, her strength restored, catches me, but the basket falls to the floor, scattering the contents, and I smell the herbs as they are crushed under our feet. The sharp rosemary – promising fidelity and romance – and the sweet marjoram – pledging to love, to honour and to bring happiness; both mix in a *bouquet-garni* of broken dreams.

'You must stop your sister from making the mistakes of young girls.' Chloe becomes the mother, helps me to the seat and bends to pick up the damaged herbs. 'Isadora, the Gift of Isis, is of an age when she should accept the disappointments of life, but I fear that her heart is still young and Fredriko...' The name catches in my throat, and I have to force it through my teeth. 'That man will bring her pain, just as my husband broke my heart.'

'I'm sorry Cecelia; I don't understand what you are saying.'

'You love your sister?'

'Of course.'

'And you, my daughter, who knows how a man can hurt a woman, will understand why it is important that she is saved from a man who has kept two beds warm.'

'What are you saying?'

I see the light of dawn begin to rise in her eyes and she

sits on the ground next to me.

'Cecelia, if there is something I should know about Fredriko, you'd better tell me. Is he married, or – worse?'

'Chloe, daughter with green life growing, as your name has meaning, so does mine. Cecelia, an ancient name, given to me by my Mama who was called Helena-Cecelia, holds meaning. Cecelia is one who is blind. I could not see Emilio, my husband, also had a name to live up to. His name was chosen before he knew its meaning but he wore it well: Emilio, the Rival.'

'So he lived up to his name, what has this to do with Isa and Fredriko?'

'Patience, daughter. I have not spoken of this to many souls. Mama knew and taught me her skill in the kitchen to save me from grieving for my son and from finding comfort in any other man, for despite Emilio's absence we were still husband and wife. I shared my heart with Marissa, and now, daughter, you must hear of an old woman's shame.'

Her hand rests on my arm, and in the warmth of her touch I begin to tell this woman, whom I want to call daughter, of how Emilio had ambition beyond this island.

'My husband left my bed, after we had buried Julio, never to warm it again. In my heart he was dead to me. It was many years later I heard he lived on the mainland and ate pasta, I also heard that this woman – who could not make soup – had a son.'

'So he was a bit of a bastard – sorry for the language. That's what most men are, you either see it or you don't.'

'This son, this man, should have been my son. He has lived, breathed, grown to be a man, while my Julio will always be a boy. I saw Emilio in his eyes the moment he stepped onto the island, and when he started to mend the boat I knew that my husband, who killed my only son, was Fredriko's father.'

'His *father*!'

My hand covers the mouth that has said too much, and I try to take the basket into the kitchen.

'Just you wait a minute.' Chloe holds my arm, refusing to let me go. 'Does he know? Does Fredriko know about his father?'

'No daughter, I thought if I made it clear to him that he

was not welcome he would leave and I would not have to look at the face which reminds me too much of my son.'

'Well, don't you think it's time he knew? At least he could then make his own decision whether to leave or stay... and what about Isa? I suppose you didn't think to tell her?'

She snatches the basket from me and I follow her into the kitchen.

'Daughter.'

'Don't you daughter me, or green-shoots-sprouting-in-my-soul me, I'm called Chloe and my sister is called Isadora, and you will tell her about Fredriko – before I do.'

I feel like a child, chastised for keeping secrets. She is right. I should have spoken before now, but I have too much of Papa in me. Secrets sit well in me, but this is one that has now been shared, and a weight I have carried for too long is lifting. I have worried for too long about my reputation, about how I am seen by others, to see what is in front of my eyes.

'Chloe, I will find your sister and explain. She has the right to know, and Julio's brother should know where he comes from.'

'Good, I'll wait here. Isa might come back. In the meantime I'll chop the herbs.'

14. Casting the nets

Isa

'Mario, I must find...' I stop, catch my breath. He's nowhere to be seen; only his boat lies abandoned on the beach. 'Have you seen Fredriko?'

The old fisherman sniffs and noisily sucks his teeth. He looks at me, his eyes dark and ancient, and I glimpse another world. He is the traveller, crossing the Mongolian plains with the Khan, a merchant carrying silks and spices from Persia, a sailor guiding his boat with the Eye of Osiris from Phoenicia. Mario bends forward, without moving his hypnotic gaze, and picks up his net, runs knowing fingers along the edge, feeling for any holes.

'No.'

Where is Fredriko? His boat rests just where we left it, abandoned halfway up the beach and surrounded by footprints, each telling their story. Mine, scattered around in my panic to get Chloe to safety; Fredriko's, steady and strong where he pulled the boat up; and Mario's, deeper than the others, carrying the weight of my sister. The boat leans at an angle and out of the sea, like a fish gasping for air, desperate to return to the water.

'Are you sure?' Surely he must know.

Mario sucks his teeth again, grunts, and leans on the side of his boat. Twice the size of Fredriko's boat, it's painted the familiar yellow and blue. The Eye is large and stares steadily ahead, solid and honest.

'He say he must go because he bring you too much sadness.'

Why? Why? Why? What does he mean, he must go? It's only a short while since it was all perfect. It's only a minute shift of time – less than twenty-four hours since Chloe came here to escape. I wanted to find something more, and both of us were strangers to each other. Fredriko wants me, I'm sure of that, and I know he is what I've been waiting for. But I was so stupid, scared to show my true feelings, frightened of being hurt the way Simon hurt me all those years ago. Dad leaving, Chloe hardening her heart and Mum dying. Why didn't I let him make love to me? Chloe would have, she wouldn't have given it a second thought. He'd be here now if I'd only...

'See...' The old man's saltwater voice cuts through my thoughts. 'I catch well today.' He reaches deep into his boat and lifts out a basket. 'All fish want to go home, but some are caught in nets and cannot escape. I pull in my net and some get away, but most stay and cannot go back.'

He lifts a large silver fish from the basket; the scales catch the afternoon sun and it shines with rainbows of light.

'The fish is happy to hunt in the sea and chase smaller fish, but out of the water it has beauty and will live again.'

I itch to tell him to just shut up about fish and tell me where Fredriko is. Why did he leave so suddenly after Cecelia had spoken to him? I watch Mario stroke the fish with hands tanned as dark as leather, caressing it gently.

'Fredriko has been free to swim where he wished. But, like this fish caught in my net, the island trapped him and landed him here.'

'He told me he came to learn how to be a fisherman.' I look at the fish, its eyes still bright. 'He said his father came from this island.'

Mario lays the fish back into a smaller basket, gently, like a father laying a baby into a crib.

'It will swim in soup tonight,' he murmurs, and I'm not sure if he's talking about me, Fredriko, or the fish.

'Did you know Fredriko's father?' Maybe if I understand more about his past perhaps I will get to know why he's so upset by Cecelia's words.

'When I was a boy, his father was also a boy. We were as close as brothers, and as brothers we learned the ways of the sea. The call was not as strong in his father as it was in me. My Papa, Alexandros, taught me well, and when he was too old to lift the oars I took the boat and filled the nets with fish. Fredriko's father thought there was more in the world; he tired of the sea, and like brothers sometimes do, we travelled different roads.'

'Who was his father?'

'Emilio Salvadori, who left the sea and stole the heart of a good woman.'

He can't be! The old man must be getting confused.

'Cecelia's husband was called Emilio, but he's got Fredriko's surname. He can't be... he's not the same one as...'

'Yes, one and the same. Emilio, betrothed to Cecelia and father of two sons. One cold in the ground, the other owns the boat lying on the sand.'

'Does Fredriko know?'

'He knows much of his father's story, but not all. Cecelia's voice is strong in the village, and those who listen to her accept her story and have made him unwelcome in the place of his father's birth.'

'You didn't, you welcomed him.'

'Fishermen are not men of the soil. It is dangerous to hold grudges, for the time will come when the sea fights, as sometimes it does, and we may have need of each other. Brother looks out for brother; that way we all return safely.'

I am more confused than ever. Is he saying that Fredriko is leaving, or staying? I've got to find him, tell him how much I want to be with him, that the words an old woman speaks are not always right. I know how the past eats you up if you let it. I'm a past master of brooding on what could have been. If Dad hadn't left I would have been free of Mum's need. If I had been a true sister to Chloe she may never have lost her way...

'Mario *please,* tell me where he is.'

He looks out to sea and absentmindedly strokes the smooth scales of a small fish, then scoops it out.

'Smell.'

Finally I know he must be mad as he thrusts the fish under my nose.

'Smell.'

I hold my breath not wanting to smell that sharp stench of dead fish. I feel the air wanting to fill my lungs and – like a drowning woman – I breathe in. The sea fills my head, salt and waves hit me, and I smell nothing, no rotting flesh, no eye-watering stink, only the fresh clean smell of the sea.

'You understand!' Mario smiles, his teeth crocked, his face cracked by spray and storm, and I bask in the old man's joy.

I understand. I understand that this fish, taken from its home, carried in a boat to the island and destined to slide into the pan and to be served in a bowl of soup, is not dead. It will live again in Cecelia's fish soup.

'Fredriko will not leave the island. He smells too much of the sea.' Mario throws the fish back into the basket. 'He is in the olive grove, getting good fortune to place on the front of his boat.'

He points towards the crossroads – where Chloe's goddess stands – with fingers bent by age and by mending nets.

'You find him.'

'Oh yes, thanks, thank you!' I hold my hand out to shake the hand of the man who has given me hope. He takes hold of it and raises it to his lips.

'Have a father's blessing. My Angelina and our child sleep peacefully. Fredriko has become a son to me, and before I take my rest next to them, I will pass on the wisdom of my father.'

Mario returns to his boat, carefully placing the largest and freshest fish into the basket. I walk up the hill, where soon he will carry his harvest to *Casa Cecelia*.

Daughter, come and sit.' Cecelia sits on the terrace and it's obvious she's waiting for me. She pats a chair, expectant and empty next to hers, placed firmly on the terrazzo, tiles blood red in the afternoon sun. 'It is good I have found you. Come, indulge an old woman with your presence.'

'I'm really sorry Cecelia, any other time, but I can't stop to chat, I have to go.'

'No, daughter, Gift of Isis, Isadora.' She reaches out to me, both arms held out, begging to be filled; implores me to join her, her face raised to mine. Her eyes shout with fear that I might pass by. 'Pray join me and listen to an old and stupid woman's confession.'

I move closer and she clasps my arm – as if she is drowning, reaching for something to keep her afloat. I am torn. If I stay I might lose my only chance and Fredriko will think I don't care about him. I look at Cecelia; in her desperation her fingers dig into my arm. This woman who hates the man I love is lost and vulnerable, and not the strong mother who is teaching Chloe and me how to make fish soup.

'Okay, only for a minute or two, then I must go.'

The chair scrapes on the tiles and I almost fall with the force of being pulled down. I can smell trepidation on her breath and she wipes, with a cloth smelling of lemon and soap, at the moisture gathering above her top lip.

'I think you have it in your heart to meet with Fredriko,' she says, so quietly I have to bend closer. 'It is time you understood where he came from.'

I raise my hand to stop her.

'I already know who his father is. Mario told me. His father is Emilio, your husband.'

She flinches as if the raised hand was going to strike her. She looks at me with hurt and anger – then, as my words sink in, confusion sweeps across her face. Cecelia passes a hand over her forehead, over her eyes, wiping slowly down, the way she washes her face in lavender soap each morning, until it covers her mouth, as if she wished to stop words from being said.

'Cecelia...' I remove the hand from her face, and hold it. 'I will find him. He has the right to know you once loved his father, and he had a brother.'

'To my shame I hated him when he arrived here,' she began. 'He brought memories of Julio close. I saw in him my son, who will never grow strong, will never love, and will never give me a grandchild to comfort my old age.'

'But all of that is not Fredriko's fault, he's innocent in all this, he didn't know his father's past.'

'It is my burden to hold too much of Papa in me,' Cecelia says. Her eyes look at the curtain and she appears to have moved into another time. 'I heard Papa one night, when Mama pealed onions. He blamed Alexandros for the mistakes of his father, in the same way I hold Emilio's son responsible for the actions of his father.'

'Why are you telling me this now? You could have told Fredriko and he would have understood.'

'Your sister shamed me and told me I must speak with you.'

Being half-drowned must have been worse than I thought – Chloe thinking about me! Well, that's a first.

'She said I must make amends with this other son of Emilio, who has the eyes of his father and looks like Julio.'

I slowly stand, and it seems natural to bend over and kiss her cheek, soft and smooth, smelling of lavender soap and cool water.

'I'll find him, bring him back. It's time for a new start for us all.'

Cecelia brushes her cheek holding on to the kiss.

'Daughter, you have been too kind to an old woman who has been blind all her life, and now when her life has almost passed her by she begins to see again. You and your sister have reminded me how a heart can sing. Go, Gift of Isis, and find your Fredriko.'

I begin to walk away but Cecelia once again calls me.

'Isadora, you must remember to honour the goddess.' She places a small pink clove of garlic into my palm and I smell the faint hint of what it could be when crushed.

'Thank you Cecelia, I will.'

'That's all she asks. Do not make the same mistake I made by dishonouring the goddess. In my passion to find love with Emilio I forgot to make the offering tradition demands, and I have had to live with her vengeance.'

It's quiet at the crossroads; even the cicadas have stopped singing, as if they are holding their breath, the way a soprano hesitates before singing the final aria. My heavy breathing makes too much noise, it fills the skies. I gulp in the hot dry air, panting after running up the hill as if I was a teenager hurrying for a first date.

I lean against the statue to catch my breath and the smell of garlic curls from my hand, sweating after all the exertion. The goddess, Hecate – her three faces carved so many years ago stare into the distance, down roads leading to different destinies. I know in which direction mine lies and – feeling a little silly – place the bulb, crushed in my haste, at the feet of the face of the young woman, virginal, looking steadfastly towards the olive grove.

When we were here earlier I didn't take any notice of the statue. I was too much in a hurry to get back, to write down the recipe, find the perfect formula for making fish soup. I ignored the effect she had on Chloe, thinking she was only doing it to be in the centre of attention, as always. Now, looking up at the stone, the faces smoothed by wind, washed by rain, and warmed by sun, I suddenly feel a spike of guilt. Perhaps I should have taken more notice of Chloe, asked her where she placed her offering, and what future she wished for.

I kneel at the feet of Hecate and look up at her, the young features, eyes open and honest, and on her lips the hint of a smile, as if she is approves the offering made and I am now blessed for honouring her.

The road to the olive grove curves, then disappears between the trees. Each step is harder to take. The heat drains energy from me, and I am afraid of what lies ahead. The ancient trunks are bent and twisted, like the old men who play dominoes in the café each evening. Each step brings me nearer. I smell thyme and see the dusty green leaves covering the ground where the road disappears into the shade. Then the coolness greets me with a breeze as fresh as a morning shower. I stop and bathe in it, and I feel the timeless calm wash away the remains of any fear.

My skirt, Indian cotton which Chloe hates so much, is dusty from the road. I stop in the shade of a tree, so ancient it is bent double as if bowing to greet the earth, and brush away the dirt.

'You will wear away the pattern if you keep beating so hard.'

'Fredriko!' My hand stops and I am frozen unable to move. 'I thought... I was frightened you'd gone, that Cecelia had...'

'It would take more than a silly old woman, no matter how much the village gossips listen to her, to get rid of me.'

He takes my hand and together we leave the dusty road and step onto a carpet of thyme, and the smell of the herb fills the grove.

'Do you really think I would let such a prize as you escape? You forget now I am a fisherman, I know how quickly a tide can change and once I have cast my nets you, my little fish, can do nothing but be pulled from the sea and land in my boat.'

His hand reaches out, sweeps my fringe to one side, and he kisses my forehead, and one cheek then the other, until I feel his breath meet mine.

'I love you Isadora…' He presses his lips onto my mouth; I forget my fears and the years of disappointments, and I return his kiss.

Eventually, when we have to stop to take breath, he looks at me with brown eyes shining with the flecks of green, and I know this time it will be all right.

'Yes.'

'Only if you…'

I put my hand over his mouth, I feel his breath against my palm; his lips hold the warmth of me and it is as much as I can do to stop myself from kissing him again.

'I'm not a girl anymore, I'm a woman who has not lived, and as a woman I know this is what I want.'

The thyme crushes beneath us as we lie down in the shade of the olive trees, and the heady perfume fills the air. I look up at Fredriko and above him the branches of silver-green leaves sway, as if reaching over to protect us.

'Isa, Isadora,' he murmurs, and kisses my neck, and I reach and pull him down on top of me.

I close my eyes and listen to the soft whisper of leaves talking to each other, carrying the news back to Hecate to tell her that I am not dishonouring her name.

We lie in the olive grove, warm breeze covering us with a blanket of kisses. Our clothes abandoned. Hands that have hauled nets and caressed fish explore my body. He cups my breast and circles it with his fingers and, as gentle as a butterfly landing on a leaf, takes it in his mouth. I feel like every woman in the world feels when they welcome love, a virgin trembling at the first touch, a lover hot with passion. I put my hand on the back of his head, sinking my fingers into the soft curls and hold him there, not wanting this feeling to end.

'Yes Fredriko...'

I welcome him inside me, and the breeze carries the news to Hecate.

After a lifetime of love we lie back, our bodies covered with the sweet smell of thyme. I place my hand over my stomach and know I have received the goddess's blessing.

15. Red Mullet – Between Death and Life

Cecelia

The sun cools and it is time for the sisters to understand how to introduce fish into the pot. I stay in the kitchen, hung with empty pans and stacked with unfilled bowls, my only company the gentle hiss of the flame simmering the soup and, like Mama after they took Papa away, I wait.

Mama had promised Papa – after the trial and before he was taken away – she would wait. She waited, with the patience of an angler watching for the tremble of a bite, and became hardened to gossips who change allegiance as it suits them – birds hopping from branch to branch.

Time passed slowly for Mama; Papa did not rattle the beads and the fish did not swim for him. The man with slicked back hair, who Mama called Francesco, my Papa with his strong dark arms, who had answered the call of the Dictator, grew old in a cell no bigger than this kitchen. When they released him he was too frail to leave the mainland. Mama packed a small battered suitcase, wiped my face with a cloth smelling of lemons and soap, kissed her grandson's soft warm cheek and left *Casa Cecelia*.

'Your Papa needs me,' she said as she took one last look at the bougainvillea.

'*I* need you,' I wept, only seeing the need I had and failing to understand how it was to love a husband so much. 'Julio needs you – what am I to do all on my own?'

I was frightened of the abyss that separated me from Emilio, and terrified that Mama would stay on the mainland.

'I will return, daughter,' she said, and carried her few possessions down the hill towards Dimitri's ferry.

I opened my mouth to call to her back, to say I loved her, and to give Papa a kiss from his daughter. But I stood with my mouth open, like a fish lying in the bottom of Mario's boat.

'I don't know how to make fish soup!' I yelled, and my voice bounced off the cobbles and rolled towards the sea.

Mama turned and was torn – pulled as puppies pull a rag – between leaving the island, leaving *Casa Cecelia*, and crossing the sea. She picked up the small battered case, walked back up the hill, and without a word disappeared into the kitchen.

I listened to her chopping onions and knew she was mourning for a husband she would never see again.

The kitchen holds too much silence, is small in the quietness after a morning of laughter and tears waiting for the afternoon to arrive. I move towards the stairs to call Chloe, her head resting in the room where I slept with Emilio and gave birth to Julio. Before I open my mouth I hear the gentle chatter of beads welcoming Mario. He brings his basket on fish soup day, carefully filled with the best, the freshest and the brightest of his catch. I move to greet him, but there is something secretive in the way the beads try to hide his entrance, and I hesitate. A thick mist, as if the easterly wind blew too hard, sits in my heart and I wait in the place I once heard Mama chopping onions, and keep my silence.

'Cecelia?' Marissa's voice slides through the air to my ears. 'No, I am sorry Mario – she said she was going to speak with Isadora to explain. I have not heard her return, although sometimes my body cannot resist sleep and she may have slipped past while I dreamed of things I cannot see when awake.'

A chair scrapes across the terrazzo and I hear a deep grunt as Mario rests a body becoming too old for fishing. He should have had a son to haul in his nets, and not keep working until it breaks him. I smell the coffee as Marissa pours it over ice, it cracks too loud for secret conversations and my mouth waters in anticipation.

'She has become obstinate in her memory, and forgets once she loved against her Mama's wishes.' His voice is liquid, and Mario speaks without knowing I hear every word. Each syllable carefully chosen cuts through me as sharp as the blade he uses to slice flesh from bone.

'You, Mario, my old friend who knew Cecelia before she became my sister – you understand. She has never been able to see further than her eyes.'

My breath sounds loud in my ears and I am sure they will soon know I have been listening, hearing words they dare not speak to my face. Mario my friend, Marissa my sister – of all the souls who have joined me during my life – they speak the words hardest to hear. They talk in tones of disrespect, not easily used on this island, and voice the thoughts only gossips and scolds should whisper.

'She has never been able to see me,' he says, his words soft and warm. 'Since she was a scrap of a child, with fire in her eyes, I have loved her, Marissa. But she could only see the light of Emilio.'

'I know,' Marissa comforts. 'My sister was never a woman to see a true heart.'

Why has he never said this to me? Mario, a man of few words and eyes of a Phoenician, has kept *this* from me? My past runs towards me, like the waves rush in at high tide. Mario, the boy with the bloodied nose and ready fists sending away those who knew what Papa was, fighting ignorant accusers of a young girl for the actions of her father. Mario, the young man who couldn't tell me how he felt, trying to prevent Emilio taking me into the olive grove. This son of Alexandros who once loved Mama was blamed, to my shame, for not stopping Julio being taken onto the sea. I cursed this old man drinking iced coffee, for allowing Emilio to escape to the mainland – leaving me in the limbo between wife and widow. Mario walks in the shadow of my life and tells my sister he loves me.

'I wait, I always wait. Cecelia, for all her faults, is her mother's daughter and my father Alexandros loved Helena-Cecelia. Such is the way of things, and like the sea women are unpredictable, they are the tide pulled by the moon, their affections wax and wane. All a man can do is wait for a calm sea.'

I press myself against the cool wall, wanting it to hide me and keep me from a future that tells the story of a different past. I am afraid of being discovered, skulking in the shade, so I paint a smile onto my face and, as loudly as my feet can walk, step onto the terrazzo. Mario stops talking, the sound of my approach silencing his thoughts as swiftly as night falls in winter.

'How long have you been with us, my sister?' Marissa knows the sound of my feet.

'I have been here as long as it takes for a sister to find a knife and an old friend to twist it.'

Mario looks at Marissa and avoids my eyes, burning with the truth of my anger and hurt. He wipes his face with a hand shining with fish scales, and his brow is covered by small rainbows sparking in the waves, holding on to the magic of the stars.

'Cecelia, I did not come here to bring you pain.' He speaks in a voice deepened over the years by salt spray and the north wind. 'I am a simple man, who brings fish for your soup, yet I can see that we are nearly at the end of our journey, and it is time we were honest with our thoughts and truthful with our words.'

I sit in the chair between them and take hold of Mario's hand.

'My old friend, you are right as always. Your Papa named you well. You hold the god of war in you, Mars, but your name is blessed by the Virgin, Our Lady, Star of the Sea, Mario. You have always been my warrior, my Star of the Sea, it is only now that these eyes, which have seen less than my sister's, can look into the night sky and with the Virgin's blessings, follow another star.'

Embarrassed by my words, he reaches down to the basket of fish and carefully lifts out a mullet, scales bright pink, matching the colour of his cheeks.

'You are a fish, beautiful in all stages of life,' he whispers as if the fish is listening. 'This red mullet, once prized more than gold, swam in the sea with a colour as bright as a fistful of rubies. When I trapped him in my net, the breath of life moved between life and death, and slowly his colour changed from ruby red to coral pink.' Mario strokes the fish. 'In the journey between death and life it is still beautiful.'

I listen to this man, who has never spoken of how he felt, laying his heart open, and I reach over to take the fish from his hand.

'My old friend,' I look into his dark eyes. 'Since the two sisters arrived to learn how to make fish soup they have been opening my eyes.' I turn the fish over and lay it on the table between us. 'Chloe, the reckless one, has the energy of spring inside her. She reminds me of when I was young, and she has awakened the part of me dead since I followed Julio to the cemetery. Demeter's daughter, Persephone, has found the mother I thought had died with my son.'

'The other sister?' asks Marissa. 'The one who will soon be returning from the olive grove with Fredriko, what do you have to say about her?'

One faltering step at a time, my sister. Marissa knows me better than anyone, but does not understand how – like a fish-bone stuck in the throat – some changes are easier to swallow.

'Hecate will decide. If Isadora has made an offering to please her, she will be blessed and I will welcome Emilio's living son.'

'It will be hard for you,' she sighs closing her unseeing eyes and hearing the resistance in my voice. 'Our names have been well chosen. You my dearest Cecelia, blinded by your name, can now be guided by Mario's star, as a true friend.'

I squeeze my sister's hand; modest in her name, she binds us together, a child of the sea.

'Come sister, we must finish preparations, fish soup will not wait, and there are cloths to be laid and candles to be lit. Mario, it would honour me if you will sit and share a bowl with me tonight.'

Mario, man of few words, lifts the basket of fish and takes it into kitchen. With the keen eye of a fisherman, and a knife sharp as a keel, he removes the sweet flesh from fish which swam in the sea a few hours ago. Patiently he pulls the needle-sharp pin bones and lays the soft fillets, ready to be added to the soup – an artist standing back from a finished canvas. Contented, he leaves *Casa Cecelia*, knowing that when he shares a bowl of fish soup with us tonight it will have part of his soul in it.

In silence, with the quiet comfort that old married couples have when they have had a lifetime of conversation, Marissa and I begin to fold the napkins as Mama had shown us. We spread the white cotton cloths over the tables, moving the worn edges so they are hidden from view. Routine tasks, simple jobs undertaken in preparation for the evening, are done without the necessity of thought and give space for the voices inside a head to talk.

My voice tells me of a woman who has not seen the good fortune she has, and tells false tales of how she wanted it to be. A history – written by the hand of the victor, as all histories generally are – of a young girl, loving her Papa, sitting on his lap while he spoke on a black telephone, ignoring the names he listed, couldn't see the men who disappeared... a Papa who was then taken from her in disgrace to the mainland. A story of how the young girl grew and watched those who had been taken return, young men turned old, thinner than they should be, blinking in the light of freedom, their youth damaged – dented like Doctor Vitrelli's old car. This girl-woman rewrote the pages to hide what she did not want to read: Emilio, unable to love her the way she had wanted him to, and Julio, her son who she could have kept beside her but in her blind anger did not see the danger he was in. The fiction of her life told her she was a happy wife with a contented husband, and did not tell of how she ignored the truth.

I place another folded napkin on the table and Marissa smiles.

'I hear many thoughts in your silence, sister.'

'Ah, my thoughts are clearing the mist of the past. The two sisters, who arrived only yesterday, seem to have been here a lifetime, and have reminded me of all the many different lives I have led. With their help the soup has been filled with the goodness of the soil and sea; the memories I have kept close to me have been added to the pot.'

'It is good. You would not see or hear the counsel of those close to you. You only saw Papa, the man who welcomed me into his home at the insistence of your Mama, as the man who hung a beaded curtain over the door. Emilio, with his fists ready to strike and feet ready to wander into another bed, you held close for too long.'

I press my sister's hand. 'Thank you, sister. Through the eyes of the two who came as strangers, I have been able to see into the past as it was, dark and muddy like the sea after a storm, and now there is a future, clear and deep.'

'Sisters do not need to thank each other,' Marissa sighs, and she kisses my cheek, then turns her head towards the door. 'I hear feet I do not recognise.'

I look through the beaded curtain, where Marissa cannot see, towards the beach, and see a man striding up the hill, his hair the colour of cinnamon, his face speckled like a hawks egg, wearing clothes made for colder weather.

'Hi, can you help me?' he speaks with the same easy voice as the sisters. 'Is this the place they call *Casa Cecelia*?'

16. In the depths

Chloe

Now what do I do? I've straightened the bed and moved the chair next to the window. The view's good, but two hours of staring at the mountains without a sign of life makes me itch inside. Isa, she would be fine with this, she'd spend her time admiring the scenery and making notes in her book. Not for me; the room's far too small to spread out in. Doctor Vitrelli said all I needed was rest, and anyway, I feel fine. It must be time to finish making Cecelia's fish soup.

I grab my trousers from the floor and hold them up to the light. The crisp linen has more lines on it than the old woman in the market square selling her vegetables, and they are stained by the tomatoes she sold. The large marks, hard and brown-red, look like blood, as if I'd escaped from a firing squad – which in some sort of way I have.

I reach into my case to take out another pair, clean. But what the hell – I'll only get them covered with something else, fish guts or worse. Time to finish what I started. I slip on the tomato-stained trousers and pull on one of Isa's extra-large T-shirts; she won't mind, and anyway I can always get her another. It'll be good to go shopping with her for a change, maybe get her out of those ethnic clothes.

A quick glance in the mirror (old habits are hard to kick) and try to pull my hair into some sort of style. It's hard, stiff with salt after being pounded by the sea. A swipe of coral on my lips and, satisfied after what's happened that I don't look too bad, I open the door, ready to get on with making soup.

'Paul!'

'Chloe!'

I stand open-mouthed, while he looks me up and down, and I step back into the room.

'You look... Um I mean, good to see you sweetie.'

'You mean I look a mess.'

He nods, then throws his head back and the air shakes with his laughter.

'You sure do look a mess, Chloe. You look like, well I don't know what you look like, a cross between a very bad chef and...'

'My sister?'

'You said it, babe.'

'What are you doing here anyway?'

'Isa called this morning. She was worried, said you and I need to talk. So I jumped on the next flight, caught that bloody awful ferry over, and voila – here I am.'

'But I tried to...'

I swallow the rest. Why should I tell him? Let him know how hard I tried to call him? Why give him the satisfaction of knowing how much I care for him?

'Yes babe? You tried to what?'

'Nothing...' I stare at him, and have to ask the question that's been standing between us ever since I opened the door. 'How's dear Helen?'

His smile fades as quickly as a summer tan and I can see I've hit a nerve.

'I thought I explained that. Babe, you've got the wrong end of the stick. Oh, what's the use?' He reaches for the door handle.

I look at his hand curl around the tarnished brass knob, knuckles white as he grips it tight, as tight as I want him to hold me. The wind blows from the mountains and cool air sweeps over me. It smells of the island, of the olive groves, of thyme and remembrance. It blows through the bougainvillea and gusts out over the sea.

'Paul, don't go,' I whisper quieter than the breeze.

He relaxes his grip and turns. My clothes are a mess, my hair flecked with grey, and if I had put on any mascara it would be running down my face with the tears dripping off my nose. I don't care anymore.

Paul takes my hand and pulls me down next to him onto Isa's neatly made bed. The sheets are pulled tight and turned over at the top, pillows plumped, and I think how cross she'll be – she won't rest until the ruffled dents made by our bodies are tidied away.

'Babe, I was trying to let her down as gently as I could. You are the only one for me. Sure, I was flattered, who wouldn't be? But it was just the once.'

'You were holding her hand. It didn't look like it was just the once to me. And it was in *our* restaurant!'

'It was the only place I could think of. Look babe, I was upset. You'd just turned me down, and that doesn't do a guy's ego much good. I wanted to ask Helen why you didn't want me. I was miserable, and she was there. It was a mistake, and I'd taken her there to tell her it was over. I wanted *you,* not her.'

Should I believe him? How much of a "mistake" is it to sleep with your girlfriend's so-called best friend? But he has travelled hundreds of miles, I'll give him that, and anyway, Helen is too much of a man-eater for him to cope with. I think back, see him holding her hand across the table... or was it her, reaching out to trap him? I remember the look of guilt and fear in his eyes when he saw me standing at the restaurant door.

'You don't want her, then?'

'No, silly!' His smile returns and lights up the room. 'I was stupid and confused and a bit pissed off that you didn't jump at the chance of marrying me.'

'Oh yes!' and I hit him squarely between the shoulders. 'As if yours has been the only offer I've turned down! What did you think? *She's* not going to get a better offer, not at her age.'

He holds tightly to my fists and pulls me closer.

'Chloe, I love you and I want us to be together. If you don't want to get married then that's fine, we'll muddle along as we have done these past few years. I won't let you go again, I've really missed you.'

'I've missed you too... try to be patient. You never know, I could change my mind.'

Paul plants a huge kiss on my forehead. I lift my face up

to his and pull his head down towards me and press his lips with mine. His mouth is a long lost friend, meeting again after being apart, taking time to get acquainted again. Soon the friendship is renewed and we lie back – crumpling more of Isa's bedclothes – and kiss until it feels we have never been apart.

After we stop to catch breath he lies back and breathes in deeply.

'Babe...' He sounds serious and I hope he's not going to spoil things by asking awkward questions. 'One thing Helen did tell me was how much you were affected by your father leaving when you were young.'

'She shouldn't have, it's none of her bloody business.'

'I'm glad she did. I'm going to make you trust again, I'm not going to leave you, no matter what.' He leans forward and presses his lips to mine, and this time I know, in our own muddled-up, messy way, we'll make it.

'I'd better go down,' I say, giving him one last kiss. 'Isa will be back soon and we have to finish making our fish soup. Tonight we'll talk properly over dinner.'

'I suppose dinner will be this soup you've come here to make?'

'Yes – and it will be the best fish soup you've ever tasted.'

'Ah, daughter of the green shoots, I thought you would stay with that handsome man.'

'What, and miss the best bit? I've squashed, sliced and stirred, and now it's time for the fish – and I'll never know how to make fish soup without that, will I?'

Cecelia stares at me, and the look of surprise and joy somehow makes me feel content, as if this is the point – standing in a kitchen stirring a pot full of soup – where my life has been leading up to.

Steam begins to rise from the red liquid, filled with the tears cried over onions, the blessings received with garlic, laughter and love squashed with each tomato and tempered with the passionate heat of chillies.

I wipe my hands and lift a large fat fillet onto the marble slab.

'Okay, so what do we do with this then?'

'A strange choice for a woman who is one of life's hunters!

This lazy fish hangs around wrecks, gorges itself on easy pickings, and is easily trapped. Unlike a mackerel, with blue and green tiger stripes, or a tuna hunting its prey, the cod is white and fat and settles for the easy life.'

'I didn't think there was such a difference with fish.'

'Oh yes, daughter, and that is the choice you have to make. You must decide what you really want out of life. Spend it racing about the sea hunting for prey until one day you make the mistake of taking a bright hook spinning though the water?' Cecelia takes the heavy fish from my hands and holds it almost reverently. 'Or, you can rest, learn to wait, swim slowly in the sea and grow fat.'

I don't know about the growing fat bit, but I can still taste Paul and hear him moving about in the room above the kitchen, and I reach to touch the cold fish.

'Not much of a choice, is it, Cecelia?'

She smiles at me and shows me how to cut the soft white flesh into pieces, making sure each one is small enough to fit onto a spoon, I have had enough of flashing through life, like a shoal of mackerel chasing sand eels. I don't want to have to start all over again, kissing frogs and hoping they will turn into handsome princes. I want Paul, I want to settle down with him, take it easy, and find calm water to rest in.

'Have you seen Isa?' I ask.

Cecelia wipes her hands and reaches up for a clove of garlic placed next to the stove. She lifts it to her nose and breathes in.

'She has gone to make her offering to the goddess, and will return with either her blessing or her anger.'

'I don't understand... you're saying she's gone to the crossroads? Why did she want to go there?'

'She is meeting with Fredriko. I listened to your words and spoke with her, she knows that he is the son of my husband and has gone to find him in the olive grove.'

I place my arm around Cecelia's shoulder and she puts the garlic back, ready to make an offering in the morning. She pats my hand and takes hold of the next fillet.

17. A pot filled

Isa

'Later.'

'Yes, later.'

I reach to touch his fingers, to hold on to Fredriko as long as possible, until the tips of our fingers part. I turn and push aside the friendly fish, sending the curtain clattering around me, and from the kitchen I hear Cecelia and Chloe, their voices accompanying a percussion of pans and ladles. I take a breath of a moment to hold onto this feeling of happiness bubbling inside and keep it mine before I have to share it. I feel warmth held in my stomach and, waiting until the last possible moment, walk into the noisy steam-filled room.

'There you are!' Chloe greets me with a kiss, pushing aside a fragment of fringe clinging to her hot forehead. 'I thought you were going to miss out on the fish bit of the day.'

'Wouldn't miss it for the world, no point making fish soup without fish, is there?'

Cecelia flaps away a rising cloud of steam from above the large soup pan and smiles across the heated room.

'Ah, Gift of Isis, you are just in time.'

She looks at me intently, looking past my eyes, as if trying to find out if I have changed. I see her searching, to discover if Hecate has spoken, and her face betrays her. Behind the gentle dark gaze, the roundness of her cheeks, I can see a jealous heart, smouldering, not wanting to admit that the goddess has answered my prayer and accepted my offering.

'You gave your gift to Hecate?'

'Yes, Cecelia.'

'She accepted it?'

'Yes,' I whisper.

She stares at me, her steady gaze plunging deep into my eyes. Eyes opened for the first time by the honesty of her love for Fredriko, and then she turns to stir the pot. The kitchen is silent, and Cecelia watches the whirlpools come and go as she stirs the pan filled with soup.

'You have pleased her,' and like a mother who cannot stay angry at a child for long she smiles at me. 'I see she has wiped away the fear from you and you have found what you have been searching for. Your eyes shine with her blessing.'

As if satisfied with that, Cecelia takes a cloth and lifts the pan from the stove.

'Daughters, now we are together we can allow the fish to become part of our soup. The pan should be hot enough to cook the fish, but not with the fierceness of flames to make it boil.'

'But how will the fish cook without heat?'

I try to remember everything I had written down, but I can't. It's hard to change, to learn without making notes, to love and trust that everything will work out all right. It's so difficult to leave behind a lifetime of depending on others to fill me up, people I'd put so much store in. Simon, on whom I'd pinned my hopes to be my salvation from Mum. I knew it was Chloe in the back of his car that night. I'd recognise her hand anywhere, I kissed it to sleep, I rubbed it better when she fell, and pressed against the steamed up windows it couldn't be anyone else. I didn't understand until now that she needed me more than I had ever imagined.

'The liquid is only a fish-bone cooler than if it were boiling, but it is the right temperature to ensure the flesh stays together and does not break into a thousand pieces.'

Cecelia takes pieces of fish and gently slides them into the pan. Chloe leans closer and I join her, and watch the translucent flesh change to opaque white, clouds floating in a blood-red sky. The bite-sized portions are added one by one, and Cecelia names them as they join each other to swim together in the pot: *Snapper, Cod, Mullet, Bass, St Peter Fish.*

I turn to Chloe concentrating on the pot, watching how it changes from a thin base into a soup as thick as a winter stew.

'You're very quiet,' I say, nudging her and bringing her out of her trance.

'I've got a lot to think about.'

'What? Finishing the soup?' I give her a quick dig in the ribs. 'I didn't think you wanted to be here?'

'Well things change, *I've* changed.' Chloe looks deep into the pot, as if she wants to jump in and immerse herself in all the flavours. 'Paul's here.'

'I'm glad he came.'

'So am I.'

'Are you okay with it, with him being here?'

'I don't know.'

'What do you mean, you don't know?'

'Oh, I'm pleased he's here, don't get me wrong. I want to make a go of it as much as he does, but...'

'But *what?*'

'Well I am worried about you Isa. This holiday, this cooking course, it... it has opened my eyes... it has been...' She hesitates, then takes a deep breath. 'The time I've spent with you has been the best, it's been so good that I don't want anything to spoil it, I don't want to spoil *us*. If we, if Paul and me, do work it out and start again, well – where does that leave you? I want us to enjoy each other and I'm frightened that you'll spend the rest of your life alone, no Mum, no sister, no-one.'

I take hold of her hand, ignore the fact that she's wearing one of my better T-shirts and it's covered in fish innards, and lead her outside into the small garden filled with herbs. The garden is cool after the heat of the kitchen, and we sit on a low wall, the stone holding the warmth of the day, the smell of the herbs held in the breeze blowing from the mountains.

'You're not to worry. We'll always be as good as sisters can get, just like Cecelia and Marissa. We'll end our days laughing about the past and putting the future into its place, and...' I can still feel Fredriko's warmth on my body and smell the bed of thyme on my skin. 'I will never be alone.' Chloe moves closer and I put my arm around her. 'Neither of us knows where all of this will take us. You might travel off to God-knows-where, but you'll always know where to find me.'

'The house? You're going to keep it then?'

'No... yes... I don't know.'

'Well, what are you going to do?' She turns and faces me, as if I've finally lost my marbles, as if the sun has affected my brain.

'You can't leave. You've lived there, well, practically forever.'

'And now it's time I broke free.'

'So where will you go? Paul's flat's far too small for you to come and stay with us.'

'I haven't decided what I'll do, where I'll go... wherever it is I know my life is starting again.'

And there is Fredriko...

18. Swimming together

Chloe

'I thought you said Paul was here,' says Isa, frantically pulling at the sheets on her bed.

'He is,' I tell her, wondering where he's gone, and add under my breath: 'Somewhere.'

She smooths the bed clothes until the white cotton cover looks like the icing on a wedding cake, then turns her attention to the pillows. With force she pounds, pummels and punches them into shape, until they resemble marshmallows sitting on top of a frothy cup of milk.

'I won't ask what you and Paul were doing on my bed.'

'Talking mainly,' I say weakly, knowing that she doesn't believe me.

'What about?'

'Him, me, Helen... everything.'

'And?'

'And he's going to stay.'

'So, *where is he then?*'

I shrug. I'd expected to find him lying on the bed with a silly grin on his face. I wanted to open the door and have someone waiting for me. Don't get me wrong, I'm happy she's found someone at last, and Fredriko will be good for her. Despite everything, I don't want her to be alone anymore.

'I thought he'd be here by now. If he doesn't come soon he'll miss...' A spike of doubt pierces deep inside me and I am suddenly afraid that Paul will never come back. 'I so want him to share our fish soup with me.'

'Well, he can't be far,' Isa says, tucking in the sheets, folding over the edges, making them as sharp as the corner of an envelope.

I turn away. No he can't be far. I sit on the edge of my own crumpled bed, the sheet flung back, and I stare at the pillow. In the middle, in the dent where my head lay and still damp where my hair dried, is a small note. The dirty hand-made paper, obviously torn out of Isa's ethnic notebook, is covered in Paul's spider-scrawled writing.

Babe, gone to have a look round the island.
Catch up with you later.
Paul.
P.S. Can't wait to taste this soup of yours.

I read it again, the same way I would read his texts. Clear at first; then I begin to find more in the words, hidden meanings. He doesn't say he loves me... and what does *catch up with you later* damn well mean? I'm not one of his casual acquaintances, someone who you see and might or might not meet up with again – or am I?

'He's gone out.'

'Oh, I was looking forward... how was it? The both of you, I mean.'

'Okay, I think. At least we're talking, and it was so good to see him again. And it's all down to you, if you hadn't called him I wouldn't have this chance.'

'It's this island. It's woven some sort of magic around us.'

'Don't be daft.' I throw a pillow at her, but as I look out at the sun setting over the olive grove I begin to think that maybe my sensible, dutiful, boring sister might be right.

'Come on, you,' she laughs, catching it, plumping it up and placing it back neatly. 'We've got to get ready. It's nearly time for the place to open and Cecelia says fish soup day is always busy.'

'What are you going to wear?'

'This, I suppose. It's practical and won't get too messy if we spill any of the soup.'

I pull a face: *not the Indian cotton skirt and tie-dye T-shirt!* I haul my case up onto her bed and wrench it open.

'Chloe, I've just tidied ...'

'Isa, for once in your life stop being so practical! Tonight you and I are going to serve fish soup looking like a million dollars.'

I tip up my case and there is a cascade of carefully-cut trousers, one-off designer skirts, silk shirts to match, T-shirts – each one costing more than Isa's entire wardrobe – and shoes. I love my shoes. Sandals with diamantes and gold thread, stilettos in killer red, hold-your-breath blue and a hypnotic shade of lime green, all ruinously expensive and ridiculously luscious.

'This... and this.' I pull out one of my more subdued skirts: cream with green spots and matching top, thin straps, low cut, for her to display those lovely round breasts. I'm sure Fredriko will appreciate that, even if she doesn't.

'Who for?'

'You of course, silly.'

'I don't think so...' She runs her hands down her skirt, a garish mix of curry powder and saffron cotton. 'I'll stick with this. It makes me feel comfortable. It's who I am, Chloe.'

'Fashion's not supposed to be comfortable.' I should know! Blisters and callouses where my feet have been shoved into tight shoes, and I think the start of a bunion!

'Well *I* like it... but I'll wear the top.'

'But Isa, it's all so... so *ethnic!*'

I despair of her, but she's adamant and the top, turmeric and gold, will match at least one of the colours in that skirt.

'Fredriko didn't think it was *ethnic*. He thought I looked nice.'

Nice! That's what you say to your granny wearing the latest thing in crimplene! I prepare for the next round, try to get my sister – who is only just the right side of middle-aged – into something with a bit of style. I think back to the conversation in the garden, remembering the smell of rosemary.

'Isa, earlier – did you mean what you said? Selling the house, moving on?'

'Every word.' Her face lights up. 'Chloe, for the first time I have found... when Mum died I thought, this is it, my life's over. I had nothing. You weren't the best help, making your queenly visits, both of you on your best behaviour, before you went off again.'

She says it without venom or spite, stating facts, and I know she's right. The last visit, I only stayed as long as I could stand the claustrophobic side ward. Couldn't put up with Isa fussing around while Mum lay there, skin iodine yellow, dipping in and out of consciousness. I couldn't stand any of it and returned to a home, which had never felt like one, with its flock-covered walls, pine-panelled ceiling and the kitchen where Mum hid the bottles – vodka, gin, wine. Whilst my mother's life was slipping away, I sat on the stairs looking through the bannister, a scared little girl, wishing with all her heart that her Daddy would scoop her up in his arms again, and that she belonged to a normal, boring family.

'Don't look at me like that, Chloe. I wouldn't change it for the world, it's made us who we are. And maybe me and Fredriko...'

Isa wraps her arm around me, holds me close, and I can feel her happiness trembling through her body and into mine.

'But you've only known Fredriko for less than eight hours; you can't be sure of anything in that short space of time.'

'I thought so too.' She takes her arms from around me and wraps them across her stomach, as if she is protecting something exquisitely precious. Her smile is not for me, or for show to make others happy. She smiles to herself, hugs herself. 'I only know how I feel at this moment. I want to be with him forever, Chloe.'

I look at the rainbow of clothes lying on the bed, a snapshot of my life, so much jumble, poured out of a suitcase which has seen too many hotel rooms, and rummage through them. The dresses bought from fashion houses, the shoes direct from Milan, and the scarves. I search for the scarf Paul haggled for with the beach seller. Proof that all of this was not wasted, that there was something tangible, a memory of good times spent with Paul, and the hope that there will be more: a future with him.

'I can't find it.'

'Can't find what?'

'The scarf, I had it on earlier, before I...'

The penny drops and I flop down on top of the mountain

of silks, cottons, linens, and burst into tears. A monsoon storm splashes on the pink, green and purple silk, spreading out over them like a flood. The hole I feel inside, a case full of nothing, no memories, nothing to connect me to anyone, just a pile of quick-fix comforts to make me feel good.

'Hey Chloe, slow down!' Isa reaches over and grabs my hand. 'Look at you! What is it? Nothing can be that bad.'

'I lost the scarf Paul bought me, the only thing he bought just for me. It must have been washed away when I fell into the sea.'

'It's only a scarf, not the end of the world.'

'I suppose...'

'And Paul is *here*. You'll have plenty of time for him to buy you new scarves.'

Isa wipes my face and I begin to think that if she can change, find love in a few hours, then there is a chance for me and Paul.

'I'm really happy for you, Isa. Ignore me; I'm feeling sorry for myself, that's all.'

'Come on, silly,' and she holds up a piece of silk for me to blow my nose on. 'Here blow.'

'You do realise that's $750 of Chinese silk!'

Isa looks at me and I look at her and we both know none of it matters any more. The cars, the hotels, the first class life; none of it. I've got all I need here, sitting next to me, my sister Isadora. Her face breaks into a huge smile and both of us tumble back, roaring with laughter.

'And how much is this?'

'$1025, Irish linen.'

She wipes her eyes on it.

'And this?'

'$300 Egyptian cotton.'

She works her way through the pile, tossing them onto the floor, while I struggle to look indignant as she trashes my wardrobe.

'Well, I reckon you've got the budget of a small country lying there on the floor.'

'Come on then.' I throw a pair of Jimmy Chews on the top of the mound. 'Let's go down, Cecelia will be waiting.'

19. Hecate's Supper

Cecelia

The offering, still to be made, itches in my hand. It is time I made my peace with her. Hecate has refused to accept every hand-warmed clove I have carried to appease her. I have walked this road in summer, when the mountains held on to the wind; in autumn, greeting the young girls and old men weighed down with olive-filled baskets; in winter, when I listened to the sea argue with the shore; and in spring, when my heart aches.

Spring was the season I loved the most. Mama celebrated my arrival into this world with pork and clams, when the trees cast off winter. Every birthday Papa would bring gifts the other girls envied – a doll with a china head and lace underwear, thin gold bracelets which rattled on my skinny arms, and, when I was too old for dolls and bangles, perfume from lands warmed by a south wind. Emilio led me to the olive grove in spring, took me for the first time and on that day I forgot to respect Hecate. It had been in this time of renewed growth, when the earth began to blossom, the sea took Julio.

I keep my thoughts to myself and try not to remember the spring day when they took Papa. In the confusion the doll with the china head was smashed, and my heart was broken into a thousand pieces. Now the biting cold of winter is my only comfort.

Hecate holds onto her anger and has thrown every offering back into my face, as the wind picks up the sand and hurls it with hatred back at the sea.

Cool air from the mountains dries my tears and I watch their shadows grow, hands spreading over the island, caressing the soil as a mother cannot help stroking the soft skin of a baby. I see the path where Emilio travelled, a winding ribbon of sun-dried dust, wrapped around the peaks before disappearing to the north.

I have often wondered, when walking this road alone and seeing the mountain tracks: if I had walked those paths with Emilio, if I had not stayed locked in the womb of the village but spread my wings – like the buzzards catch warm currents, lazy and content – and joined my husband in his travels, perhaps I could have escaped Hecate's reproach. The past is easy to change when looked back on, and I was too frightened to step on any road other than those my feet fitted, and Emilio had to travel alone.

The village hugs itself behind me. The houses lean close together, gossiping and scolding, and I step onto the empty road. I pass Dr. Vitrelli's house, the garden filled with herbs and healing plants, and tighten the grip on my offering. I look back and allow the loneliness I have felt all these years to wash over me. Alone as a daughter of a Papa who sent good men away for no reason other than that they disagreed with him. A lonely wife who, once she felt the movement inside her belly, forgot to understand the needs of her husband.

Stones crunch under my feet, reminding me of where my steps are taking me. My knees throb with the climb and I have to stop and listen to the cicadas. They are a choir singing an opera; as each one closes its wings, as the day cools, duets are sung on each tree until finally, from the olive grove, one last soloist fills the air.

The sounds of the day finally slip into the evening, and the cicadas will not be heard again today. The quiet covers me like the cerecloth covering Julio, and I feel the same emptiness each time I take the road to visit him. Today is different, there is a lightness in the air which I have not felt before. It came across the waves in Dimitri's boat and walked into *Casa Cecelia*. The sisters blew in as the spring wind blows over the mountains, and filled the spaces inside me where loneliness gathered.

I smell the garlic in my hand and encourage my knees to

walk to where Hecate waits. I feel the same way Papa must have felt when they took him away. It was done, not as he once arranged these things – under the cover of darkness stealing lives. No, Papa was visited by a man in a crumpled suit and whose hair appeared to be having a different conversation with his head. He explained to Papa all about reconciliation and justice. He told Papa that, although things were different now, he must answer for what he has done. It was, of course, done in an open and honest way. But they still took Papa and locked him away. I never saw my Papa again, to tell him his daughter forgave and loved him.

The goddess glows in the evening sun, and holds high a torch ready to greet the dark. It lights the path for souls who have no choice in the road they travel. I reach out and the heat from the stone warms my hand. The folds of her gown, delicately carved, are worn smooth by pilgrims' hands asking for blessings. The stone shines with their touch, the way hair shines after being rinsed in rosemary water, and feels as smooth as silk.

'I have come,' I say to her.

What do you want daughter?

'Forgiveness,' I answer, but cannot look into her face; my eyes can only gaze at the hem of her robe. I wait for her reply, for her to say, *Come daughter and rest a while.* But she is silent.

'Hi, Cecelia, I thought you would be back at the *Casa* making the soup my Chloe's been bending my ear about.'

The silence is broken and I drop my offering. I had not heard his footsteps, this man who has helped Chloe to finally spring into bloom. He walks up to me, then looks at Hecate.

'Who's the statue?'

'Hecate. The goddess who watches over the crossroads.'

'Mmm, pretty impressive. Anyway, thought I'd come up and take a look. Chloe said she came here this morning. It seems to have made quite an impression on her.'

'She understands the power the goddess holds.'

He scratches the back of his neck, sucks in the cool air and holds onto it for what seems like an eternity.

'Tell me,' he says, the air rushing out with the words.

'Chloe, my Chloe... I sense she's not the same woman I knew before. She's different, more relaxed. The Chloe I knew was always busy, ready to skip off on an adventure, but today... well there's something about her... I can't put it my finger on it... it's as if she has...'

'Come home?'

'That's it! It's as if she's found where she belongs.'

'Chloe, your Chloe, has travelled a great distance. This morning she made the traditional offering of garlic, Hecate's supper, and the goddess accepted it.' I look up and in the fading light it is difficult to see the faces Hecate shows to us. 'She keeps her favours for those she knows will accept them.'

Paul looks thoughtful. He sits down on the edge of the road and looks up at the statue. He puts his head on one side and I can see why Chloe loves this man. He has the easy charm travellers have, able to make their home any place their feet take them.

'So this goddess, this Hecate – you say she is very powerful?'

I nod at this stranger to our island, who the land greets like an old friend, and raise my eyes to stare at the goddess. For the years I have breathed on this island I have made offerings to her, and she gave her blessings willingly. Until I fell for Emilo, forgot to honour her, and lay under the olive trees.

The offering lies in the dust. I bend, pick it up, and it sits in my palm. Paul stretches out on the dry grass which struggles to grow on the edge of the dusty road, and he lies as if the ground were a feather bed. I hear the single cicada finish his solo; the silence can be tasted, as a spoonful of cream covers the tongue. I see this easy man who watches me out of the corner of his eye, eager to know more; curiosity shines from under his lashes. His intrusion interrupts my conversation with Hecate and this annoys me.

I move and look up at the face I have not dared to raise my eyes to for so many years. When Julio left this world with only eight birthdays celebrated I made my offering to the face of the goddess who watches over the cemetery, the old woman, who has been vilified by time, mistakenly been called witch and sorceress, feared as one who only deals in the dark arts. They do not see that Hecate, the distant one, goddess of shepherds and sailors, holding her torch high to light the way for souls to ease their journey.

'Why so scared?' he asks. 'It's nothing more than a beautifully carved piece of marble, put here to frighten the superstitious.'

I want to argue, to say that Hecate, the goddess of women, has powers he would not begin to dream of. I look up at the face I had ignored in my hurry to become a mother, the face of the virgin, the maiden who I angered all those years ago. He is right, she is beautiful and she is carved from marble and made by a man. But the goddess is more than the skill of a mason's chisel; her spirit surrounds the island.

'You may be right in what you say, the statue is nothing more than stone, but those who know her will feel her presence and she brings me comfort.'

I have spent a lifetime in fear of this statue, a block of stone I believed could change my past by the offering of garlic; I blamed the anger of a marble statue for events I had it in my own power to alter. This traveller has opened my eyes. I do not need to placate Hecate; she will always be with me.

Paul seems reluctant to leave his resting place, but eventually he stands and faces the village.

'Come on Cecelia, it's getting dark. We should be getting back.'

He holds out his hand and, taking one last look at Hecate, stony in her silence, I place the garlic in my pocket.

20. The rites of Dionysus

Isa

Chloe sits next to the door. She's worried. She folds and unfolds the napkin, a bishop's mitre on the table, it is carefully smoothed and then, as if unsatisfied with the lay of it, she carefully folds it again, making sure every crease is perfect. All the time my sister keeps her fingers busy, her eyes fixed on the door, waiting for Paul.

Chairs are pulled back as each new guest appears, and everyone receives a greeting from the beaded curtain. It clatters briskly around a group of chattering tourists, who pull tables together and huddle, talking and laughing with the freedom of sun and wine. Chloe doesn't give them a second glance. She hardly hears the curtains rattle a welcome to Marissa and Stephanos, she ignores the fish swim with Mario as he joins them, and she barely smiles when I lift the jug and fill her glass with a wine the colour of ruby.

'Hey, Chloe,' I say, taking a sip. 'Come on, he'll be here soon.'

I take the napkin from her fingers and push the wine towards her. She shakes herself, as if casting off a demon clinging to her back, and holds up her glass.

'Cheers, Isa,' and our glasses ring together. 'Here's to us, to sisters, to *Casa Cecelia* and fish soup.'

I'm as nervous as my sister, but try not to show it. Even so, each time the curtain announces another guest, I can't help my heart from jumping and I have to rescue it from the bottom of my stomach where it has plunged with disappointment.

A flock of chicks pecks its way in. They sit, clucking excitedly to each other, young women dressed in skimpy tops and short skirts, and eye up the cockerels in the room.

Chloe waits for Paul and I wait with her, for Fredriko to walk up the hill. Together we stare at the curtain; the faded blue, white and sea-green beads sway in the gentle wind of evening, the fish sparkles and moves lazily in the candlelight, and Chloe tops up my glass. The heat of the summer, trapped in the grapes, is released with each gulp. I feel it rise from my neck and begin to burn my face.

'You never could hold your booze,' my sister laughs as I try to fan my face with my napkin.

'I've never wanted to drink too much. I saw what it can do, saw how it destroyed her.'

'Sorry, didn't think,' Chloe says, putting down her glass.

I always felt Chloe had deserted us, that she didn't *want* to know what it was really like for me, and now as she twists the napkin in her fingers I know she never meant to hurt me. And I know I will never tell her how it was at the end.

At first Mum just looked as if she had been on a good holiday, her skin glowing with a golden tan, and I really thought she'd turned a corner. She was looking fit and healthy. Then the gold began to tarnish and turn to a dark amber as her liver gradually gave in to the years of abuse she had given it. They were very caring at the hospital, making her as comfortable as possible, but the end was inevitable. No-one warns you that jaundice poisons the brain, and that was the hardest challenge as she slipped into a coma, her body fighting every step of the way, until they gave enough medication to stop the fits. No, Chloe will remember her as she saw her last, sober, happy and a mother to both of her daughters.

'There's no point beating yourself up about it, Chloe.' I reach over and take hold of her hand. 'We've both made mistakes, you with Mum, and me? Well, I cut myself off. I just wanted it to be me and her, not to share her with you. No wonder you went off and did your own thing.'

I hear the beads gently embrace a new friend to *Casa*

Cecelia and my heart hovers, beating like a hummingbird's wings trapped in my chest. Fredriko looks terrified, as if at any moment Cecelia could appear and chase him away – a lioness protecting her cubs, flinging barbed words to stick in his back, accusing him, telling everyone how men from the mainland can only bring misery to the island. But Cecelia hasn't returned from the crossroads and Fredriko slumps down in the chair next to me, as if the relief is too much to hold him upright.

'Hello you,' I say, and slip my hand into his.

He squeezes a greeting for me, smiling his smile, and holds on tightly, as if to reassure himself everything is all right.

'Are you well now?' he says turning to Chloe.

She stops mid-fold, the napkin taking up her full attention again, and turns to look at the curtain hanging still and silent.

'Yes. I think so.'

'You look upset.'

'It's nothing,' Chloe says, the wobble in her voice betraying her.

'No, it's nothing,' I say to Fredriko. Nothing he needs to know about, not yet, not until I feel strong enough to tell him all about Chloe and me.

'He should've been here by now,' she says staring out into the night beyond the curtain.

'Who should be here by now?' Fredriko asks. I squeeze his hand again, willing him to stop asking awkward questions.

'Paul.'

A strong gust of wind whistles around the corner and blows at the curtain, sending the beads into a frenzy, and through the jangle Cecelia and Paul part the curtain and walk into the candlelit room. They stand for a moment, as if both had lost their way. Cecelia stares at Fredriko and disappears into the kitchen. Paul spots Chloe and waves.

'Hi babe,' he says, stooping down to give Chloe a kiss, but she turns her head and his lips are firmly planted on her ear.

'Where have you been?'

'At the crossroads with Cecelia, we lost track of time,

that's all. I'm sorry.'

Chloe pats the seat next to her. Paul sits down and she allows him to give her the kiss this time. I introduce him to Fredriko, and then he faces me and smiles.

'Thanks Isa.'

'For what? I haven't done anything.'

'You've done more than you know. You brought Chloe here, and now look at her.'

Chloe grins, her whole face suddenly happy, from the lines at the edge of her eyes, the wrinkle of her nose, and her mouth as wide as the dawn spreading across the sea. In that moment I see what Cecelia has meant, calling her Chloe of the green shoots. My sister, who has grown up with a desert inside and turned into a woman moving so fast through life that roots could not take hold, has been left behind and I can see that the real Chloe has bloomed on this island. She has slowed down, allowed the green shoots which were lying dormant to grow, and is welcoming her future, coming into bloom.

'Me, Chloe, Cecelia, this island... it doesn't matter what has changed.' I reach over, Chloe uncurls her arm, our hands meet in the middle of the table and we know it will be a good evening.

We leave Paul and Fredriko and join Cecelia in the kitchen.

Fresh soft bread should be only for the table, to break as the priest takes bread for communion, and enjoyed warm from the baker's oven.' Cecelia reaches over and lifts the basket. 'Alexandros's granddaughter brings bread each morning and when it has forgotten the warmth of the baker's hand and has become hard at the edge, it is perfect for fish soup.'

Cecelia hands us a small loaf each and we begin to slice. Hard crusts flake on to the floor and we put a slice into the bowls lined up on the table ready to be filled.

'It is now time,' she says, as she takes hold of a spoon, dips it into the soup and waves it in front of us. 'Now, daughters, what can you taste and smell?'

I glance at Chloe. She wafts her hand towards her, as if trying to steal the smell of the soup. I also breathe it in deeply, then blow the hot liquid cool. The metallic tang of the spoon is soon forgotten as soup flows over my tongue and slides down my throat.

'Fish, onions, garlic, tomatoes,' I say, hoping I'm saying the right thing when all I can taste is soup.

'Oh Isa, you must be able to taste more than that!' Chloe says, still waving her hand over the spoon, as though it is incense, purifying her before meditation. She closes her eyes and opens her mouth. 'It's smooth with olive oil, keeping the garlic and onion from drowning the other ingredients.'

Cecelia encourages her with another spoonful.

'Oh, tomatoes!' she exclaims, as if she is shocked by the revelation. 'I can feel them filling the space between the bites of fish melting in my mouth.' She swallows. 'And then, only then, when I think it has gone and am ready for another spoonful, there is a tingle of chilli on my lips, waking up my mouth... and it begs for another taste.'

Cecelia puts down the spoon and takes down a large ladle hanging above the steaming pan.

'Daughters, you have done well. Isa, Gift of Isis...'

'Yes, Cecelia?'

'You have much more to learn, but I think you will not travel far from *Casa Cecelia*.' She looks to where Fredriko is deep in conversation with Paul. 'You are a welcome guest at any time, you will come and learn more, and discover the secrets held in fish soup.'

I feel a bit disappointed; after all, it was my idea to come and learn how to make the soup, me who's written it all down, made sure I followed every step, and now it looks as if Chloe's taking the limelight again.

'Daughter, don't be upset.' Cecelia reads my face as easily as an open book. 'You are cautious and take your time to find what you want. Caution is a good thing, it will keep you safe. It will help you choose wisely, show you where your heart is to rest. It is well-known a cautious cook will never spoil the soup.'

Cecelia turns to my sister.

'Chloe, my daughter of green shoots. You understand the depths underneath my soup, and now with your own soup you can awaken. You will always, wherever you travel

– because this island will never hold on to you – understand, by tasting, by smelling, by feeling what is hidden in the depths of any soup.'

Cecelia takes the spoon from her hand and places a gentle kiss on Chloe's forehead. I feel confused, mixed up inside, fed up I didn't make the grade on the soup front, but glad for my sister, who I have never seen so happy before. The disappointment, tinged with more than a little jealousy, is soon forgotten. I hear Fredriko laughing and know I have plenty of time to make more soup.

'Daughters it is time.' Cecelia plunges the ladle deep into the soup; she lifts it and carefully tips the liquid onto the bread. The dry crust greedily sucks in the liquid. Cecelia waits until the bread has drunk its fill and then adds another ladleful, until the bowl is brimming with the thick liquid, deep red from tomatoes and chilli, and floating with bite-sized pieces of fish. She repeats, ladle, bread, ladle, bowl, until there are all but eight bowls filled.

'You've missed these,' I point out to her, only to receive a smile and a shake of her head.

'All good cooks serve their guests first, and these bowls have been filled for all of those who have heard that *Casa Cecelia* serves only the best soup. We will fill our own bowls later, when the candles have burnt down and the tables have been cleared.'

I look to where the group of tourists are toasting their good fortune of being together, hear the girls giggle with the fun of flirting, see the couple no-one notices sitting quietly holding hands. The candlelight softens the woman's features, smooths out the wrinkles around the eyes she cannot take off the old man sitting opposite. I watch them and want with all my heart for it to be me and Fredriko sat at that table, holding hands, with the conversations of a lifetime between us.

One by one bowls are placed on the tables. The old man, hands dark with age spots, thanks me, rises from the table and places a napkin on the lap of his companion. Then, comfortable in their own company together, they dip their spoons into the soup. Chloe laughs and jokes with the girls, and then collects another tray filled with more of the steaming bowls.

I follow her to where tables have been pulled together and occupied by a large and very vocal gathering. Faces red from beer and sun seem to glow in the dark, and they call for more wine.

'Keep your hands to yourself!' I move quickly to avoid the groping hands pinching my bottom.

'I beg your forgiveness,' the owner of the hand slurs, his accent as heavy as the hand he uses to slap my bum.

'Better watch that lot, they've had far too much already,' I warn Chloe, and turn to make my escape back to the kitchen.

The raucous outbursts from the table get louder, glasses crash against each other and more and more of the heavy red wine flows easily down throats unused to its strength. They cheer as Chloe – head down, concentrating on keeping the tray steady – approaches the table. She carefully puts her load down, then begins to place the bowls in front of the overeager diners.

'Ah, the tiger,' is shouted across the table and I recognise the voice as being the owner of the generously hard hand.

Chloe stops, a bowl of hot steaming soup held in her hand, and I see the colour drain from her face. She slams the bowl onto the table, spilling soup all over the white cloth. I watch as she stares at the soup as if it were blood from an open wound seeping across the table. She turns and I see how terrified she is.

'Not so fast. I think, as you say, we have unfinished business.'

A large bronze arm reaches out and grabs her wrist. She pulls away, but he tightens his grip and I see the square bronze face move closer to her.

'Leave me alone, Wilfred,' Chloe looks like a trapped animal.

From the other side of the room a chair falls to the floor.

'Let her go,' Paul slaps away the hand and takes hold of Chloe.

If it wasn't for the panic in my sister's eyes the scene would look like something out of a farce. Paul with his arm around Chloe's waist and the drunken square-headed bronze German pulling at her arm, like two small boys fighting over the same toy. The grip on her arm is loosened and Chloe turns to bury her head in Paul's shoulder.

'What's going on?' he asks holding her tight.

She looks up at him, rubs her arm where finger marks are beginning to turn into bruises and runs outside, leaving the beads rattling. Inside there is an expectant silence, the calm before the storm, and Paul – mouth tight and eyes narrow – looks down at his adversary.

'Right pal, you better start explaining. Or do you just take some sort of pleasure in groping any woman who comes in reach.'

As if knowing when he was beaten and unable to do anything else, a smile creeps over his face. 'You are welcome to her. You had better give this back.' He reaches into his pocket, pulls out Chloe's batik scarf and waves it at Paul.

I see Paul stiffen. The scarf, waved in front of him as a matador waves a red flag to a bull, is torn from the vice-like grip, and with one last laugh the German raises a glass to the departing Paul.

I go to follow Paul. Chloe will need me. She won't be able to deal with this alone, not after everything she's been through today.

'No – they have to do this alone,' says Fredriko, and blocks my exit.

'But she might go and do something stupid – you don't know my sister.'

'I don't know her, but I do know you, my Isa,' he says and guides me back to my chair. 'And it is time you began to think of yourself and not everyone else. Chloe and Paul will sort themselves out.'

I begin to protest again, but I know he's right. Chloe has lived her own life for so long I feel silly thinking, imagining, that my sister still needs me to oversee her. It is hard letting go, putting myself first, but I look at Fredriko and begin to set myself free.

21. Plenty more fish in the sea?

Chloe

'How dare you, after all the grief you gave me about Helen!'

'I didn't... Paul, *please*!' I feel a gut-wrenching sickness, as though his hand is reaching inside, twisting, and I can't stop the pain.

Paul turns, and without a backward glance strides down the hill and is swallowed up into the dark. I stand there, feeling like a car crash; each second slows until it feels like an hour. I watch the debris of my life fly around me; so much shrapnel to dodge, so many shards of glass ready to pierce and draw blood. I want it to stop. I want none of it to have happened, for it not to be real. At that moment I want to be the old Chloe again, the one who doesn't give a damn, who would shrug her shoulders and tell herself there are plenty more fish in the sea.

I can still hear his feet slap angrily on the concrete, but fading, and then the night takes him from me as he disappears onto the silent sand. I listen. Listen to the sea, the waves stroking the beach, enticing me; the wind, blowing from the mountains, pushes me forward, and when eventually all the noise in my head quietens, I listen to another voice.

It is the soft voice that I listened to while making the soup, as it whispered each ingredient until it changed me and made me understand that on my own, there is no flavour. It showed me how to stop and hear Cecelia's voice. It was so quiet at first, because I wasn't listening to her;

then her voice, rich and full of the taste of the life, told me to take a chance and never to let the soup go cold.

The hours rush back into seconds, and I run. Run down the hill, leaving *Casa Cecelia* behind, candles glowing and tables ready for fish soup day. I pass the small square building covered with posters, sulking in the shadows, the boarded windows staring like blinded eyes. I brush past Fredriko's boat resting on the slipway, waiting for the dawn and a high tide, and run until my feet sink into the cool sand.

I peer into the darkness. Clouds cover the stars and blackness rolls over me. I can't see him, but I know he must be there. He didn't turn back and walk past me. The houses are built close together and there are no hidden passageways, no secret routes where smugglers could run; the island is honest and open.

'Paul,' I shout. 'Let me explain.'

But only the sea answers, ruffling the sand like a father's hand on a child's head, the same way Dad used to mess my hair, and as he will have done to his new son when he couldn't reach mine anymore. In my desperation to speak to Paul my mind begins to remember things I wanted to forget, and I feel the bitterness of losing Dad to his new family.

The sea continues to soothe the sand and I begin to hear a different voice, telling me to stop blaming everyone else for making me feel bad, and this time I answer and promise that when I get back, when I have finished making soup, I will get in touch with Dad and see if there's some way we can forget the past. After all, Isa and I have two brothers we don't even know.

I feel the wind strengthen; it blows the clouds away, letting moonlight scatter across the sea. I see the white-topped waves splash on the shore, and in the cold blue light see Paul kick at the sand.

'Paul!'

He turns, glares at me; the clouds cover the moon and he is swallowed up into the night again. This time I don't hesitate. I place my feet in the hollows left by his feet and follow him down the beach.

'Paul, darling – at least *listen* to what I've got to say.'

I reach out to him but he keeps his distance. I haven't seen him so upset before and if it wasn't so dark I would swear there were tears on his cheek. He holds me at arm's length, as if he doesn't want to touch me, as if I was damaged goods. Dangling in his fingers is the scarf. It flutters in the wind and I want to reach over and tear it from his grasp, fling it into the sea and let it sink without a trace or memory.

I touch his arm and he turns to me. The look on his face is unbearable: disappointment, hurt, jealousy and fear, all roll together into one despairing look.

'Paul,' I whisper his name and he stops and listens. 'I didn't do anything. He...'

'He *what?*' he snaps, and dangles the scarf in front of my eyes. 'He didn't come up to your usual high standard?'

'I'd had too much to drink.'

Paul snorts a laugh with none of his usual good humour in it.

'Okay, okay so I never can have just the one, I was angry, annoyed that you didn't answer any of my calls.'

'Don't you pin this on me! You couldn't get me because stupidly I was trying to get here. To say I was sorry for hurting you. More fool me!'

'How was I to know?' I'm angry at him for doing the right thing, for me not trusting. 'It's was just... listening to your answerphone message. Well, I thought you didn't want anything to do with me again.'

It all sounds so desperate, as if I am making excuses for myself. I push my fingers where tears are starting to well up. I'm not going to cry this time, it would be the last straw and Paul would only feel sorry for me. No, not this time. I take a deep breath and the sea smells different, the fear held in the mix of seaweed and cold salt spray starts to disappear and the cold, dark waves splash a freshness onto the beach.

'I really thought you didn't want to speak to me again.'

'So you went out on the pull,' he sneers.

'Sort of.'

'You did or you didn't.'

'Okay so I thought, *what the hell, if he can do it so can I.* But it went all wrong.'

Paul looks at me and I can see he is searching for some clue, some sign of repentance. Well, he won't be getting that from me. I might have changed but not that much, not enough to beg for forgiveness. Chloe – as Cecelia calls me, the one of the green shoots – has bloomed and yes, my sister and I have become closer. Paul will have to like me for who I am, or he can damn well lump it.

'How did it go all wrong?' he asks, the acid bite to his questioning beginning to dilute. 'What are you trying to say?'

'I'm saying I didn't do anything. I went to his room to try and sober up, then I had every intention of leaving.'

'And?'

'And he...'

I can't help it, the memory of Wilfred's hands mauling me, holding me down, the feeling of helplessness... all my resolve to not show any emotion disappears as quickly as the clouds scud across the sky.

'I was so scared! I couldn't stop him, couldn't do anything – he... he...' I feel the lump in my throat strangling the words. 'He was too strong. He wouldn't listen when I told him no.'

Paul stares at me and in a voice as tight as a boxer's fist speaks the words he dreads saying.

'Did he rape you?'

'No.' I shake my head and miserably wipe my dripping nose. I roll up my sleeve and show Paul the bruises left where I was held down. 'He tried, but I managed to...'

I think back to Wilfred rolling on the floor, clutching himself, red faced and white lipped, and I begin to laugh hysterically. Paul looks at me as if I have finally lost my mind. When I calm down I tell him how close Wilfred came to succeeding, and how I fought back.

'I imagine he's been finding it difficult to walk since you sank those talons of yours into his precious jewels,' smiles Paul, and he bends down and kisses the finger marks on my arm and strokes the bruises as if he could make it all better.

'Come on babe,' he says, wrapping me in his arms, and I let him take charge, knowing I've got to sometimes let the old Chloe go. 'We're a bit of a mess, you and me, and it's about time we sorted each other out.'

'I do love you, Paul.'

'I know you do babe, and I love you, but hey, let's take things one step at a time.'

I nod and allow him to lead me back to *Casa Cecelia*. His fingers are empty and the scarf is being carried out to sea.

Isa waits on the terrace. I see her staring into the dark, listening for our footsteps, and she trips over herself in her hurry to greet me.

'I've got something I have to do babe,' Paul says, and disappears inside, leaving the beads to untangle themselves with a clatter.

'Are you all right, Chloe?' Isa asks.

'Yes.'

Paul strides past her and pulls the curtain with such force the beads don't have time to make any noise.

'And Paul?'

'I think we're getting there.' Raised voices tumble out onto the terrace. 'It's not going to be easy. We've both got to learn to trust each other again.'

My sister wraps me in her arms and hugs me. She asks no questions and I tell no lies. We stand in the cool air, with the sound of the sea calmly stroking the shore, while from inside *Casa Cecelia* is the clamour: Paul roaring like a wounded beast, Wilfred's staccato machine gun replying and getting louder with each volley, a wind circling until it becomes a hurricane.

'Get out,' I hear Cecelia shouting, her voice drowning in the uproar breaking out around her. 'You disrespect my Mama's house, out, out, out!'

'What on earth is this all about?' Isa aks, reaching out to me. I take her hand and briefly tell her about Wilfred, and the child in me who stopped growing up sitting on the stairs watching Dad leave; how I think that now the little girl who was tucked into bed by her big sister, promising everything would be all right in the morning, is finally able to grow up.

Isa pulls me close and holds me, stroking my hair a moment before the giggles come. 'It sounds to me that this Wilfred is getting his comeuppance,' she says, against the cacophony from within.

A sudden explosion of beads scattering indignantly, and we have to jump to avoid the whirlwind as Wilfred staggers past us, swiftly followed by Paul and a furious Cecelia wielding Stephanos's broom.

'You, pal,' Paul shouts at the stunned red face, 'you are not welcome here!'

'*Nein*, you cannot...'

Wilfred has a look of confused innocence as Paul pokes and pushes him along the terrace. Each step backwards knocks the smooth slime out of him. I look at the square face, remembering how he sweated and panted over me, and see the hand that held me down. I rub my arms, the bruises darkening, and I can still feel the stab of his fingers as he tried to force his way into me.

Now he pulls those fingers into a tight ball.

'Watch out, Paul!' I reach out and grab the arm that's ready to jab at Paul's head.

The face of the man who turned my life upside down is twisted with the contempt of a man who usually gets what he wants. He brushes me off as if I were a horsefly buzzing around him, and I fall onto the terrace. Paul lashes out, grabs hold, ripping him away from me along with the Hawaiian garden shirt. The thin, bright fabric which should only be worn on south sea beaches hangs in tatters from shoulders still bearing the scratch marks I tattooed on them.

'As I said,' Paul pants, forcing out the words, the fight, the anger, leaving him breathless as if he has run a marathon. 'You are not welcome here, and if you think you can get away with what you did to my fiancée, then *pal* you'll find what she did to your balls is nothing like what I'll do to them if you ever show your face around here again!'

Wilfred takes a step forward and squares up to Paul, towers over him, in for the kill. He looks at me struggling to stand, then back at Paul, and hisses through his teeth: 'Too thin anyway,' and, giving me a wide berth, disappears back to his stark white apartment.

Cecelia snorts, brushes the terrazzo as if cleaning away the remains of the battle and then, pushing the beaded curtain aside, returns the broom to Stephanos.

'Come on babe,' says Paul. He tucks his hand under my arm and leads me to a chair. We sit on the edge of the terrazzo, and he takes hold of my hand.

'Yes,' I whisper as he sits next to me.

'Yes what, babe?'

'Yes, I'll marry you.'

22. Salt to close the wound

Isa

An awkward silence covers the tables as I slide in. I hear Wilfred's name whispered past the empty bowl where he had been sitting. The others in his party concentrate on eating their soup, heads down, embarrassed. Occasionally they glance outside, waiting for Paul to come back to accuse them too, guilt by association. The hen-chicks have lost interest; finishing their bowls hastily, they cluck and clatter out to find something else to fill their evening.

I see Chloe and Paul sat outside, on the edge between light and dark, the candlelight spilling out over the terrazzo until it's eaten up by the night. At first I didn't see Cecelia, sat opposite Fredriko. She perches on the edge of the chair as if ready to escape at the smallest excuse.

'Fredriko Salvadori, your name is one that hurts my tongue when I speak.'

Fredriko opens his mouth, but Cecelia pulls him into silence with the spike of a finger, and the cut of her hand sweeps across the air. She turns and looks at me with soft eyes, then turns to Fredriko and they become as hard as a steel knife as she throws her words across the table.

'Isadora, this woman who was a girl inside, a Gift brought by Isis to this island, has fallen for your charms. In the hours which have made less than a day, you have stolen her from me by using words your father used many years ago.'

Cecelia is talking as if I have left the room; she doesn't

see me any longer. I sidle in next to Fredriko, unsure what to do. If it were Chloe sat here she would demand to be heard, wouldn't let the man she loves be spoken to in that way. But I can see the need Cecelia has to say these words. So I sit quietly and allow Fredriko and Cecelia to draw their battle lines, and hope in the deepest corners of my heart that no-one wins.

Cecelia keeps her gaze firmly locked on Fredriko, and I reach under the table to hold his hand. It is cold and there is the barest tremble in his fingers. The silence between the words is like the mist rolling in from the sea, cold and impenetrable. Cecelia searches Fredriko's face, as if she's looking for a chink in his armour, seeking the place she can hurt him more than Emilio hurt her.

'Emilio Salvadori was my husband. But I have chosen not to recognise that name as part of mine when my son, Julio Salvadori, was killed by his father's stupidity. You have that name and hold it too proudly.'

Fredriko's jaw tightens and he grasps my hand. His knuckles are as white as bone but his face burns like the setting sun boils into the sea.

'Madam *Salvadori*,' he begins through gritted teeth, and Cecelia's eyes widen with rage as he uses the name she refuses to acknowledge. 'I love my Papa. Whatever the injustice you think he has done you, he will always be the man I look up to, and the man I am proud to have call me *son.*'

'Before he was *your* father,' Cecelia flings back, 'he was my husband, and the Papa of my child.'

Cecelia pulls herself to her full height as if she could make herself so tall that she would be able to look down onto Fredriko. Her back is as straight as the roads in the village are crooked, and she sits in the chair tall and stiff.

'I did not want to tell you how your father had hurt me. But he would never hear my voice and you, his son, would also not listen. You have, to the pain in my heart, refused to leave the island as I had wished.'

I am torn between them, and reach over the table to stop this war from being fought any further. Inside my stomach is churning and I am once again a ten-year-old, grown up before her time, pleading with Mum to stop crying, stop fighting with Dad. But a small, fat little girl just wanting to be noticed failed miserably, and here I am again, in the middle of two people I love, trying to make peace.

My hands shake with fear of what is going to happen, as it happened before: Cecelia will hate me, Fredriko will leave, and I will be alone again.

I lean over, trying to hold on to both of them. It's the smallest of touches, a pot – placed on every table – filled with salt. It wobbles and the salt is scattered across the white table cloth.

Cecelia starts to brush the grains together, as if they were gold dust, into the centre of the table. Fredriko absentmindedly joins her, methodically gathering each bright white crystal with his fingers. Together they brush and scrape until every last grain is found and placed in a small pile in the middle of the table.

'Cecelia,' he says quietly, licking his fingers. 'My Papa lives his life in the past. He talks of you constantly.'

'What do you mean, *talks?*' she snaps at him, and drops a pinch of the salt back into the bowl. 'You are telling me that Emilio, who has been dead to me for more years than I knew him – this man from whom I have not heard for longer than you have lived – is still *alive* in this world?'

'My Papa, Emilio Salvadori, who was once your husband, has been a good father to me. He does live, but not in this world any more. His thoughts are confused, and inside his head he mixes the past with the present.'

Fredriko sprinkles a few grains of salt into the dish and I look at his hand, the hand that held mine in the sand, explored the Eye of Osiris, and held me so gently in the olive grove. I want to reach out and grasp it, never let it go, but I know I must allow him and Cecelia to sort it out together. So I clasp my own hands together under the table to prevent them from interrupting, and sit back.

'Papa,' Fredriko says, pushing the salt with his finger, forming a circle of small diamonds glittering in candlelight. 'As the past became more real to him he spoke of a woman, from this island, whom he once loved. At these times he becomes sad and cannot prevent tears from being shed each time he speaks of her.'

Cecelia gathers the rest of the salt into a rough pile.

'He has no right to sadness,' she says beginning to separate each grain. 'This Papa of yours left me when I was so deeply hidden in my grief that the wounds caused by him have never healed.'

'Papa often mistook me for his old friend Mario,' continues Fredriko, choosing to ignore Cecelia's anger. 'We would talk about fishing, of how the sea had made him the man he was and how he had once lived a simple life. He spoke of the Eye of Osiris and how, as a young man, he was too arrogant to keep it painted.'

Cecelia snorts, scattering grains across the table.

'It is a pity that *your* Papa was not so concerned when he took *my* son onto that sea he loved so much.'

They continue to gather and scatter the salt across the table, and I see this war of words needs to be resolved. Unlocking my hands, I begin to scrape the grains into the centre of the table. Satisfied at last, I reach over the white, white pile, looking like the snow which refuses to melt on the top of mountains, and grasp Cecelia's hand.

'Cecelia.' I look into her dark brown eyes, see the anger in them smouldering, and hold onto to her hand, which is shaking with indignation and fury.

'Fredriko,' I whisper, savouring his name, and feel my fingers tingle as I reach for his hand. He wraps his fingers around mine. His thumb gently strokes my palm and it's as much as I can do not to bring it to my lips and kiss it.

I take a deep breath. 'You've both scattered too many words, like these grains of salt, and instead of it healing and purifying, you have chosen to throw it over the table.'

Cecelia nods and, letting go of my hand, she scoops at salt, harvesting it pinch by pinch until it is safely placed into the bowl. 'Mama used salt sparingly. She would add just enough to give a dish flavour, but not too much for it to overpower the taste.'

Fredriko caresses my palm then, and I sink into his touch, and feel the loss when he lets go and joins Cecelia in placing the remaining salt into the small bowl, roughly made, spring-meadow green with rich black olives painted around the rim.

'My Mama said salt was a precious gift from the sea. She would offer a prayer to St Paul, who taught the value of salt to the righteous, and treated it with respect.'

'Your Mama seems to be a prudent housewife,' Cecelia concedes, looking directly at Fredriko, challenging him. 'Does she love Emilio?'

'With all her heart,' Fredriko says without hesitation, smiling at his memories. 'She told me when she first met Papa he carried the weight of his past. Over the years she helped to heal his wounds and never asked why, when she chopped onions, his eyes held tears.'

Cecelia sits back and I watch as she licks her fingers, as if the salt could change the taste of them.

'Fredriko,' she says, and seems to savour his name as if it had been sprinkled with salt. 'The wounds Emilio left me with will be difficult to heal. I hear from your words that your Mama is as strong in you as your Papa.'

She presses her lips together and as she leans forward the look on her face changes. The anger has been replaced by... well, I'm not quite sure how to describe it, one of resignation and acceptance – as if she has found a truce, a piece of no-man's-land where the hurt she has felt for too many years can be left behind.

I wait, keeping as still as possible, and time slows until all I can hear is Fredriko's breath, not the excited breathing of when he showed me his boat, not the deep inward suck as he pulled at the oars, or the whisper of a sigh on my ear as he told me he loved me in the olive grove... this is the breathing of a man who has run a race and can see the finish line.

Cecelia reaches over and takes hold of Fredriko's hand. She carefully turns it over.

'It is time for us to heal some wounds,' she begins, and with her other hand takes hold of a measured pinch of salt. 'You have, running through your veins, the same blood as my precious Julio. As his brother, I offer you peace.'

As if she is adding flavour to a favourite dish, Cecelia sprinkles salt into Fredriko's upturned palm. Then, satisfied, she lets go of his hand and time rushes back into the room, shaking the beaded curtain until it can't help but rattle as if the fish wants to swim in the salty air.

Fredriko slowly raises his hand to his mouth, all the time looking at Cecelia. He licks the salt from his hand and when it has all gone he smiles across the table.

'Thank you,' I whisper to Cecelia.

'You have healing hands, Gift of Isis,' she says, rubbing her knee and pushing her chair back. 'Always remember to season your soup well. Tonight I welcome the brother of Julio at our table.'

23. Marissa and Stephanos

Cecelia

I greet the sisters, hold my arms as wide as the island is small, and welcome them back into the kitchen.

'Your return is welcome to me.' It is right they are here, I know now they belong here. 'We will all eat together.'

The sisters have stirred feelings that I had forgotten, the concerns a mother has for her children. Chloe made my heart anxious when she rushed to follow her traveller. I feared after all she had discovered, everything she had begun to understand, it would all be undone, like the scarf she wore when she left at midday.

I dip the ladle into the pan, to where the best fish hides and where the strongest flavour gathers.

'Come on Cecelia,' says Chloe. It warms a heart to hear her. 'We've made the soup together and now together we will serve it.'

Bowls are filled and placed on the tables. Paul waits for Chloe and Fredrik for Isadora. Marissa and Stephanos accept their soup with gentle thanks. The final two bowls are filled and I watch the bread greedily drink and thicken the soup. I turn, the bowls of soup hot in my hand. Chloe and Isadora stand together and reach out to take them from me.

I am unable to speak; my head shouts too loud with all the changes it has accepted. The sisters lead me into the warm glow of candlelight where I can rest and rub my knees with the cloth smelling of soap and lemon. A bowl is filled with soup for Mario, and one for me.

Stephanos sweeps the soup into his mouth the way he cleans the cobbles, fast and with a great deal of noise. Chloe turns, and in her forthright way asks me what the road sweeper's story is.

'When we have finished our soup daughter, you will hear a tale of patience and of love.'

Satisfied, she continues to eat her soup.

'Cecelia?'

'Yes, my Gift of Isis.'

'It would mean the world to me if you would give your blessing to me and Fredriko, now that he knows whose son he is.'

'I understand what you are asking, Isadora.' I wait for the hurt to bite into my soul, for his name to fight with the son I bore, and to feel the lump, as solid as any gnawing cancer. But I cannot find it inside, no matter how much I search into every hidden corner for the hate and hurt.

I look at the man sitting next to Isadora. He is not his father, he is not my Emilio and he is not here to banish Julio from my heart. This half-brother to my son adores the Gift of Isis who, like the goddess she was named after, did not give up and found the Eye of Osiris. 'You have both helped to open these old stupid eyes, clouded when I lost Julio, and I have wasted too much time blaming others for my blindness.'

Isadora bites her lip hard and turns away as if afraid to speak.

'What's wrong, Isa?' Chloe asks.

'Nothing, just happy I guess.'

'You don't look it.'

'Happy or sad. Sometimes it's like they feel the same inside.' Isadora sniffs, then smiles at Chloe. 'I feel mixed up, this happiness, this joy, is so overwhelming it hurts more than anything. I'm so frightened it won't last.' She turns back and smiles at me. 'It will last won't it Cecelia?'

'Yes daughter,' I reassure her and dip my spoon into the soup. A soup with the solid base Mama taught me to make. It has the taste of all the soups I have served at *Casa Cecelia* during all my lonely years, but yet it holds something new and different. It has the breath of new flavours. Of Chloe, who could have made it taste bitter; she arrived sour-faced and angry with her sister for bringing her here, and blaming herself for her stubbornness. Of Isadora, who would have made the soup too bland with her eagerness to remain unchanged, keeping love at a distance. The soup has changed with them; it has a delicacy of touch, sweetened by the growing and blossoming Chloe and lightness of taste of the Gift of Isis. The sisters have given my fish soup a new flavour, and everyone who tastes it will ask for a second bowl.

The soup has woven its spell, and the last guest has left, filled with its warmth and thanking the beaded fish for its welcome, and *Casa Cecelia* lapses into silence as friends and lovers eat their soup. Mario keeps his eyes firmly on his bowl, scooping up mouthfuls as if casting his net onto the sea. Marissa smells and tastes the soup, while Stephanos keeps watch, ready to guide her hand. I see the conversation of lovers as Isadora and Fredriko dip their spoons, as if in a mirror, lifting the soup to their mouths while all the time their eyes are devouring each other. And there is Chloe, eating her soup slowly, savouring every mouthful, and describing each one to Paul.

'Under all of these flavours – can you taste it?' she asks him, pushing a spoon into his mouth.

'I taste an excellent soup, big in taste, nothing more than that.'

'I can see I'm going to have to educate you,' she laughs, and scoops another spoonful. 'Don't gulp it down like you were a condemned man eating his last meal... right, *now what can you taste*?'

'Fish.'

'Yes, and...?'

'Fish.'

Chloe laughs, drops the spoon back into her bowl and flicks him with her napkin.

'I've got my work cut out with you, haven't I?'

'Work in progress, that's me.' He finishes his soup, leans over and kisses Chloe. She responds as if just as delighted as in every spoonful of soup, and returns his kisses as if he were her last meal. I feel a spike of jealousy in my breast. It was mine once, when I lay under the olive trees with Emilio, that wonderful feeling of sinking so deeply into someone that nothing else mattered. He strokes her face and combs her hair with his fingers, and even though *my* moment for such love disappeared in the time it took to walk past Hecate, hers will last. Chloe fills the air with the sweet scent of blossom, the green shoots no longer hidden inside, and I bask in her happiness.

'Cecelia...' Chloe glances at me. 'You haven't forgotten about Marissa and Stephanos's story, have you?'

I reach over and squeeze Marissa's arm. 'May I tell these sisters your story?'

Marissa smiles, pats my hand and nods.

'My sister, who sits here as she always does on fish soup day, has a long story. You have been told how she became my sister, and that despite her blindness she can see more of this world than I have been able to. When Mama joined Julio in the warm ground protected by rosemary, my sister who had lived with us ever since the sea brought her to us, decided that she would move into a small house at the edge of the square. I had sunk into a pit, all-consumed with my own loneliness. Mama had left me, Emilio had taken my hopes to the mainland, and Julio was as cold as the deepest sea cave. In all of this I did not see the need Marissa had to live her own life.

'It was difficult for her, and the road from the square was uneven and had more holes than a moth can make in a blanket. Marissa, sure-footed, knew the paths she had always trod, began to become unsteady and would often trip, grazing her knees and elbows.'

'What about Stephanos?' Chloe demands, looking at the road sweeper, who smiles at the sound of his name, and Marissa whispers gently to him that we are telling their story.

'Patience daughter, if a story is worth telling it has to start somewhere. Stephanos's grandpapa swept the road when Mama was a girl. He would begin his day at the old woman's house, where Dr. Vitrelli now lives, sweep through the square – remembering to offer a prayer to the virgin, stop at *Casa Cecelia* for a bowl of soup, and then down to where the cobbles of the slipway meet the sea.

'When Stephanos's grandpapa had worn his broom down he decided it was time to play dominoes with the old men. His son, Stephanos's father, replaced the bristles and continued the work of keeping our road clean. The village had changed but as diligently as his father had done before him, Stephanos's father made sure the dust of the day was swept into the sea. He watched the men who left the island under the cloud of suspicion, and carefully swept the step of the small square building where Papa sat answering the black telephone. Stephanos's father eventually cleared the path when the men who had survived their imprisonment on the mainland returned. He was there when the old regime sank into oblivion and, as his father did before him, kept his silence.

'They had asked him to testify against Papa, to say all he had seen in the days when men only whispered their thoughts, but – to Mama's everlasting gratitude – he refused to speak other than to say he did not see anything other than the dust his broom raised. After they had taken Papa, Mama rewarded Stephanos's father by keeping a place laid at the table where Stephanos and Marissa are now sitting.'

I hesitate to carry on, but Marissa encourages me. Stephanos fills her glass and places it in her hand.

'Stephanos is the last of his line. His broom is the same as the one his grandpapa used; the bristles have worn and been replaced, and still it is the same as his Papa used. The wooden handle has broken many times and Christofe – the boat builder – has fashioned new ones each time. But still, the broom Stephanos uses is the same one his father and grandpapa swept the road with.'

'Yes, but what about...?'

I stop Chloe before she has time to become impatient. Stories told too quickly have no happy ending. 'Stephanos would lean on his new broom and watch Marissa. He saw how easily she missed her footing. Every day he swept the road from Dr. Vitrelli's house, through the square – offering a prayer to the virgin – and down the hill towards *Casa Cecelia*. Each morning, before my sister had opened her shutters to let the light into her room, and before the faithful had been called to prayer, Stephanos – having noted the places Marissa stumbled – filled the holes in the road and kept clean the path leading from her front door to *Casa Cecelia*. Each evening I would repay him for his kindness to my sister by serving him chicken and rice, pork and clams, stews made from the tender mountain goats, and of course fish soup.

'Stephanos, who will not mind me saying so, is a quiet, modest man. The months grew into years and the bristles of his broom had been replaced more than once. He wiped his plate with bread made by Alexandros's granddaughter and asked me, "Cecelia, do you think if I asked...?" and I nodded, because I knew my sister was weary of walking up the hill on her own, with no-one to guide her.'

Marissa reaches for Stephanos's hand and while he listens to his story he smiles with pleasure and encourages me to finish. 'So it has been, and the road remains constant. Stephanos brushes it from Dr. Vitrelli's house down to the sea. But when he turns his back on the slipway and walks back up the hill, he stops at *Casa Cecelia.* He waits, and after Marissa has finished folding the cloths, he helps her feet find their way home. With Stephanos at her elbow, he guides and catches her when she stumbles. Making a note of where to repair the road, he prevents her from falling. Together they walk up the hill and stop at a small bright green door opening onto the market square. Stephanos places his broom next to the door, allowing it to rest until the morning is allowed past the shutters, the faithful have been called to prayer, and it is time to sweep the road.'

'Oh what a lovely story! Don't you think so, Fredriko?'

The story curls around the room and the Gift of Isis rests against the man she has set her heart on. I warm to this man I had held so much hate for as he wraps his arms around her and buries his nose in her hair – as though breathing the scent of her is keeping him alive.

Stephanos takes hold of Marissa's hand and whispers his thanks to her for allowing him to keep her path clear.

The story continues its journey around the room and rests on Chloe's head. I search her eyes but she is shielding her emotions, as though if she let them show then all too soon they might crash around her, and she would never be able to pick up the pieces again. This daughter of the green shoots, the blossoms not as bright as they should be, looks at Paul. He lifts his spoon, his mind as empty as his bowl; he circles around the edge, glancing at Chloe from time to time as if seeing her for the first time. They have made promises to each other and the gulf they held between them, as wide as the sea between the island and the mainland, has narrowed. These two separate souls needed time to find each other again, but they have eaten fish soup together and that is a good beginning for them.

'It is getting late, daughters. In the morning Dimitri will have to leave on a good tide and you must be ready to say goodbye to this island.'

The sisters reluctantly agree, and begin to gather the bowls and spoons, and I return to the kitchen to clean the pan Mama lifted every day. The kitchen is still and quiet, as if glad the heat and the cooking has finished, and I let its calmness flow over me.

These walls once held the anger of Mama, who hid her tears with onions. They have heard the clash of her head hitting her heart as she chose to love Papa. Like those who follow blindly, I allowed Mama's anger to seep into these white-painted walls to fester inside my own heart, to boil like a spoiled stock. I only looked backwards, and lived in a past I should have left behind. But the walls forgot their fury with the arrival of the sisters; they have allowed me to release it with each telling of my story, and the sour taste it left behind has been washed out of my mouth.

I pat the wall and hear Mama sigh; she is tired and should have the rest I have not allowed her to take, keeping her near me in the walls, in the heat and flames, in the pan filled with fish soup every week, needing to keep her with me here at *Casa Cecelia*. But these sisters, Isadora the Gift of Isis, Chloe with green shoots sprouting, these two who I would call daughters, have filled the gaps I refused to fill and Mama knows she can leave. She can sleep next to Julio and be able to close her watchful eyes.

It is late and the evening weighs heavy. The darkness closes in around me and I hear the call of a bed covered with a bedspread made by Mama's grandmother, with needles as fine as fish bones. I lift the pan and, despite its weight, hold it and wonder what the light of tomorrow will bring. The cicadas will sing the day awake; that is how it has always been. I will soak my bread in olive oil, the sea will wash the sand and the wind will blow fresh life into the olive grove. But the sisters are to leave in the morning. Isadora will leave her heart here, and it lightens my own heart knowing she will return. Chloe has a different road to travel, but the island is strong in her and she will carry it with her. I will miss these daughters, and a piece of my heart will leave with Dimitri's boat, but my eyes are now open and I can watch their departure clearly.

A crash of iron fills my ears and my head begins to smoulder, as if a badly-laid fire had been lit in it. I cannot feel the pan in my hands, the tiles rush to meet me and I hear the crack of bone. The embers spark into a flame; it burns into my head and I call out. But my mouth has twisted; pulled out of shape, it droops down and the words I hear inside refuse to be spoken, they mix on my tongue and trip over themselves.

I try to lift myself, but the fire roaring inside stops my arms and legs from working and, as the black clouds rush down the mountain before a storm, I know I am leaving the island.

I claw away from this burning darkness and the ends of my fingers touch the last of the fish soup crawling across the floor, dregs of a good day spilled from the upturned pan, as cold as rain falling onto a grave.

24. Cold Soup

Isa

'What was that?' Chloe jumps, looking towards the kitchen.

'I don't know. I think she's dropped something.'

'I'll go and help,' announces my sister, and I let her go. I'm wrapped up in Fredriko and don't want to let a moment waste before I have to leave him.

Paul reaches for her hand, to pull her back. Then he looks at her face and the hand drops.

'Don't be long, babe.'

Chloe smiles at him and disappears into the kitchen; then:

'ISA! Come here – QUICKLY!'

All eyes turn. The cry has to be answered, and my chair crashes to the floor in my haste. It hits the curtain and sends the beads into frenzy as they smash against each other.

Like a car crash, every moment slows until each minuscule moment is locked into separate cameos – the pan lying on its side, cold congealed soup spilling across the tiles, onions and garlic stalactites hanging from the ceiling, ladle rocking on the edge of the cooker. Then I look down.

Death, familiar to me, watching Mum disappear into all its different stages – but the sight of Cecelia, lying on the floor with her eyes open in terror, shakes me to the core.

'No! Oh God – Chloe, what on earth happened?'

'I don't know, but it looks really bad.'

Cecelia's mouth opens and shuts, as if she was a fish

pulled from the sea, desperately trying to speak.

'Can you understand what she is saying?' Chloe says, putting her ears close to the constantly moving mouth.

The small kitchen begins to fill. Stephanos leads Marissa to her sister's side and she kneels down, and gently lifts Cecelia's head onto her lap.

Mario stands in the doorway. He takes one look at Cecelia, and turns to Fredriko and Paul. 'We will get Dr. Vitrelli,' he orders, and the three of them disappear into the night.

Marissa lifts the cloth, smelling of soap and lemons, from Cecelia's hand and begins to wipe the soup from her fingers, and I see a different death. *The nurses wash Mum, lifting her arms, unresponsive and limp, care for her like a child and prepare her body for its final journey.*

I grip on to Chloe. I have to feel the warmth of life spark through me. She wraps her arms around me and together we take comfort in each other. Chloe is trembling, and under her breath keeps murmuring, as if in prayer.

'Please let her be all right, *please let her be all right,* please let it be all right...'

'The doctor won't be long,' I try to reassure her, and keep my torn emotions silent. They keep babbling under the surface – a shoal of fish disturbing the calm of an evening sea – and I try not to listen, nor to hear the raw slice of words cutting away, begging me to turn to Fredriko and leave this place which smells of the grave. It is creeping along the floor, like a snake wrapping around my ankles, and at that moment I want to be selfish, do what makes me feel best inside.

Guilty spears jerk me back and I know if I run, leave Chloe here alone, I will be the same as Cecelia, wanting to take revenge on all of those who have hurt me. I can't do it, because eventually it would eat me inside, and I know the fragile love I have for Fredriko will disappear as quickly as I welcomed it.

'You all right?' Chloe shakes my shoulder. She's finished intoning her prayers and turns to face me. Her hands cup my face gently and she looks at me with her deep fondant-chocolate eyes which are filled with such love I can't help crying.

'Hey, hey, big sis. What's all this then?'
'Oh Chloe, it's all going to fall apart again, isn't it?'
'What are you on about? Come here.'
She takes my hand and leads me outside, leaving Marissa to comfort her sister. The curtain and beads rattle quietly behind us, as if it also doesn't want to think of the impossible, of *Casa Cecelia* without Cecelia.
The wind blows from the sea and I feel the force of it against my face. Chloe and I, sisters together, stand in silence and let the cold air wash over us.
'Now, what's all this about it all going wrong?'
'I'd planned it out, spent all day getting it right. You know me Chloe, lists for everything and this list, the one for my future, was all sorted out.'
'Do I know you and your lists!' Chloe laughs. 'Which particular list was this one?'
'My *What Happens Next* list – it was almost complete, all here inside my head. Not a long one – go back and sell the house; return here to the island; be with Fredriko; learn how to cook fish soup like Cecelia; live happily ever after.'
'Sounds okay to me. What's your problem?'
Chloe doesn't understand. This impulsive sister of mine has winged her way through life, walked a tightrope between destiny and disaster, and by the skin of her teeth has hung on and survived. She'll never know the importance of making plans and following them through. Except, when I think back – I've never managed to tick every box, follow things through to the end. If I tear up the list, this fixed vision I have of how my life must be, will it all collapse around me? Or maybe, just maybe...?
'It can't happen now,' I begin to explain. 'If Cecelia can't teach me how to cook, if she...'
'Sssh... don't say it.'
'If she isn't here then the happily ever after can't happen.'
'Is that it?' Chloe takes hold of me as if she wants to shake me. 'You think your life will be ruined because one of the boxes on your list can't be ticked?'
'Don't make fun of me Chloe.' I knew she'd never understand. 'I've *had* to be like that, making lists, it's how I got through it all.'
Chloe looks down at her feet, concentrating on her flimsy

fool's-gold sandals sparkling with diamantes, nothing real.

'You and me, we've really messed up our lives, haven't we, Isa? You making lists, and me? I've tried to break every rule in the book.' Chloe raises her chin and stares into the dark, as if she wants it to swallow her up. 'I think, Isa, it's time.'

'Time for what?'

'Time for us to be what we always should have been but never bothered to try for.'

'What's that?'

'Sisters, just plain boring sisters, not bothering if the occasional rule is broken or list not completed, we've got each other to make sure everything ends up all right.'

I take hold of Chloe's hand. 'We'd better go back inside.'

'Yes, we'd better.'

Dr. Vitrelli, his head beaded with sweat, puffing with the effort of keeping up with an insistent Mario, rushes into the kitchen. He flaps his hands at the crowded room.

'Out, out,' he commands. 'This will not do, not do at all. How can a doctor work with all these eyes on him?'

We slink into the restaurant, like naughty children. I sit next to Fredriko; he strokes my hair and I rest my head on his shoulder. I think back to earlier that evening, savouring every mouthful of soup, conversations which have fallen silent. Of Cecelia, her chair empty. It doesn't seem right that she's not sat next to Mario, or fussing to make sure her fish soup tastes the best it can be. A lump sits just above my heart, the heart that had beaten so fast in Fredriko's arms; he filled it full of love and hope but now, turned over like a sand clock, the place he had filled begins to empty as Cecelia's life runs out of her.

All eyes are fixed, turned towards the kitchen. Marissa gently wipes Cecelia's face and Dr. Vitrelli bends over her, his battered bag open, the contents spilling out over the floor. I'm a stranger, intruding in the most intimate moment of Cecelia's life, her fight to stay in this world, but can't tear my gaze away from watching. Dr. Vitrelli listens intently with the stethoscope hanging around his neck like a talisman, before he plunges a syringe into a small sage-green bottle. He draws up the contents, rich and gold, until the glass is filled and then, with a professional tap to remove any air bubbles, he carefully injects it into Cecelia's arm.

I look down at the cloth under my elbow. It's grubby and stained with wine, bread and soup, and I want to grab Cecelia, tell her that her Mama would have not allowed them to remain on the tables. I want to shout at the prone body in the kitchen to get up and be the Cecelia we all need; Cecelia who showed Chloe how to stop running away, Cecelia who opened her arms and welcomed me as a daughter when I needed a mother to wrap around me.

Chloe, her head bent, is engrossed in conversation with Paul. She's talking with an earnestness that at first takes him by surprise, and I can see from his face it's something he has wanted for so long. Some of her words float across the table, flat pebbles skimming over the water, bounced snatches of her dreams.

'It might take a couple of years and...'

'India, then Thailand to find the...'

I strain my ears to catch more, but words sink, like stones always do. She looks at me and gives me a smile, not one of those ear to ear grins splitting her face, more of a shrug of a smile, a mixture of happiness at being with Paul, an acknowledgment of our conversation on the terrace, and worry for the woman who helped this all to come about. The woman on the kitchen floor is not our Cecelia. The doctor talks to her gently, like an old friend or lover. She gently sinks into unconsciousness, helped by the sedative he has injected into her arm.

Fredriko is very quiet and, while Chloe carries on talking with Paul, we sit without saying a word to each other, until:

'Isa.' His voice gently breaks the silence.

'Yes?'

'Have you changed your feelings?'

'What do you mean?'

'Has your heart cooled? We had our passion in the heat of midday, but now it is evening you appear to have become colder.'

This is not what I expect. Without any hesitation I wrap my arms around his neck. 'Oh, no, no, no, Fredriko. I want to be with you with every part of my being. It's just...' I look over at Chloe. 'It's just I had to find my sister before I could let her go again, before I could belong to someone else.'

Fredriko's body remains still, tenses for a moment, and then I feel the muscles in his neck soften and relax as he allows me to pull him towards me.

'But,' he whispers, 'you leave tomorrow and I do not want you to go. Would you... could you ever consider staying?'

I check the list in my head and that one wasn't on it – at least, not till the house is sold. Stay here on the island, not go back? I think of *Casa Cecelia*, and how it will be without Cecelia – and if she does recover, she'll need help. I look once again at Chloe, at Cecelia lying on the floor, at the tables waiting to be cleared, and make the only choice I can.

'Yes, I'll stay.'

The rest of the list can be sorted out later.

Cecelia must be taken to the mainland,' announces Dr. Vitrelli. He snaps shut his bag and places a hand on Mario's shoulder. 'Good friend, go quickly and fetch Dimitri. Tell him to get his boat ready.'

Mario glances into the kitchen and his dark eyes are a bottomless pool. He pinches his nose as if the water would overflow, and with a shake of his head leaves *Casa Cecelia* to go and speak to Dimitri.

'You two...' Dr. Vitrelli jabs a finger at Paul and Fredriko. 'Upstairs, and bring down a mattress and some blankets. We must make her as comfortable as possible. The crossing to the mainland is not going to be swift or smooth.'

I study Dr. Vitrelli. He fiddles with his cuffs, his hands twitching and fussing as if he is a nervous bridegroom, and it begins to dawn on me how serious this is.

'What's wrong with Cecelia?'

The doctor has one last tug at his cuff and then pulls at the lapels of his jacket. 'I think... in these cases a doctor from a small island will need a second opinion, but I think Cecelia has had what is generally understood to be a stroke.'

I feel a lump harden inside, and I should cry but I can't. It's always at times like these, when I should show, and others expect, some sort of reaction. It had been my saviour and my curse. This knot which ties just above my heart at the base of my throat stops me from falling apart when

I have to be strong. The first time was when Chloe – far too young to understand – needed me to be her rock and make up for a father who couldn't stay. It strengthened each time Mum fell ill and – with all good intention – the nurse, who was with us during her last hours and tried to comfort me, was surprised that a daughter who had lost a mother couldn't cry. I remember how Cecelia welcomed us, making soup and surrounding us with the smell of the goodness held in this island, and I feel the knot untie and the relief of tears trickle down my cheek.

Dr. Vitrelli waves his hands like a policeman in the middle of the road, directing Fredriko and Paul as they struggle down the tight stairs with the mattress. It is laid next to Cecelia and, under the direction of the good doctor, gentle hands lift her onto it. Marissa carefully covers her sister with the finely-knitted bedspread, and this seems to comfort Cecelia. Her fingers stroke the edge of the soft cotton and I am sure I see her lips move. They twist with the effort, as if somewhere deep down Cecelia still exists, and it almost looks as if she's smiling.

The doctor checks Cecelia is secure. He takes her pulse, and then strokes her face with the gentleness of someone who has more than professional feelings towards her. The mattress is lifted. Mario, red faced from running up to the square to drag Dimitri away from his game of dominoes, lifts one corner. Stephanos, arms strong from sweeping the streets for over forty years, takes another, and Paul and Fredriko willingly take hold of the last two. Together they manoeuvre their burden out of the kitchen, keeping Cecelia as level as possible, past the tables waiting to be cleared and through the beaded curtain.

Marissa holds onto her sister's hand, silent tears washing her eyes, as Cecelia moans with every jerk and jolt of the mattress. I stand with Chloe and watch the curtain gently fold back; each strand of blue and turquoise beads glistens and shimmers around Cecelia, and a shaft of moonlight brings the fish alive. It swims across her face, and then Cecelia is taken from her Casa into another world, a deeper world, one where the sea welcomes her.

The sea is unkind. If all this had happened earlier Dimitri would have had a smooth crossing, but the wind has picked up and the waves run up the beach like the wheels of a runaway train. Again and again it smashes over the sand and then creeps out with a whisper, as if hoping to take the beach unawares next time. I hear the wind catch the masts of the yachts, shaking them at their complacent moorings; it whistles and screams through the metal spars which slap and jangle, accompanying the unrelenting, pounding beat of the waves.

'It's going to be hard,' Dimitri says, sucking what is left of his teeth.

'Cecelia has to go *now,'* insists Dr. Vitrelli. 'Marissa, come, she needs you to be with her.'

Marissa stands back, her feet remaining on the cobbles, refusing to set foot on the concrete slipway. She turns her face towards the wind and I see her shudder. Her face is as pale as the plaster virgin, and her feet seem to be frozen to the cobbled street. Stephanos whispers in her ear and tries to encourage her forward, but she remains as still as Hecate at the crossroads.

'Hurry, hurry,' Dimitri shouts, trying to keep the boat still while the waves rise higher, splashing over the side while the doctor kneels in the boat trying to protect Cecelia from the worst of the brewing storm.

Out of the corner of my eye I see Chloe move. She strides up the slipway and stands next to Marissa.

'I know you're frightened,' she says, and slips an arm around the terrified woman's waist. The wind dies down for a moment, as if it too wants Marissa to hear Chloe's words. 'We all get frightened about things that have happened in the past, and it's so difficult to take the first step.'

Marissa turns her head towards Chloe and it is as if she can see her beyond the darkness in her eyes. Slowly she raises one foot and places it onto the slipway, clinging on to Chloe as though if she let go she would be flung into the waves again, blinded again.

Step by slow step she keeps moving. At first it is as if the concrete will burn her feet; then she moves forward, more and more determined to reach Dimitri's boat bobbing on the waves. He struggles to keep it even as Chloe and

Marissa reach the vessel and – as if she has left her past back on the cobbled street – she climbs into the boat. I lose sight of her as she disappears into the bottom to be with her sister, and I smile as mine walks back to join me.

The small engine begins to pop into life, and with a couple of hard pulls on the oars the boat is released from the shallows. I watch as the waves welcome this tiny ship as it dips and dives like a cormorant, with Dimitri standing at the stern steering it towards the mainland. The steady sound of the engine is slowly swallowed up by the sound of the wind, and they disappear into the blackness.

'These boats need pulling further up,' Fredriko shouts to Mario. 'This wind will blow the waves high onto the slipway.'

He points to where the sea has already flung weed onto the concrete, littering it with tangled heaps of strong-smelling brown and green strands. Mario bends and scoops up a handful of the pungent weed, and flings it back into the sea.

'Here – I'll help with the boats,' Paul shouts.

Fredriko, Mario and Paul begin to heave and pull the old fisherman's boat, inch by inch, up the slipway. We can do no more to help, and together Chloe and I walk up the hill to *Casa Cecelia*.

The beaded curtain has once again faded and lost its sparkle. It rattles at us, old bones giving a cold welcome. The life seems to have been sucked out of *Casa Cecelia*. The tiles on the terrazzo show their age once again. Every crack and chip a chasm, a gulf between the day when the cracks had been smoothed over simply by making fish soup, and this night of doubt and fear of what the morning will bring.

'What do you think we should to do?' whispers Chloe.

'I don't know.'

I look around at the tables. They stand like mourners around a grave, covered with their tablecloth shrouds stained with the happiness of the evening. Soup spilled from overfull bowls and dripped from overeager spoons mixes with the marks where empty wine glasses stood, and crumbs of broken bread are scattered on the floor.

Then I know exactly what to do, what Cecelia would expect her daughters to do.

'Come on Chloe.' I grab a tablecloth. 'We've got to get *Casa Cecelia* ready.'

Chloe looks at me and confusion crosses her face, as if the evening had brought me to the edge of madness. She runs her hand over the table where she sat with Paul, smiles, and I see she begins to understand.

'Yes,' she says, picking up the empty bowls and brushing crumbs onto the floor. 'Cecelia wouldn't rest until it was all cleared.'

Together we wash the bowls and glasses, clean the kitchen until the floor shines, put the stained white cotton cloths in a pan to boil and, with a cloth smelling of soap and lemon, we wipe down the tables. Working in silence, we listen to the sound of *Casa Cecelia* as it begins to prepare for days to come. Chicken stew with rice served when the wind blows from the north and men mend their nets; pork and clams, for days to celebrate; dishes to be served with the comfort of yesterday and the promise of tomorrow. Dishes waiting to be served tomorrow, because today is over, fish soup day is over.

PART THREE : A SECOND HELPING

'Behold Lucius I am come, thy weeping and prayers have moved me to succour thee. I am she that is the natural mother of all things, mistress and governess of all the elements, the initial progeny of worlds, chief of powers divine, Queen of heaven, the principal of the Gods celestial, the light of the goddesses: at my will the planets of the air, the wholesome winds of the Seas, and the silences of hell be disposed; my name, my divinity is adored throughout all the world in divers manners, in variable customs and in many names, for the Phrygians call me Pessinuntica, the mother of the Gods: the Athenians call me Cecropian Artemis: the Cyprians, Paphian Aphrodite: the Candians, Dictyanna: the Sicilians, Stygian Proserpine: and the Eleusians call me Mother of the Corn. Some call me Juno, others Bellona of the Battles, and still others Hecate. Principally the Ethiopians which dwell in the Orient, and the Egyptians which are excellent in all kind of ancient doctrine, and by their proper ceremonies accustomed to worship me, do call me Queen Isis. Behold I am come to take pity of thy fortune and tribulation, behold I am present to favour and aid thee. Leave off thy weeping and lamentation, put away thy sorrow, for behold the healthful day which is ordained by my providence, therefore be ready to attend to my commandment'

– *Lucius Apuleius: Metamorphoses*, or *The Golden Ass*, Book 11, Chap 47. Adapted by Paul Halsall from the translation by Adlington 1566 in comparison with Robert Graves translation of 1951.

Olivia

'Mama...'

'Yes, Olivia-Cecelia?'

'It will be soon, won't it Mama?'

'Yes, soon my daughter.'

Mama's hands, much larger than mine, fold the tablecloths and I sit near the curtain Papa mended when the fish forgot to swim, and where Grandmama once sat. I fold the napkins, small squares of stiff white cotton. Grandmama showed me how to lift one corner, pull it over until it covers the other, then tuck the point in so it is neat and flat.

'That's good,' Mama says, and gives me a smile, a hug of a smile to wrap around me.

I put the folded napkin on top of a pile to be placed on the tables. Mama tells me the cotton is much older than me; she shows me the holes where the iron worked hard to smooth every crease, and where hands have folded them. She said they belonged to another Cecelia, many years ago.

'Mama?'

'Yes, Olivia-Cecelia?'

'I've finished Mama. Can I stir the pot now?'

Mama hugs me with another smile and lifts me onto a chair. Steam wets my face and I lean over the large pot to breathe it in.

'Careful daughter, you don't want to fall into the soup and be like one of Papa's fish.'

Through the kitchen door, past the tables waiting patiently to be dressed, the beaded fish rattles a welcome as Papa brings the fish for the soup.

'Olivia-Cecelia.'

'Yes Mama?'

'Come, it's now time to stir the soup.'

Mama places her hand over mine; together we grasp the large wooden spoon and begin to stir. I smell the onions and remember how they made Mama cry. Garlic tickles my nose, and I think about the offering we will make at the crossroads. I try to hide the stains on my dress from the tomatoes we squashed with our hands.

'Is the soup ready?' Mama asks, dipping a small spoon into the broth. She lifts it to my mouth and I feel the warm soup cover my tongue. I wait for the spark of fire.

'It isn't the same as last time, is it Mama?'

'Do you think it needs a little more fire, to warm from inside?'

I nod and Mama reaches up to the shelves, the ones I'm not tall enough to get to, and fetches down a small jar.

'The honey jar!'

'Careful, Olivia-Cecelia,' Mama says, steadying me as I wobble on the chair. 'Yes, it's the honey jar.' She twists open the top and the jar, with a faded picture of a honey bee, is filled with small fiery flakes. 'Take a pinch, like this, between your finger and thumb. Now sprinkle the chilli into the pan.'

I watch the feather-light flakes land on top of the red liquid and float on the surface, as if they were driftwood on the sea. Mama helps me to stir the soup, and gradually the chilli begins to disappear into the depths.

'Now we must let it simmer and absorb the heat. Can you see, Cecelia? It has to cook so gently that you have to look hard to see the soup move.'

I look hard and watch the liquid in the pan; it moves like the sea after a boat has disturbed it, and I remember that the soup has to be filled with flavour before the fish can be introduced.

'Mama.'

'Yes?'

'Is it time to add the fish yet?'

Mama's hugging smile changes to the one she saves for Papa, and she stirs the soup.

Cecelia

The days are too long for the hours they hold. I have waited too long for today; I sit on the terrazzo and listen to the beads rattle and chatter with excitement.

Once, only my knee complained and was easily soothed with a cloth smelling of soap and lemon. It was here I welcomed the daughters who, for a blink of time, I taught how to make fish soup. This chair is now hard on my bones, and I shift to silence their noise.

Marissa will walk down the hill, before they arrive. She will rest at the corner, lean on Stephanos's arm, and together they will join me to sit and wait. The streets are swept clean by Thomas – son of Maria – to whom Stephanos, in his generosity, donated the broom. Thomas changed the bristles and fitted a new handle, but it is the same broom that Stephanos inherited from his father and grandfather.

I wait with patience I did not ask for. Under such a hard teacher I have learned to endure the time I thought I would not have, and wait for Julio's brother to bring fish, as did Mario, only choosing the best of his catch for today's soup. It took time for me to welcome him. Like all fishermen, he waited and kept casting his nets until I was ready to be caught.

'Grandmama?'

The child's voice sings in my ears; it reminds me of a song sung many years ago by the man who was to become her grandpapa.

'Yes Olivia-Cecelia?'

'Mama says they will be here very soon. Papa is taking us to greet them.'

'Your Mama is very wise. A daughter must welcome her Mama's sister.'

She skips across the terrazzo, as the sunlight chases shadows in the olive grove. She stops, as if the wind has held its breath, and looks at me.

'Grandmama.'

'Yes Olivia-Cecelia.'

'Why can't you come and welcome them?'

I rub my knee. It has ached for so long that even when it is not painful the gesture makes me feel better.

'I am waiting for my own sister.'

Her eyes are the colour of thyme flowers, as blue as the Virgin's robe. She smiles at me with the same smile Julio once smiled, and I see her Mama in her eyes.

'Olivia-Cecelia, are you ready?'

'That's my Mama. She needs me to guide her to the sea.'

'I know. You had better go.'

I feel her breath, and she kisses me like a feather brushing my skin. Then, as if a shadow was chasing her, she runs to be with her Mama.

Chloe

How are you feeling babe?'

'How do you damn well think? I feel like I'm in the middle of a bloody hurricane.' I know I am snapping at him, wanting him to shut up and stop being so bloody superior in the boat. But if I open my mouth I'll know I'll be sick again, so I keep quiet.

'How much longer, Dimitri?'

Dimitri sucks what remains of his teeth. His mouth has more gaps than the last time I saw him. 'See the rocks, Mr Paul?' he says, jerking his head towards a large outcrop. 'Just past there and we arrive.'

I concentrate on keeping my churning stomach under control and study the line of shark-toothed rocks. They point out to sea, waiting to trap the unwary and drag them down. I see the place where I lost my footing and fought to survive, and shudder at how close I came to losing the future. If Isa had not fallen under the island's spell it could have been so different.

I feel cold, and reach over to stroke Paul's leg and to feel the warmth of him. It reassures me, and I offer a silent prayer to the goddess at the crossroads for bringing me back here safely.

'Come on babe, it's not that bad.'

I reach over to swipe the smug look off his face. He dodges and sends the boat rocking from side to side. I sink back into my seat and try to hold onto the maelstrom rumbling away inside.

'It might look calm to you,' I mutter, trying my hardest to be angry but failing miserably, 'but I can assure you that I can feel every ripple and wave under this boat.'

Then it hits me, another wave of nausea. My face feels as hot as the sun rising higher into the sky from behind the mountains. I lean over the side, wishing the ferry crossing from the mainland was very much shorter.

'Here babe,' Paul says gently, and hands me a cloth to wipe my face.

'Thanks.' I feel guilty for giving him such a hard time. 'Sorry for being such a bitch. You know me and boats.'

Paul dabs the edge of my mouth and plants a kiss on my

sweating forehead. 'If you weren't such a bitch I wouldn't love you so much.' He puts his arm around me and together we watch Dimitri skilfully guide the boat past the jagged rocks.

'I'd forgotten how wonderful the island is.'

'Me too babe.'

The sun, nearing as high as it can get, has chased away the dark shadows from the mountains. The tall peaks hold tints of French lavender and deep plum in the places where the sun is unable to reach. These soft, gentle mountains, smoothed by wind and rain, wrap their arms around the island, protecting it as a father protects his child from harm.

'Can you see them yet?'

I shade my eyes. The beach sweeps along the shore like a blanket, a golden fleece in the bright sun. *Villa Nova,* once fondant-fancy-pink, has now mellowed to a soft marsh-mallow, and a forest of frilled beach umbrellas flap in the breeze. From here, in the bottom of Dimitri's boat, my eyes hurting with the light glaring from the sea, I still can't see *Casa Cecelia*

'Hey Chloe, is that them?'

Paul tugs at my arm and points. I feel like a mariner looking through a telescope as I follow the line of his arm. Where the sand ends and the village begins, the concrete slipway dives into the sea. I can see the boats with their bright yellow and blue paint, and I know each one will have the Eye of Osiris painted on the front, just as Dimitri has carefully painted an Eye on his ferry.

Beyond the boats, where the sea meets the land and the concrete gives way to cobbled streets, I see them. Fredriko, skin dark from sun and salt; Isadora next to him, a smile as broad as the island; and between them, skipping to the sea to greet me, the blessing which will always bring me back to the island.

While I am glad, there is an empty space where Cecelia should be. I hold on to hope. I have waited so long for this.

Isa

It's a good catch today.' My husband – how good that is to my ears! – holds a basket filled with rainbows.

'Put them over there,' as I make space next to the pan.

Fredriko reaches for the knife, kept as sharp as when Mario filleted the fish for Cecelia. 'I miss him.'

'I know you do.'

He lifts a fish, as if he was holding a newborn baby, and runs his hand along the scales. At first he strokes it with the blade, as if all he wanted to do was to touch it. Then with a flash of steel he slices under the gills, turns the knife and cuts off a fillet just the right size for our soup.

'He was the last link to Papa,' he says, laying down the fillet. 'If I didn't have you and our little Cecelia...'

There are those who only hold onto love briefly before it turns its back and finds new hearts to break, but this pain is swiftly replaced and the bruised hurt fades into memory. But the pain Fredriko feels for the loss of Mario endures. It is the same desolation I hold onto for Mum, leaving a space that can never be filled.

'You'll always have us,' I reassure him, and touch his arm.

My Fredriko smiles, and I know the joy our daughter brings sweeps through him and the hollow gaps are forgotten, hidden by the busyness of life, only felt in the quiet times. In those times sadness steals in, washing through like a waterfall cold after the snow has melted. It starts with the face, the muscles frozen, as if they are unable to look happy or sad. Then the feeling overwhelms, plunging down, a dread realisation that the love has gone and the loss sits just below the heart. At these times the whole body aches with a longing to be filled, but is empty with the famine of loss.

'Come on,' I whisper to him. 'We have fish to prepare.'

The need to speak is lost in our silence. We both know of our starvation. I long to be able to hold onto a mother, not only in the dreams in which she visits me, happy and healthy – I long be a daughter again. Fredriko mourns for a father who in the end couldn't recognise him as a son, and whose mind was replaced by an impostor, a thief of his very essence. But the sadness my sweet Fredriko feels today is for Mario.

The old man taught him how to fish as if he had been born to it. When he was satisfied that Fredriko was as good as the son who lies with Angelina in the cemetery, he was pleased the son of Emilio had truly become a fisherman. Mario sold his boat, turned his back on the sea, and spent his days sat on the terrazzo with Cecelia, encouraging her to speak again, helping her to use the useless side of her body.

When our daughter swept in to this world like a whirlwind and Mario knew Cecelia had a purpose to live, he started to slip from this world. On a day when the sea was calm and the wind brushed the leaves in the olive grove, Mario travelled to the crossroad, turned to the left and joined Angelina and his son.

Chloe

'C*hloe!*,' I hear her shout. My sister's voice skips over the waves and I stand to wave to her.

'Shit.' One final lurch and I end up on my back, staring up at the sky in the bottom of Dimitri's boat. Not the elegant arrival I had planned – the one with me standing at the front of the boat, scarf gently blowing in the breeze, Paul by my side. Instead I'm like a cargo of rags, tangled up in my scarf and lying flat on my back with Paul grinning like a catfish.

'Take it easy babe, I know you're excited.'

I haul myself up and ignore him. The shore is so close I can taste the island. Fredriko raises his hand and next to him my little niece jumps up and down and hops from one foot to the other. My sister holds firmly onto her hand and together they wave, like castaways waiting to be rescued, and Dimitri's boat scrapes onto the sand.

Isa

Mama, Mama they're here!'

'Yes, they are.'

Fredriko wades into the sea and takes hold of the rope Dimitri throws with practiced accuracy.

'Come on Paul, it's about time you got your feet wet.'

Chloe wobbles in the boat. The small distance separating us at this moment could be a chasm as wide as the sea. Paul jumps over the side and, knee-deep in water, joins Fredriko.

'Bloody hell mate, you could have told me the water was this cold.'

Fredriko laughs. 'The sea needs the summer to warm it. It holds onto winter late this year.'

Paul grabs the rope and together they get ready to haul Dimitri's boat onto the sand.

'Paul, come on, help me out,' orders Chloe, impatient as usual.

She climbs onto the edge of the boat and holds onto Paul, trying too hard not to get her feet wet. The boat gives one last lurch in the sea before being calmed by the land, and I watch as my sister disappears over the side.

'Chloe,' I call as the sea covers her. The sight of her being swallowed by the waves again is too much to bear, and I wade in to rescue her. But she pops up, drenched from head to toe and coughing with laughter.

'Mama, Auntie Chloe has fallen in.'

'Yes Olivia-Cecelia,' I say, wringing out my skirt and feeling a little stupid for panicking.

'So much for the graceful return of the prodigal,' Chloe laughs.

She slops onto the land and drips up the slipway. I look at the grossly expensive and now-ruined silk trousers and wonder how this island manages to do it – welcome everyone in the way best suited to them.

'Auntie Chloe, Auntie Chloe!'

'Hey, haven't you grown!' Chloe says, bending down until she's face to face with my daughter.

'Do you know what day it is?'

'Mmm, let me think... is it Let's Go Swimming In Our

Clothes day? Or is it something else?'

'You're silly,' giggles my daughter. 'It's a double, double special day. I'm five today and it is also fish soup day.'

'I know darling, I was only teasing. That's why Uncle Paul and I are here, we couldn't miss fish soup day.'

'And my birthday,' Olivia-Cecelia says, pouting with the beginning of a sulk.

Chloe scrapes my daughter off the ground and holds her tight.

'Come on, Cecelia, you show me where Auntie Chloe is going to stay.'

'Olivia-Cecelia is my name,' she says, and wriggles so much that her feet are placed back onto the ground.

I can't help but smile at my daughter. She reminds me of so much of Chloe, never able to stay in one place for a moment. She holds a part of us all and carries our story in her name. Cecelia, the name that called Chloe and me to the island... without that name I wouldn't have fallen in love with the man pulling Dimitri's boat to shore, the man who gives me a flower every evening. And Olivia, chosen to celebrate the first time I walked in the olive grove with Fredriko, and where I found peace, and fell in love with her Papa.

'Hi sis.' Chloe turns and reaches out. I wrap my arms around my sister and she buries her head in my shoulder. If I didn't know her so well I would swear I could feel the tremble of a sob.

'How is she?' Chloe asks, wiping her nose with the back of her hand.

'Good days and bad.'

'Can't wait to see her.'

'Soon, Chloe, soon.'

Chloe

'Come on babe, hurry up.'

Paul taps his watch. A damn annoying habit picked up when we started travelling, tapping at the departure lounge, tapping when we hopped from island to island, and now tapping because he can't wait to taste another bowl of fish soup.

'Five minutes, just five.'

There are some days that have to be just right, and tonight is one of them. He gives me one of his *how long does it take for one woman to get ready?* looks and then flops down on the bed.

Lipstick, and I'm nearly done. I check the mirror and see Paul stretched out behind me, and I'm glad we came back. Isa's worked a miracle with this place. The last time I saw it I was nursing a stubbed toe and the windows were covered in old ragged posters. I remember the inside was a wreck; table turned upside down and phone wires dangling from the wall.

'Hope you like it,' Isa had said, showing us the small square building halfway between the sea and *Casa Cecelia*. 'We had to do something. *Casa Cecelia* can't accommodate everyone who wants to make fish soup after the book was such a success.'

Paul glances at his watch again. He's got to understand it's not about him, this is about me, the island, Isa and fish soup.

'The green dress, what do you think?'

'As if you've ever listened to me when it comes to what you're going to wear,' he sighs, and closes his eyes.

Green, like spring, like green shoots, yes – the green silk dress will be perfect. I slip it over my head and turn towards Paul.

'Well?'

'Great, can we go now?'

'And you're staying in those?' I point to his jeans, still damp from wading in the sea.

'So?'

I reach for the nearest thing to hand and fling my hair-brush at him. It rockets through the air and hits him squarely between the eyes.

'Why, you...'

I jump on the bed and rub the egg shaped bump appearing on his forehead, and he grabs my hand and pulls me on top of him.

'Mind the dress.'

'Sod the dress.'

He's hot, despite the wind blowing off the sea. I feel his breath on my face and he rolls on top of me, presses his lips against mine, and I know why we are right for each other. The island slows us down, wraps itself around us – just as it did five years ago when I stopped rushing and it showed me how to grow – and then while we make love time stands still.

Olivia

The soup is almost ready. Mama stirs and tastes, dips a spoon into the pot, testing for flavour, and as with every spoonful she closes her eyes, smells the air the way Grandmama taught her, never forgetting to taste, always taste.

'Go Olivia-Cecelia, sit with your Grandmama.' Mama gives me one last smiling hug and flaps me away, with a cloth smelling of soap and lemon.

Grandmama Cecelia sits on the terrazzo. She always sits here. She once told me she did so because she was warming herself to be ready for the day to arrive, like a bright salamander absorbing the sun; she's "warming her old bones". I take hold of her fingers, rub the cold out of her hand and, while Mama is busy rattling pans in the kitchen, I know Grandmama Cecelia is worried.

'I might have to leave,' she tells me, and I rub her hands some more.

'Not yet Grandmama Cecelia. Not on fish soup day.'

My Grandmama waits for her sister to arrive. Each day she sits with Auntie Marissa and they talk, and don't even notice me tucked under one of the tables, hidden by a large cotton cloth. I listen to them telling stories of names I have not lived long enough to forget, of Cecelia's Mama, her Papa who hung the beaded curtain over the door, and faces I have not smiled at, Mario who left before I could walk, and of the times before she was my Mama and was called Isadora, who gave an offering to Hecate.

'Grandmama.'

She squeezes my hand and I see my reflection sparkling in her eyes.

'Today has taken a long time to get here.'

She nods, and looks far into the distance. I feel her thoughts slip back to times few in the village now remember. We sit and listen to each other's thoughts and enjoy the breeze blowing from the mountains.

'Grandmama.'

'Yes Olivia-Cecelia?'

She says my name and it makes me laugh; I love my Grandmama because she has the same name as me.

'When they arrive, we are going to have a special fish soup day.'

'Every fish soup day is special, Cecelia.'

Cecelia

Chloe of the green shoots arrives like a bloom waiting to burst open as soon as it is warmed by the spring.

'Hello Cecelia.'

She smells of freshly-picked herbs; she sits next to me and places a bouquet of thyme, marjoram and rosemary in my hand. My words sometimes will not come and I have to search for them. Chloe waits with a patience she had forgotten before she came here. I feel my mind remember, sort the jumble inside and my mouth begins to work again.

'Your sister tells me you have written a book.'

'Yes, Cecelia, it was written for you.'

This daughter from another land has become as dear to me as the child I had carried. She reaches over and hands me a small but heavy book. It rests on my lap and my fingers, hesitant after the bolt of lightning took my strength. The cover is smooth to the touch and I remember Mama saying, "Cecelia, you have fingers and hands for the kitchen," and how she stroked them, preparing me for the time I had to make fish soup without her.

The fire, the stroke which burned through my body, has left me weak. One side of my body refuses to cooperate; my left side useless, the rest of me unable to compensate for the harm done.

I stroke the shiny book and look at a woman stirring a pot, the Orient shining in her eyes. 'It is a good book,' I say, and the woman smiles at a world beyond the camera, steam from the pot curling around her head as if she is being caressed by its contents.

Chloe stares into the woman's face. 'She is from Vietnam, she's showing me how to make fish soup on a small island no bigger than this one.'

'You have travelled many miles, daughter.'

'Yes, I have...' Chloe looks up at the sky as if she wants to join the clouds rolling from the mountains towards the sea. 'Many, many miles, but I've always kept this island in my heart.'

'Why did you not stay, like your sister?'

'Isa was born to live here, and I'm not my sister. It's why we, Paul and I, wanted to write the book. We... I had to find my own fish soup, and... I know this sounds silly, I needed to find *Casa Cecelia* wherever I travelled.'

The book, heavy with pots held inside the covers, begins to feel lighter in my hands. All the hundreds of bowls of soup served in its pages come together and I smell them, each one: hot and sour; spicy and sweet; thick and creamy; clear and light. Each bowl filled with the warmth of the soil and holding the taste of the sea.

'Cecelia.'

'Yes, daughter?'

'Look inside the front cover.'

I carefully turn the cover until I cannot see the woman living far to the east, and look at a photograph of *Casa Cecelia*.

'See,' Chloe points with the excitement of a child. 'The book is dedicated to you, to Cecelia and *Casa Cecelia*.'

'I am a famous woman now.'

'Yes,' she laughs.

I hold the open book on my lap and I know that Mama's fish soup will fill bowls in places far beyond this island.

Chloe

I gently take *Fish Soup* from Cecelia's hands and she murmurs in her sleep. She is older than I had expected, and the excitement of today, of our arrival, of seeing the book, has exhausted her.

The curtain welcomes me like an old friend and I help Marissa lay the cloths while Olivia-Cecelia places a napkin and a spoon for each chair. I hear Isa busy crashing and banging pans in the kitchen and, not wanting to disturb her, I sit down.

'Auntie Chloe?'

'Yes Olivia-Cecelia?' I reach out and lift her onto my knee.

'One day, when I am as big as Mama, I'm going to make fish soup.'

'I know you will.'

I hold her warm body and feel the breeze blow from the mountains rattling the curtain, and the bougainvillea blushes in the sun. The smell of fish soup curls from the kitchen, and Olivia-Cecelia sits on my lap filled with the excitement of growing up to be just like her Mama. Cecelia is asleep on the terrazzo, and I know *Casa Cecelia* will always celebrate fish soup day.

Cecelia

Mama...'

'Yes Cecelia?'

'I think it is time.'

I feel the breath of wind blow from the crossroads. Hecate stands and waits to welcome me, and the pain in my heart is soothed by the smell of rosemary for remembrance, and the olive trees whisper their farewell.

'Mama...'

'Yes, Cecelia.'

'I am a little frightened.'

A warm glow runs through me as Mama takes my hand and leads me up the hill. We pass through the square where vegetables are sold, smelling of the soil, and Dimitri sits playing dominoes; past the Virgin smiling her encouragement, and then we walk out of the village. The road, dusty with pilgrims' feet taking offerings of garlic to Hecate, winds past Dr. Vitrelli's house, where he sits in his retirement and smells the herbs in his garden. I hesitate, and it is difficult to move forward,

'Don't be worried Cecelia,' Mama whispers. 'It is only a different road, no more frightening than the road you have already walked.'

I feel a small hand creep into mine and, together with Mama and Julio, I take the left fork under the loving gaze of Hecate.

THE END

ABOUT THE AUTHOR

Michelle Heatley always dreamed of writing a novel. As a child she wrote horror stories in ghoulish black italic script, and penned articles for the local newspaper on litter, abandoned railways, and school bullies. In 2009 Michelle was featured in the Stratford Literary Festival Anthology with her one-page story *Fish Soup Day*. Inspired by this success she began writing short stories, and is widely published in UK and Australian magazines.

Born in leafy Warwickshire – Shakespeare's own county – as far from the sea as it is possible to be, Michelle married Brian and raised her two sons, Robert and Benn. After the nest was emptied she listened to the call of the sea and moved to the picturesque South Devon fishing port of Brixham with her husband and Molly, a lovely but not very bright Border Terrier.

Michelle has a Diploma in Literature and Creative Writing with the Open University and is a member of Brixham Writers, a group of well-published writers and authors. The ever-changing sea is the inspiration for Michelle's writing, and she can be found scribbling in her notebooks (she has more notebooks than WH Smith!) on the beach or on the back of *Her Outdoors,* a 25ft fishing boat. The novel *Fish Soup* is filled with the sights, smells and taste of the sea that Michelle loves.

Web: http://fishsoupnovel.blogspot.co.uk/

Facebook: www.facebook.com/pages/Michelle-J-Heatley-Author/526367587382603

Twitter: @fishsoupwriting

A Whisper
on the
Mediterranean

TONIA PARRONCHI

A WHISPER on the Mediterranean
Tonia Parronchi

Prologue

I must explain from the start that I cannot claim to be a real sailor. What I know about sailing I learnt after we had set off on our journey around the Mediterranean on our beautiful 42ft ketch *Whisper,* and the technical terminology I picked up is all in Italian. However, not knowing the correct sailing terms for the ropes, rigging and toilets didn't hinder me at all and I hope that this book will be as much fun to read for those who already love sailing as for those who are terrified by the thought of it, or who get seasick looking through the porthole of a washing machine. Whether you are a reluctant sailor like me or a professional, I hope that the book will make you laugh, make you dream and maybe encourage you to try this wonderful way of life.

Buying a boat was my husband's idea, but I followed him into this adventure with great enthusiasm, mingled with some trepidation; mostly for fear of exposing our baby son to situations where I was unsure of my ability to protect and care for him properly. When Guido gets an idea it is usually on a grand scale, so we weren't intending to potter around on the water for the occasional day trip but to embark on a real odyssey, exploring the Mediterranean while I learnt what I could about sailing – with the final goal being to eventually sail around the world.

We set about making the boat into a home for an indeterminate length of time, paring down non-essentials to make room for the provisions and safety equipment. Not for us the life of the weekend sailor, wearing designer deck-shoes and sipping champagne, whilst moored in Costa Smeralda waiting to be admired. I watched in dismay as Guido vetoed my high-heeled sandals and half of my chosen wardrobe, then gave me a smile of surprised pleasure when he found the old, bleach-stained T-shirt I wear for cleaning, which I had absolutely no intention of taking but that had got into the pile by mistake.

Adjusting to this new way of life took some time. Even tasks usually taken for granted become difficult in a constantly moving boat, full of hard, sharp corners to bump into. The simplest of things, such as cooking, making a bed, even standing upright or having a wee, needed a whole new set of muscles to be coordinated in order to get it right.

It wasn't all plain sailing either. The Mediterranean is notorious for the unpredictability of its weather, something I had no idea about when Guido first described his idyllic plans to me. Violent storms, hair-raising scrapes, seasickness and sunburn were among the many adversities that we had to endure. You may think it exaggerated to call sunburn an adversity, but tell that to the girl who burnt her bottom so badly she couldn't sit down for a week.

We were all changed by these challenges, becoming stronger, both physically and mentally, as we confronted our own fears and conquered them. By the end of the summer I had learnt to know myself better and for the first time in my life I was content to sit in silence, in tune with the simple rhythms of the natural world in which we were immersed. I had discovered the inner peace that I had always been searching for.

There is a dream of adventure in all of us and the sea has a magical lure all of its own. You don't have to be the sporty type to harbour dreams of life on the ocean wave. Even hapless dreamers, like our friend Gianfranco, respond to the siren's song at some point in their life, although his love affair with the sea was short lived. He bought himself a small motorboat, with the idea of idle days fishing from it in the lee of the coast. On the second day as proud owner of his vessel he found a tempting little bay in which to settle down for an hour or two, with his captain's hat set at a jaunty angle and his fishing rod in his hand. In his fertile imagination he saw himself as a cross between 'The Old Man and the Sea' and Captains Ahab, Bligh and Findus – but his dream was shattered when he threw out the anchor, forgetting to let go of its rope, and took an unexpected plunge.

I don't think I will ever qualify as a proper sailor but I have come to love sailing. I still snort with laughter when I hear someone discussing the merits of wind-buggers and think that it is very rude when the Italians shout at me to *cazzare le vele*, which could be misinterpreted as doing unmentionable things with the sails. I still hate the overriding smell of damp and engine grease that lingers in your clothes, so that on your sporadic trips to dry land for provisions people cast sideways glances at you and move away quickly. However there is nothing quite as wonderful as life on the move, the absolute freedom to go wherever you choose or to drop anchor in places unreachable if not by boat, while you watch the sun turning the waves to the colour of molten bronze as it gradually sinks below the horizon.

When I started writing this book it soon became clear to me that my sailing memories were all linked to the different tastes of the food and wine from each beautiful place that we visited, and for this reason I decided to put recipes at the end of each chapter. This isn't a cookery book; there are so many people better qualified than myself in this respect, but when living in Italy it is impossible not to get passionately involved with food and I found the fact that I managed to feed my family, in spite of high seas and gale force winds, quite inspirational. To be able to cook in such conditions means that these recipes must be foolproof and worth passing on!

That first summer of sailing soon became a way of life. Winters were spent planning and dreaming about our next itinerary, spring was when *Whisper* was lovingly prepared and overhauled and then, when summer arrived, we sailed away. Exploring the lesser-known Italian islands and keeping off the well-trodden tourist routes meant that we were able to discover an Italy that is timelessly beautiful. I hope that reading this book inspires you set sail yourselves; to experience Italy's islands, remote coasts and the unpredictable, endlessly fascinating sea; so that you too can immerse yourselves in the tastes, the heat, the perfumes and the warm friendliness of its people and discover your own magical Mediterranean world.

Chapter 1

The Dream

The year that changed my life, filling it with adventure, exhilarating new experiences and an occasional moment of sheer terror, began in a rather mundane way. I was completely unaware of the schemes and dreams that were boiling in my husband's brain, keeping him awake at night as he worked out financial and technical possibilities. In fact I wasn't aware of anything Guido did after my head had touched the pillow because, with a tiny baby around, I was grabbing any sleep I could get.

That morning started just like any other. I woke up, feeling that my chest was going to explode, at around 6.30am. As usual, this uncomfortable sensation was followed seconds afterwards by James's hungry screams, shattering the morning silence and bringing me wide awake.

There is a strange kind of telepathy between mother and child in the early months, allowing the mother's milk to be ready even before the baby wakes up and realises that it is hungry, which caused havoc to my clothes and put me in countless embarrassing situations!

Of course Guido was thrilled that I was breast feeding because it meant that he never had to get up early to prepare a bottle, so he acknowledged his son's cry with a sympathetic grunt, then rolled over and got comfortable again.

I clambered out of bed, pulled on some pyjamas and staggered into James's room, then picked him up and staggered on to the kitchen, where I put the starving child to my breast and peace returned to the household. When the little darling had gone back to sleep, but I was wide awake, I made a coffee and took it onto the balcony of our apartment in Ostia, Rome, to enjoy the early morning tranquillity and some time all to myself. Usually James would now sleep for another two hours and my husband for at least four – he's not good in the morning!

Sometimes, if I got up really early, I would share my morning reverie with the mad woman who lived in an apartment across from ours. She liked to pace up and down on her balcony and shout out loud, sometimes obscene, abuse about our caretaker, Vincenzo. Her most frequently repeated phrase was "Vincenzo, go to jail!" – and maybe she wasn't so crazy after all, because a few years later that is exactly what he did.

On this particular morning, as I sipped my coffee, I was surprised to hear movement from our bedroom, and moments later an amazingly alert-looking Guido appeared in the kitchen. One look at him was enough to establish that he wasn't feeling ill, but I really couldn't imagine what else could have dragged him from his bed so early.

He grinned at me and said "I've had an idea."

There was nothing strange about that, apart from the timing. One of the reasons why I love Guido is that he is full of unusual ideas, plans and schemes. However, this idea seemed to be particularly exciting, and I was very glad, because since he had taken early retirement three months before, he had been getting restless and fed up at home and it was obvious that he needed something to keep him occupied.

As he sat at the table and explained his idea my forty-seven year old husband looked more like a boy of ten, all shiny eyes and glowing cheeks, as he talked for more than an hour without a pause. When he finally stopped and asked me triumphantly what I thought about his plan, I had to agree that it was great, since by that time his enthusiasm had rubbed off on me too; and so it was that we first decided to buy a sailing boat and spend a summer exploring the Mediterranean.

I have a rather unusual husband. My best friend calls him the "Italian Action Man", which is quite an apt description. He left home at sixteen to go travelling and never stopped. In his time he has done such varied jobs as singing in a Parisian nightclub, waiting in various restaurants around Europe, and being part of a photographic troupe in a Congo war zone. Then he returned briefly to his home in Italy to do his military service, where he chose to go into the parachute corps and was asked to stay on as an instructor – but declined, as his feet were itching again.

He set off once more, this time to South Africa for a while, where he was the assistant manager of a hotel. Then he went off on a round-the-world trip and finally settled down (if one can call it that, given all the travelling involved in the job) to work for Alitalia airlines as a steward, a job that he did for the next 24 years. This gave him time to indulge in his two main passions of flying and sailing. He got his Private Pilot Licence and bought his first small sailing boat.

When I met him (in Greece, but that's another story) he was finishing building his own microlight aeroplane from a kit, but was temporarily without a boat of his own. Our first date however took place on board his friend's boat, so I knew what I was getting myself into.

I, on the other hand, have done most of my travelling through books, and have had my most exciting adventures the same way. I am not unadventurous, just a bit of a coward! I had never sailed on a boat smaller than the Channel ferry and had never felt the slightest desire to do so, but now I found myself plunged into a completely unknown nautical world. I had to learn a whole new language, and since I had never learnt the English technical terms for boat parts (I knew that toilets were called heads but never could bring myself to call them that), I learnt them all in Italian. Throughout this book you will doubtless be aware of the complete absence of correct sailing terminology, but I am afraid that for me a bed is a bed and not a bunk and since the boat was to be my home, I decided that it was fine to call the galley the kitchen if I felt like it.

Guido bought me books on the art of sailing and I looked at them, I promise. Then James would come and crawl over them and smear something horribly sticky on the pages so that I just couldn't read them properly!

The fact is that I *was* caught up in Guido's dream of

the joys of life at sea, but I was a bit apprehensive too and worried, in particular, about how I would cope with the baby on board. However, having lived in Italy for five years, the novelty of having no job and being on a constant holiday had rather worn off. Added to that was the day to day effort of coping with overly excitable people (Guido is the only calm Italian I know!), irritating relatives and Italian bureaucracy, and doing all that in a foreign language was becoming stressful.

The inevitable lack of sleep that comes with the birth of your child wasn't helping either and, although being a mother should be considered a full time job, I still felt a sense of guilt about staying at home and wanted to do something that would contribute to the family finances. So far, though, I had been unable to find an interesting job, so I really liked the idea that Guido and I could work as a team on the boat project. We decided to enjoy our first summer aboard together, then use the boat to do charters for a few months each year – and, when we were ready, set off to sail around the world.

A couple of months later another change in our lives gave me an even bigger reason for being excited about a whole summer away together on a boat. After Guido retired we decided that we should leave our small, sunny apartment in Rome and move to Guido's large family home in Tuscany. There I would have to share a house with Guido's mother. This idea filled me with icy dread every time I thought about it, and I knew that by the time we set off I would be ready to go around the world in a bathtub if it meant that I could escape.

So, before we packed up and moved home I kept myself going by feeding my dreams with images of myself, all bronzed after weeks at sea, hauling up billowing sails as we plunged through turquoise waves and watched dolphins playing under our prow. I tried to push aside irritating, niggling thoughts such as, "I am always more lobster-coloured than bronze", "Will the baby be screaming while I struggle to haul a sail up, because he hates being tied up in his safety harness?", and "Will I ever be able to relax when the baby is on deck, in case he slips overboard?"

I joined in enthusiastically with Guido as he spread

countless faxes and pictures of potential boats on the kitchen table, pointing out their collective good and bad points. To me they all looked the same and the only ones I could get excited about were the brochures of fantastic modern yachts that we collected from the stands at the Genoa Boat Show; the ones with polished wood interiors that glowed golden in the sunlight and had tiny vases of flowers decorating tables that were laid with crystal glasses and expensive crockery.

I drove Guido mad with comments on what cutlery we should get, the pretty candles I'd seen to create a romantic atmosphere, and dainty little curtains for the cabins. They struck me as homely touches, but for him were completely pointless and unnecessary. He is already convinced that we British are obsessed with putting curtains everywhere instead of functional Italian shutters that actually keep out the light!

We had a few day trips out that autumn to look at various boats that Guido thought might do for us, but none of them were quite right. I was beginning to be impressed by the warm cosy atmosphere on board, even if some boats we viewed were rather cramped. With the heating on and the smell of coffee in the air I could imagine how they could really become a home. Then we got a call from Alessandro, our yacht broker, to say we should come and see a boat that he had in Fiumicino.

My first sight of *Whisper* was on a cold, November morning, in dry dock. As I climbed awkwardly up the rickety ladder, clutching thirteen-month-old James with one arm, I couldn't help being less than impressed by her rust-coloured hull, obviously in need of some hard work.

As Guido steadied me from behind and Alessandro yanked me and the baby on deck, the reality of the situation hit hard for the first time. This was no cosy floating home or spotless, pristine craft, like those seen at the boat show. This was a real sailing boat, a Ferretti Altura 424 that had been in dry dock for a few months and was covered in autumn leaves, dirt and sand, blown up by the sea winds. There was a sense of dereliction and abandonment about her, and my unease grew as Alessandro opened her up and ushered us inside.

As I passed James down to his daddy and negotiated the steep steps into the cabin, I was hit by a smell that would become all too familiar – the smell of BOAT. It is a strange mixture of damp, mould, and engine grease, which permeates everything and allows one to tell another boat owner from a distance, if the wind is blowing in the right direction!

Guido breathed deeply and grinned at me, looking like a little boy on bonfire night. I knew that he was thinking how lovely everything was, and sure enough, off he went, straight down into the hole under the floorboards to look at the engines, enthusing about the twin 72-horsepower Mercedes beasts down there.

I sat down and looked around the main cabin. There was a small galley at the end, a central lightwood table flanked by two settees then a step up to the chart table, instrument panels and the fold-down stairs to the outside.

The cockpit descended down into the cabin above the table, so that when standing the view of the other side of the room was cut off, although when sitting this wasn't so obvious. I breathed in the dank smell, quietened James who had suddenly decided he was hungry, and tried to recapture the romantic, exciting images of life on board that I had set out with that morning.

Guido hauled himself out of the engine hole, happily wiping grease off his hands, and shouted at me to come and view the rest. A couple of steps down from the dinette and we were in a narrow corridor. Two small cabins with bunk beds lay on either side, then a tiny bathroom. A main, double cabin with en-suite bathroom was at the stern. The smell here was much worse. The bathrooms were mouldy and when I peeked underneath, so were the mattresses.

Guido's eyes gleamed!

Later that evening, with James fed, bathed and finally put to bed, Guido and I discussed the boat. By the end of a plate of red-hot *penne all'arrabbiata*, washed down with a litre of strong red wine from our vineyard, I was almost convinced again.

Guido finally won me round by overfilling my brandy glass and taking me out onto the balcony. It was cold but the sky was bright with stars as we leant together on the railing. While the brandy hit the spot, Guido pointed to the stars shining so fiercely above and told me how much bigger and closer they would seem in the open sea with no man-made lights to take away their splendour. I have always been a sucker for a bit of romance – I was hooked, again!

The next day, as I supervised Jamie's breakfast to make sure that some of his cereal actually made its way into his mouth, Guido phoned Alessandro and made an offer for the boat. Then followed two nerve-racking weeks while we waited to see if our offer would be accepted. The wait was nerve-racking for Guido because he couldn't wait to get his hands on the boat, but more so for me because I couldn't decide if I wanted us to get it or not.

We both love Christmas and always put our tree up so early that we have to have a fake one, because the real thing would shed its needles long before the big day. Putting up the decorations this year with James "helping" was however proving to be quite a trial, although James was blissfully unaware of the chaos he was causing and was having the most wonderful time. It was 1st December and we were immersed in tinsel and fairy lights while James helped with the baubles, seeing how high they could bounce (I had grabbed the breakable ones away from him and already stuck them at the very top of the tree!), when the phone rang.

"Can you get it?" Guido and I called simultaneously, before both charging to answer. Guido got there first and I sank down on the settee to get my breath back. All at once my man's face changed. Every trace of tiredness vanished and he turned to me grinning.

The boat was ours.

James howled loudly as he got his foot tangled up in a length of tinsel and fell over. Guido laughed and started singing loudly as he swept up both baby and me and danced us around the room. There was no turning back now. It was time for this landlubber to start learning to sail!

(Turn over for the first of the recipes contained in *"A Whisper On The Mediterranean".*)

Penne all'Arrabbiata

This is a delicious pasta dish for those who love hot, spicy food and is the ideal dish to accompany the making of exciting plans!

The dish is typically Roman. The hot chilli peppers love the climate there and are often seen growing in small pots on balconies, alongside other fragrant herbs such as basil and rosemary. Guido and I grew lots of plants and picked the chillies fresh whenever we needed them, either to cook with or to cut up fresh and sprinkle on top of our food for a blast of real heat. We found that they freeze really well, so that even in the winter months we are ensured a constant supply.

Even if you do not like your food as hot as we do, a delicious sauce can be made by modifying the quantity of chilli to suit your own tastes.

500g penne
1 small tin of peeled tomatoes
3 cloves of garlic
2 chillies
salt
sugar
fresh chopped parsley
olive oil

Cut up the garlic and one chilli and fry them in a little olive oil until just browning. Add the tin of whole tomatoes. Don't worry about chopping them much, as they will break up anyway when cooking and they give a better taste and texture than the ready-chopped ones. If you have fresh tomatoes in the summer you can make a sauce using them that will be lighter in colour and have a more delicate taste.

Add half a tin of water, salt to taste, and half a teaspoon of sugar to take away the slight bitterness you sometimes get with the tinned tomatoes. Let the sauce boil for 10-15 minutes until it has reduced and the tomatoes are cooked well.

Boil the pasta in salted water until it is cooked, then run a little cold water from the tap into the pan before straining the pasta. This ensures that the pasta doesn't get over cooked but remains *al dente*.

Toss the pasta with the sauce and add the parsley. Chop the remaining chilli and put it on the table so that those who like it really hot can help themselves.

END OF SAMPLE

"A Whisper on the Mediterranean" by Tonia Parronchi can be purchased from all good online stores, or better still, ask for it from your local independent or chain book store.

SUNPENNY
PUBLISHING
GROUP
ROSE & CROWN, BLUE JEANS, BOATHOOKS, SUNBERRY, CHRISTLIGHT, and EPTA Books

COMING SOON:

30 Days to Take-Off, by KC Lemmer
A Devil's Ransom, by Adele Jones
Bon Voyage, Sophie Topfeather, by Sonja Anderson
Brandy Butter on Christmas Canal, by Shae O'Brien
Broken Shells, by Debbie Roome
Heart of the Hobo, by Shae O'Brien
The Lost Crown of Apollo, by Suzanne Cordatos
Raglands, by JS Holloway
Sudoku for Bird Lovers (full colour illustrated gift book)
Sudoku for Horse Lovers (full colour illustrated gift book)
Sudoku for Sailors (full colour illustrated gift book)
Sudoku for Stitchers (full colour illustrated gift book)